Caffeine Ni

Top Dog

Now a Major Film

Dougie Brimson

...ion aimed at the heart and the head…

Published by Caffeine Nights Publishing 2014

Published in Great Britain by Caffeine Nights Publishing

www.caffeine-nights.com

British Library Cataloguing in Publication Data.
A CIP catalogue record for this book is available from the British Library

ISBN: 978-1-907565-45-8

Cover design by

Mark (Wills) Williams
Image of Leo Gregory by Julia Underwood

Everything else by
Default, Luck and Accident

For Tina.

Essex girl supreme.

Acknowledgements

Huge thanks to Leo Gregory, Jonathan Sothcott, Martin Kemp, Richard Thompson and Darren Laws for making magic things happen.

I would also like to give a special mention to Neil Stevenson and Gary Lawrence for being genuinely top blokes and thank every single person who helped and took part in the making of the movie.

You were all quite simply awesome.

Introduction

Martin Kemp, Director of Top Dog

It was a quiet day in LA, the sun was washing the walls of my hotel room a distinct shade of California when my Mac went ping as an email dropped into its box. I love that sound, it's the sound of possibility....and this time I wasn't disappointed. I opened up the email and attached was a script with the title TOP DOG. In small print underneath, it said, 'This is the ultimate lads' movie!' I was intrigued, not just 'a' lads' movie but the *ultimate*. I grabbed a bottle of beer from the fridge, pulled up a chair and started to read, and bit by bit was sucked into every twist and turn of the journey Mr Brimson had sent me on. By the end I felt like I knew the ins and outs of Billy Evans and his Cockney Suicide Squad that rule over at Upton Park with an iron fist. I love it when a story engulfs me like that, and I hate it when I get to the end, realising my two hours of fantasy have come to an abrupt halt. What I didn't realise at that moment was that this was the beginning of an adventure that would envelop the next six months of my life.

The next day, I had arranged a Skype call back to England to chat with Leo Gregory, who was to play the part of Billy Evans, and Dougie Brimson, the writer. Now I had heard of Dougie and Leo, I loved their work on *Green Street* like every other football fan, but we had never met. Then suddenly my

Mac screen flashed to life telling me I was connected, a quick 'hi' and an introduction and then the technology let us down, our twenty-first century face-to-face would have to wait, but we spoke, and we spoke for ages about *Top Dog* and the possibilities it held. Billy's life, his background, his family, his mates and of course the violence that surrounds him. To me, *Top Dog* held more than just the kick and tell story that was visible on the surface, I wanted to get to the human story behind it. I wanted to know how it affected Billy, how it affected his family and the people he called his friends. I wanted to get to know the CSS and find the vulnerability behind the bravado.

I have always been fascinated with people who reach the top of the pile, people who think as themselves as the 'Top Dog' in any walk of life. It's a dangerous place to be, there is nowhere else to go apart from down, once you put your head above the parapet and call yourself 'the leader', don't be surprised that there are others waiting to bring you down, there's only one person everyone points at when it all goes tits up.

When I got home from, LA, Dougie and I spent hours together and many a cup of coffee turning *Top Dog* into a movie that we could both be proud of.

Top Dog is the dog's bollocks..... Enjoy!

Martin Kemp, 2014

Top Dog

Billy Evans drew heavily on his freshly lit Benson & Hedges, closed his eyes and sank into the leather luxury of his Range Rover as the sound of Al Green singing 'How Can You Mend a Broken Heart' drifted from the stereo.

To Billy, brought up on a diet of seventies and eighties soul, Al Green was god. He'd even named the first of his two boys after the great man as a mark of respect, although Samantha hadn't thought *Al* Evans had gone together, forcing him to settle on Alfie as a compromise.

But this song was more important to him than most. It was the track he'd played to Samantha as he drove her home the night they met at The Goldmine on Canvey Island, and the song they'd had their first dance to at their wedding reception. It was their song. And he never, ever tired of it.

Six minutes and twenty-four seconds later, with the hairs on the back of his neck still vibrating, he leant forward, and with a barely audible 'fuck it' pressed repeat, cranked the volume up two notches and sank back into his seat with a grin.

He was just settling into the second verse when a tap on the window broke into his meditation. Instinctively, and without even opening his eyes, he raised his fist and extended two fingers. He had a good idea who it was. And they could wait.

Outside, Graham Hawkins tried to peer through the blacked out windows and then, with a curse, gave up and walked back across the car park to four smartly dressed men leaning against a silver Mercedes. Years of travelling to games with Billy meant that he knew each and every note of each and every Al Green song by heart. As a result, he hated Al Green with a passion.

'D'you know, that cunt spent nearly £800 on that stereo and all he does is listen to fuckin' spade music. He should have been a bastard darkie.' He took a brief drag on his cigarette, more for comic effect than anything, and then, with a nod at

13

the tall, slim black man standing in front of him added, 'No offence, Stretch.' They both burst out laughing.

'None taken, Hawk. I prefer a bit of Abba myself. That's good old-fashioned white music.'

Hawkins smiled and flicked his dog-end in the direction of the black Range Rover. 'You'd never make a decent honkey Stretch. Your knob's too small.'

'That's not what your mum says.'

'Funny that,' said Hawkins, lighting another cigarette. 'Yours does!'

One of the other men moved forward, unconsciously smoothing down the front of his new Burberry jacket as he did so. 'Hawk, for fuck's sake hurry him up. The fuckin' Boleyn'll be rammed by the time we get there.'

Hawkins stared at him for a moment and slowly shook his head. 'Fuck me, PJ. Didn't you just see me go over there and bang on the window? What the fuck else am I supposed to do? You know what he's like. Besides, by my reckoning,' he said, pausing and listening attentively to the music throbbing from the car across the road, 'he'll be out in about forty-odd seconds.' Unconsciously, a few of the group looked at their watches and then at the Range Rover.

Exactly forty-seven seconds later, Billy pushed open the door and stepped out into the road as a loud 'Yes!' erupted, followed by uncontrolled laughter. 'What the fuck's up with you lot?' he asked as he crossed the road.

'You, you daft twat.'

'What?' he asked, holding his arms out in front of him, a gesture of mock surrender.

'You had to be here,' said Hawkins. 'Which of course you weren't, because we've been stood here waiting for you as fucking usual. Now, are we going for a beer or not? We're gagging here.'

Billy looked at the familiar faces and shook his head like a disapproving father. 'What, d'you need me to hold your bloody hands? Or are all you Cockney Suicide Squad boys afraid of those nasty Southampton fans?'

'Yeah right-oh.' A tall blond-haired man stepped forward, his cockney accent reeking with sarcasm. 'I'm shitting it at the thought of all those fucking inbreds.' Billy looked at him and frowned.

'Fuck me, Darren, who rattled your cage? And where'd you get that shit jacket? Oxfam?'

'Oi, it's fucking Stone Island this. A proper fucking lads' label, not like some of that poncey stuff you faggots are wearing.' PJ looked at him and shook his head.

'He always was about three years behind the times. He was making plans for France '98 the other day.'

'Yeah, I was gonna buy your bird a new pair of pyjamas.' The entire group burst out laughing. It was a half-day spent shopping for a birthday present in France during one of West Ham's all-too-infrequent European excursions that had earned PJ his nickname.

'Look, girls. Are we going for a pint or what?' asked Hawkins, the tone in his voice becoming increasingly irritated. 'In case no one's noticed, it is nearly five o'clock already.'

'Well, I'm waiting for you cunts,' said Billy without a trace of irony. 'But you won't stop gassing. Speaking of which...' He turned to face a short, round-faced man still leaning against the Mercedes, his voice suddenly serious rather than jovial. 'We sorted for Chelsea, Geoff?'

'No problem,' he said, pushing himself off the car. 'I just got some canisters over from Belgium. It's top stuff. The Rent Boys won't know what hit 'em.' Billy nodded. Geoff was sound as a pound. That's why everything was kept at his place. Including all their mobiles.

'Good. We've got a few days yet. So, PJ, give 'em a bell tomorrow and find out if they're actually gonna show for once.'

'And tell them to try and keep it from the Old Bill this time,' interrupted Darren. 'Fuckin' club must have more leaks than a Tory cabinet.'

Billy looked at him and smiled. He was glad to be back among the day-to-day banter of the firm. It had been a while. 'I'm a bit snowed under this week, so any chance we can have a plot-up meet next Thursday?' He looked around, and when no one indicated otherwise, added, 'Top. But not at the Boleyn. Best use somewhere a bit less obvious for this one.'

'How about the St George?' said Stretch. 'I know it's a bit of a scarfers pub, but we ain't been there for a while.'

Billy nodded. 'Seems sound to me. About 8.30 then. Now are we going for a beer or what? Hawk's buying.'

Within a few minutes, the small group were strolling down Green Street in the direction of the Boleyn, their favoured match-day pub. To the uninformed, they were simply six lads having a laugh on their way to football but to those in the know, they were much more; they were faces, their expensive clothes and inherent arrogance as much a uniform as the one worn by the policemen who kept a wary eye on them as they walked.

Suddenly, Billy stopped and let out a stream of expletives. 'I've only left me bloody phone in the car. You go on, I'll catch you up.'

'Have you noticed how he always pulls a stunt like this?' laughed Stretch. 'Anything to get out of buying the first round.'

Billy looked at him and feigned offence. 'You cheeky bastard. Here ...' He reached into his pocket for his wallet but found it empty, the realisation that he'd left that in the car as well hitting home with tragic irony. 'Lend us a score, Hawk?'

The others fell about. 'Fuck me,' roared Geoff. 'He's even pulling doubles now. Ain't you got no shame, Evans?'

Billy waited until the laughter had died down a bit before he held out his hands in surrender. 'What can I say? Go on, sod off the lot of you.' He turned away from them and headed back towards the car park, shaking his head and mentally kicking himself. Sure in the knowledge that their piss-taking would continue all night.

He was just about to cross the road when a white minibus slowed to a crawl directly in front of him, the nervous occupants staring out through the misted windows as it became trapped in the early evening congestion. Billy instinctively knew who and what they were, and so he stood and returned their stare, smiling to himself as he imagined what they were thinking. Anywhere else, with some wanker outside giving them the large one and odds of at least ten to one, they'd be out of the van and having a pop. But not this time, not if they wanted to go home in one piece. Step out of line around here and anything could happen. The place was hard as nails, worse than Newcastle even.

Billy caught the eye of a lad sitting at the back and stared at him for a second, catching the obvious unease in his eyes. He was almost tempted to jump forward and shout, 'BOO!' But in the end, he settled for a broad wink, laughing out loud as the lad recoiled slightly and looked away. 'Fucking bumpkins,' he thought.

The traffic began crawling again and Billy gave the lads in the van a wave of his hand before darting out behind it and making his way across the road. As he did so, he noted the address of the hire firm painted across the rear of the bus, which confirmed his instincts that they were boys up from the south coast. But as he was almost at the kerb, he was astonished to hear the distinctive sound of a metal door slamming behind him and turned to look. He smiled at the sight of four lads trying desperately to lose themselves among the pedestrians on the opposite pavement, while all the time keeping their eyes fixed firmly on him. 'You've got to be fucking kidding!' he said out loud. 'Cheeky bastards!'

The blast of a car horn made him jump and, with a wave of apology, he stepped back on to the kerb to allow a car to pass. Glancing up again, he saw one of the Southampton lads break out from the crowd and make his way across the road, not directly towards him, but at enough of an angle to cut off any chance of escape to his left. And then another came, cutting off his right. Billy suddenly realised he was in big trouble. These were obviously no mugs, they were game lads. And a kicking from some south coast bumpkins hurt just the same as a kicking from anyone else.

He glanced around and caught sight of the two men on his side of the road working their way through the unknowing throng towards him. Billy realised with not a little irritation that there was no one but commuters and the odd scarfer in sight. 'Fuck it!' he muttered angrily as he tried to work out what to do for the best. 'This could be embarrassing.' He daren't go for either of them; the number of pedestrians would prevent anything other than a wrestling match and he'd almost certainly end up on the ground, with obvious consequences. That left him only one option and he took it without hesitation, stepping out into the road to give himself some space. Forcing the traffic to slow to a halt, but ignoring the irritated blasts of a dozen car horns, he spun around to get his bearings. He was more indignant than angry now. It had been a long time since any lads from any club had come to Upton Park and had the effrontery to have a pop at anyone this close to the ground. The fact that it was a pop at him made it even worse. These bastards would pay, one way or another. Maybe tonight, maybe next season. But they *would* pay.

When the first of the four men followed his lead and walked out into the traffic, Billy focused every ounce of his attention on him. He took in every detail of his face, his clothing and his manner. Logging it into his memory for future reference as everything else became a blur, London drifting out of focus as the early evening noise receded into the distance as if someone had turned the volume down.

'You cheeky fucker!' barked Billy, as he began walking towards him. His movements were relaxed, his arms held down but slightly forward. Ready. 'You have no idea what shit you're in.'

Ray Jackson manoeuvred his motorcycle through the early evening traffic until he saw exactly what the hold-up was. He accelerated the final few metres and then pulled the bike to a halt, flicking down the side-stand and hitting the switch on the panel in front of him even as he climbed off. The loud whooping of his siren had the desired effect and the two men confronting each other in the road turned to look at him as he flicked up his visor and walked towards them. The closest face was instantly recognisable from a hundred pre-match briefings.

'You,' he barked angrily, 'piss off now or I'll nick you.'

'Oh, is that fucking right?' replied Billy cockily.

'Yes it bloody is! Piss off! And you ...' he added, pointing at the second man and cocking his finger. 'Here, now!'

He held Evans' stare for a second and then relaxed as, with a final angry glance, Billy turned and began to make his way through the traffic and into the distance. The fact that he was moving away from the ground was irrelevant. As long as there was no trouble, Ray didn't give a shit.

With Evans on his way, he grabbed the second man and dragged him over to the side of the road, pushing him firmly against the wall with a thud and ignoring his protests.

'Listen, I don't give a shit what that was all about, but it stops. OK?' He waited until the man nodded and the aggression had begun to ease from his face, then smiled at him. 'You should be thanking me, sunshine. Have you any idea who that was?'

Billy cruised along the A12 in his Range Rover and silently seethed. Despite the 2-0 win, he'd had a shit night. For if there was one thing he hated, even though it was a part and parcel of the Saturday scene, it was people taking the piss out of him. And tonight he'd had it in spades. Never mind the fact that he had fronted up four obviously game lads, as far as his lot had been concerned, the Old Bill had saved his arse. It wasn't even as if he'd been able to go out looking for revenge. The copper must have put word out about what had happened and, as a result, the filth had been all over the Boleyn, keeping an eye on the CSS to make sure they behaved. And now he'd have to wait until next season. Would he make those fuckers suffer or what?

He lit a cigarette and picked up his phone, dialling the number without even looking. 'Hi babe, it's me. I'll be about ten minutes, OK?'

'Billy...' she said, her voice oozing out of the phone and bringing an instant smile to his face.

'Yes?'

'Nip into the Chinky and get me a mushroom Foo Yung, will you. I'm desperate.'

He paused for a second, his smile increasing as he waited. 'How desperate?'

The response was exactly as he'd expected. A giggling voice and a sarcastic dig. 'Just do it tubs, you know I'll make it worth your while.'

'Sounds interesting. Let's see, a Foo Yung costs about £2.40, what would I get for that, then?'

'That's for me to know and you to find out,' she replied, before lowering her voice and whispering in a sultry tone, 'But you know I'm good value.'

Billy laughed out loud and after telling her to ring up and order what she wanted, adding that he'd have a curry and expect a decent tip for delivery, headed off in the direction of his favourite takeaway.

'Mister Evans, your meal.'

Billy stood up and with a smile, walked over to take the white plastic bag from the young Chinese girl behind the counter. 'Thanks love, I'll...' He was interrupted by a sharp, almost abrasive voice which ripped across the small shop like a blade.

'Hang on a fucking minute!' Billy turned to look at the only other person in the takeaway: a young lad, nineteen at most, his face twisted with the arrogance of self-importance as he stood up and walked over. 'I was here before this geezer. Where's my fuckin' food then?'

'This gentleman phoned his order through sir,' answered the girl nervously, almost bowing her head in apology as she spoke. 'I'm sure your meal will be here in a minute. I will go and check.'

The young lad gave a grunt of satisfaction and then turned to Billy who was eyeing him up and down. 'What's your fucking problem, fat boy?'

Without saying a word, Billy stuck out his bottom lip and slowly shook his head as the hairs on the back of his head began to tingle with anticipation.

'Well, why don't you fuck off then?' added the youth, unwittingly sealing his fate as he spoke. 'Before you end up wearing that shit instead of eating it.'

Billy smiled and nodded before walking out. The opportunity to off-load an entire evening's irritation in one fell swoop had just presented itself.

With his own food sitting safely on the passenger seat, Billy was leaning against the front of his Range Rover with his arms crossed when the youth came out. Billy watched silently until he'd ripped the top from a foil container and taken a mouthful of food, then pushed himself off the car, the youth catching sight of him as he did so and freezing on the spot as he realised that this bloke wasn't the average middle-class coward he'd had him pegged as. He was trouble.

'Now then...' said Billy, rubbing his chin and glancing around to make sure no one was nearby as he walked slowly across the semi-lit pavement. 'There are certain things that really piss me off: Chelsea, Tony Blair, people carriers ... and mouthy little cunts like you.'

'Oh, is that right?' stuttered the youth, his arrogance evaporating as he tried to work out what to do. 'Well, unless you want me to ...'

'Save it,' said Billy, raising his hand to stop him but closing the gap between them with each syllable. 'I ain't interested in what some little arse-wipe like you's got to say.'

When he was less than an arm's length, Billy stopped and smiled. 'Word of warning for you, son: never diss people you don't know. You never know what might happen. Understand?'

The youth nodded slowly but even as he did so, Billy's right hand shot out and struck him full in the throat. The splayed fingers caught the Adam's apple perfectly, shunting it back into his windpipe and instantly blocking both his breath and the power of speech. The youth let out an involuntary gasp and staggered backwards but before he could take a full step, Billy was on him, grabbing hold of the back of his head with his left hand and the container of food with his right before driving the silver foil into the youth's face, filling his nose and eyes with boiling hot liquid. Billy held it there for a second to muffle what noises the youth was able to make and then, with an expertise that only a seasoned street fighter could ever exhibit, pulled his right hand away and grabbed the youth's collar with his left. He dragged him across the path as the silver foil fell away, and slammed the scalded face against the roof of a car with such force that it dented the rain gutter.

Again, Billy held him for a second before taking his left hand away and delivering a crushing and perfectly targeted blow to the kidneys with his right. He smiled with grim satisfaction as the youth let out an involuntary yelp and slid to the floor, first to his knees and then on to all fours as his body fought desperately to draw in breath.

'Just think yourself lucky I don't want my grub to get cold,' smirked Billy as he stood over him. 'Or I'd really lose my rag.' He went to walk off but then stopped and looked down at his jacket. It was covered in sticky brown liquid and, with, a curse, he turned back.

'You cunt,' he growled. 'Look what you've fucking done! D'you know how much this cost?' He paused for a second and studied the body as he worked out where and how to inflict the most damage. Stepping forward once he'd decided, he ground the fragile fingers of the youth's right hand into the unforgiving tarmac.

Only when the soft crunching noises came less often did he lift his foot away. With a final glance around, Billy headed for his car and his takeaway.

Within a few short minutes, he was home, tucking into his chicken curry and rice without a care in the world as Samantha devoured her desperately craved Foo Yung.

'What're you so happy about?' she asked as she ate. 'You look like you lost a fiver and found a tenner.'

'Nothing...' he said, grinning at her. 'I'm just thinking about how you're gonna pay me for this.'

Part One

CHAPTER 1
Thursday 16 March 2000
18.45

Billy stood across the narrow street from the St George and glanced at his watch. He was way too early for the others. But having been at an auction all afternoon, it hadn't been worth the hassle of driving out to Romford at this time of night only to have to come back in later on. Especially with traffic being as bad as it had been lately. Besides, a trip down memory lane once in a while never hurt anyone. And the St George had always served up a decent pint of Fullers.

He looked around for a moment and then lit the latest in a seemingly endless conveyer belt of cigarettes. He loved this place, loved it. Sure, it was a shit hole to look at, but there was something about the East End at this time of night. A feeling. Like the darkness was returning to reclaim its empire. And here in the back streets, built on a tradition of crime and violence that stretched back way before the Krays and even Jack the Ripper, it was at its most atmospheric. The lengthening shadows looked almost real, solid black shapes which carried along with them a sense of anarchy and menace that grabbed hold of you and told you to fuck off out if you didn't belong there or something bad would happen.

But Billy belonged. This was home. He might live out in Romford now, but he'd been born two streets from where he was standing and the almost sacred rules and values of the old East End still coursed through his veins. He could almost hear his old man saying them: honour the family above everything and, no matter what the circumstances, do what you have to do to keep your self-respect. If that meant bending the law once in a while, then so be it. It was their way.

The door of the pub swung open and a couple walked out into the half-light. Billy smiled to himself as he watched them go, heading off in the direction of Upton Park tube station and away. They didn't belong. He could tell it a mile off. Even from the way they walked.

He waited until they had turned the corner and vanished from sight before returning his gaze to the front of the pub. He had a soft spot for the St George. It might be hidden away in a dark and dingy back street, but before the old man had finally had enough of the immigrants and followed the East End exodus to Essex, it had been his local. And the two of them had spent many a happy Sunday lunchtime in there. Putting the world, and The Hammers, to rights over a pint or two. It was a good place, with good memories.

The idea of a drink finally galvanised him into action and he crossed the road and walked inside. It was like stepping back in time, all sixties decor and light brown walls. But it was the smell; a heady cocktail of beer, old wood and dust mixed with the pungent odour of stale smoke that hit him like a right-hander.

'Billy Evans! Well fuck me. How you doin'? And how's your dad?' Billy smiled and crossed the floor to grasp the outstretched hand of the middle-aged man standing behind the bar.

'He's good, Steve. Still moaning, but what can you do with the old cunt?'

Despite the fact that there were at least four other people waiting to be served, the landlord reached up, grabbed a tall glass and began pouring Billy a pint of Fullers. 'Fucking diamond, your old man. A proper gent. What you doin' round here then? We ain't seen you for a while.'

'Just visiting, meeting some people. You know how it is,' he said, reaching into his pocket.

Steve held up his hand. He did indeed know how it was.

'On me, Billy. Heard about the Rome thing a couple of months back. Bit rough weren't it?'

Billy glanced around and smiled. He'd known Steve long enough to know that if he'd heard anything, he'd heard almost everything. 'Yeah, it was a fucking nightmare,' he said sarcastically. 'Got me some tidy breathing space with Old Bill, though.'

'Always useful. Especially in your game.'

Billy nodded, although in truth, things had been fairly quiet for a while now. It had been almost six months since, under the umbrella of an England away game, he'd used a load of football lads to 'export' almost thirty stolen cars to Italy. And, although he knew almost straight away that he'd got away with it, he hadn't taken any chances since. Every single aspect of the business had been kept totally legit, just in case the Old Bill had decided to pay him another visit.

The other big worry for him had been the court case in Italy involving the National Football Intelligence Unit. Setting up an undercover copper to take the fall for his mate Fitch's stabbing had been a masterstroke. And Billy had known right from the off that if the copper did get sent down, he'd be almost untouchable, which is another reason why he'd kept a low profile at Upton Park. He knew the coppers had been watching him and trying to trip him up. So he'd stayed away from anything that might have ended up with him getting a tug; not only to ensure his credibility as a prosecution witness had remained unharmed, but also to avoid ending up in court himself and possibly picking up a ban.

But the court case in Italy had ended six weeks ago, and with the copper now in jail and the NFIU discredited and disbanded, Billy knew he was finally in the clear. The time had come to get back to work. Not just with the motors, but also at football. And, with the European championships coming up, he had decided that the time had come to give the profile of the CSS a timely boost. Chelsea would provide the first real opportunity to do that, and he didn't intend to waste it. If he could turn over their main boys, word would spread through the scene like wildfire and ensure that West Ham would be given the respect their reputation and history demanded.

'Listen, Steve, any chance I could use upstairs for a couple of hours later? I've got a few mates comin' over and we'd like a bit of privacy. And have you got any grub on? I'm bloody starving.'

'No worries, old son. Take a seat and I'll get Sal to bring you over a menu. Just give us a nod when you want to go through.'

Billy smiled, took his drink and walked over to an empty booth. It was like he'd never been away. He half expected his dad to come bursting through the door, cracking jokes and singing shite songs.

'Billy!' A short, round, dark-haired woman came scurrying towards him, her arms outstretched and a huge smile on her face. 'How are you, my darlin'?'

He stood up and put his arms around her. 'Good, Sal. Really good. You look fantastic as always. How come you're still living with that old git?'

She laughed out loud and put a hand on his cheek. 'I'm waiting for you lover. I always have been, you know that.' She looked into his eyes for a second and then slowly dropped her hand. 'How're Sam and the kids? When you gonna bring them down to see us again? And bring your bloody mum and dad as well. I ain't seen 'em for ages. They still in Leigh on Sea?' She rattled off a stream of questions like an ack-ack gun.

'Soon, Sal. I promise.'

She looked at him and raised an eyebrow. 'You're a lying little fucker, Billy Evans. Here,' she said, dropping a menu on the table in front of him. 'And don't piss off without saying goodbye.'

Billy watched as she headed back to the kitchen. Sal was a true cockney bird - all heart and laughs, but hard as nails. He'd lost count of the number of times he'd seen her sorting out rucks in here. She'd even chased him up the road once.

Daft cow. He'd been about seventeen and had lost her after about two minutes. But when he'd walked back, he'd found her sitting on the kerb having a smoke. She'd been so knackered she'd just stopped and sat down. Once she'd convinced him he was safe, he'd sat down next to her and the two of them had ended up sitting there for half an hour laughing like drains. She'd still given him a right-hander when they'd stood up though; and a threat that if he ever threw a punch in her pub again she'd have his bollocks on a plate. But she hadn't said a word to the old man when they'd come in together on the Sunday. Just given him a wink. He smiled at the memory, scanned through the menu and, having chosen what he wanted, stood up and walked over to the bar.

He was about to call out to her when the door opened behind him and he turned to see two men enter. Billy looked at them for a moment and, after taking in as much information as possible, turned back to face the bar. He didn't need a sixth sense to know that these two weren't punters; they were trouble. And he knew better than to make eye contact with lads like them because they hit hard, fast and first. And then, if they could be arsed, they asked questions.

But they were just bullies. Thick fuckers who wore their black jeans and black bomber jackets as a uniform and earned their living using their brawn wherever and whenever it was needed, be it security, debt-collecting or dishing out the occasional straightener for someone with more money than bottle. Billy knew a hundred of them. Yet he also knew that their type weren't exactly social animals. And if they were here, it was for a reason. He reached forward and picked up his glass. If it was him they were after, he was taking at least one of them down with him.

Suddenly, a hand slammed down on the bar beside him and Billy turned his head to find himself looking into a pale, thin face, a smug, almost mocking grin on the lips and the dark eyes staring at him. 'All right, mate?'

Billy stared back into the eyes and smiled. 'Yeah, top thanks. You?'

The head nodded slowly, but the dark eyes were gleaming and it didn't take much to see that he was on something, speed probably. And he was ready to go at even the slightest invitation. 'Yeah, I'm good too. We're both good, ain't we, Dave?'

Billy turned his head slightly to look at the other man. He was broader across the shoulders and slightly taller. Billy guessed he did weights. Lots of weights. 'I know you,' he said.

'Is that right?'

'Yeah, I'm sure of it. Can't place from where though. But it'll come to me. I never forget a face'

Billy smiled. 'Sorry, mate, can't help you. I've never seen you before in my life. I'd have remembered.' He turned back to face the bar and drained his glass. Play it cool. If it was going to kick off, let them force the pace. He was about to call out to Steve when the dark-eyed man beat him to it.

'Oi, landlord! Over here.'

Steve came hurrying along the bar. If Billy hadn't known better, he'd have sworn his old friend looked almost nervous. 'All right, lads. Come through to the back, Barry, and I'll sort you out. Won't be a minute, Billy. I'll send Sal through.'

Billy stood back as the dark-eyed man pushed past him. The expression on his face seemed even more arrogant than before.

The second man, Dave, clicked his fingers. 'Got it! You're the geezer off the telly. You was involved with that court case where the copper got sent down for murder. Well fuck me! Good to meet you, mate. Fucking filth, think they can get away with anything.'

Billy almost laughed at the irony of the situation. He had suddenly realised what was going on and was instantly irritated. 'Yeah, cheers.'

'What you after, Billy?' Sal had come out of the kitchen, the smile on her face as beaming as it had ever been. For the first time since he had known her, Billy wondered if it was all an act. Even with him.

'Just another pint, Sal. And take one for yourself.'

'You not eatin', then?' she asked as she took his glass and. began pouring.

'No thanks. Lost me appetite. Maybe later.' He turned his head as the two men returned from the back room. He felt almost sick.

'Here, Barry, d'you know who this is? He's one of the geezers who got the copper sent down in Italy. Remember? Couple of months back.'

Barry with the dark eyes looked at him and sneered. 'Is that right?' he said, hardly even attempting to disguise the mocking tone in his voice. 'Bit of a hard man then?'

Billy returned his stare and smiled. 'Not me. I just got involved with something I shouldn't have. You know how it is.'

'Here, Billy, your pint.' Sal thumped the glass down on the counter. She could sense when things were beginning to turn nasty; in her line of work, it was essential. And the process had definitely started here. She might not have seen Billy for a while, but she knew better than most who and what he was. And you didn't get to be top dog at West Ham by stepping back from a fight, even if the odds were stacked against you. She looked at the two men in their black jackets. 'You two not got places to be?'

After a pause, dark eyes smiled and nodded. 'Yeah. Nice to meet you ... erm ...' He paused, inviting Billy to say his name; gain that tiny piece of one-upmanship.

'You too,' said Billy, not rising to the bait. 'And be lucky.' He turned back to the bar and lifted his pint. It was only when he heard the door swing shut that he relaxed.

'How long's that been going on, Sal?' he asked.

She shrugged her shoulders, the smile suddenly absent. 'About six months,' she said, avoiding his gaze at first but eventually relenting and looking at him. 'Come on, Billy, you know the score, it happens. It's a legitimate business expense round here. Always has been.'

'How much?'

'One hundred and fifty quid a week. For that we get to keep the furniture in one piece and the windows in their frames. And they say they'll deal with any problems we might have.'

Billy shook his head. 'A hundred and fifty for a back street pub! Shit, that's steep. Who are they?'

'New firm. You won't know 'em.'

'Fuck off, Sal. There are no "new" firms. Not in the protection game anyway.'

Sal let out a sigh and looked along the bar at Steve, who was busy serving a small group of women. Their coarse laughter filled the bar. She leant forward and in a hushed voice whispered, 'We only see the two goons, but I heard it was Mickey James.'

Billy almost choked. 'That little runt! You're having me on! I used to go to school with him, ain't seen 'im for a couple of years though. But I heard he'd been banged up. Something to do with smuggling in illegals.'

'He got out... by coincidence, about six months ago. Word is that when he was inside, he got pally with some serious faces from up west. They taught him a few things, lent him some muscle. You know how it works.'

Billy leant forward, his elbows on the bar. 'Has he got a toe in all the pubs round here then?'

She nodded. 'Seems like it. They even tried it on at the Boleyn, which shows they ain't none too clever. You know Pat, he's well connected and don't take no shit from no one. Told 'em to fuck off.'

'You don't have to take it, Sal,' Billy whispered. 'You know that. Say the word and I'll put our mark on this pub. They won't come near you again.'

She reached forward and touched his cheek again. 'This ain't a game, Billy. They don't piss about.'

'You think I do?'

She shook her head and looked up the bar at Steve. He was laughing and joking with two young women. 'Look at him, silly fucker. He honestly thinks he's in there.'

'Say the word, Sal.'

She looked back at him and sighed. She hated what these scum were doing to her: walking into her pub and taking hard-earned money out of their pockets. She felt like she'd been abused each time they brought their filth into her pub. Her face broke into a half-smile but her eyes blazed with the thought of retaliation. 'You do what you gotta do, Billy.'

'What the fuck is wrong with you? You been quiet all night.'

Billy looked across the dusty table at Hawkins and shook his head. 'Nothin'. I've got a few things on my mind that's all. I'll tell you after.'

'It is *after*, Billy,' said PJ. 'I reckon we're well sorted for the Rent Boys on Saturday.'

Billy looked at him and then at the others. Eleven of his closest mates, collectively, and jokingly, referred to as The Cabinet, because they planned everything. These men were the inner circle of The Squad, and Billy trusted each of them totally and without question. 'I've got some business. It ain't strictly football but it does concern The Squad.'

The others looked at him, their faces a mixed bag of expressions ranging from bewilderment to apathy. They might all be key players in the CSS, but even though he'd drifted away from the scene for a few months last year, Billy was still their man and he was back now. He'd called the tune since the day he'd become top dog over four years ago, and they were more than happy with the situation.

'Does it involve me gettin' deported again?' asked Hawk jokingly. ' 'Cause I gotta say my old lady weren't none too thrilled last time.'

Billy and the others laughed. 'No, son, it don't involve you gettin' deported. But what it does involve... is this place.' He glanced around the room and then returned his gaze to the others. 'Someone's putting the squeeze on it and I can't let that happen.'

'Why the fuck not?' asked Stretch. 'It's just a pokey back street boozer.'

'No, Stretch. It's more than that. I've got history here. And besides, this place is now the official pub of the CSS.'

'Who decided that then?'

'I did. Anyone got any problem with that?' Another sweep around the faces. 'Good. Now, first things first. If this is gonna be our new home, we gotta stop people takin' liberties. And that means sorting out these chancers draining the till. So, I'll need some troops here next Thursday. Who's in?'

Billy took a deep breath and strode purposefully up the road towards the St George. He was looking forward to tonight.

Saturday, and the visit of Chelsea, had been a wash-out. Another in an ever-growing list of victories for the police in what was becoming an increasingly tedious game. If someone had told him five years ago that Chelsea would come to Upton Park and hardly a punch would be thrown in anger, he'd have laughed at them. But that's exactly what had happened on Saturday. The police had been all over both mobs from the start and, although a few half-hearted charges had taken place, the coppers had called up the horses and that had been it. Once they were out and about on the streets, it was game over.

That was the norm these days. The large-scale battles that had been a part and parcel of football when his dad had first taken him, and which eventually had sucked him into the scene, had all but gone. Wiped out by segregation, oppressive policing and closed-circuit television. These days, things were different - much different. For the most part, what fun there was to be had at Upton Park came from the cat-and-mouse side of the contest: thinking on your feet and trying to outwit Old Bill while still trying to get one over on the opposition. It was like a real-life computer game, Theme Hooligan. He still got a buzz from it though, but not the same buzz. And he wasn't alone. The scene was dying on its arse, although that wasn't always down to the police. From his many trips abroad with England, he'd become good mates with lads from almost every major firm in the country and when they came to town it was usually a case of meet up and beer up. If there was any scrapping to be done, let the young lads do it.

There was the odd exception of course, especially with some of the London clubs; although that was when the tube came into its own. Get a couple of decent firms down there and it was game on. But more often than not, if anything did kick off, it was always away, usually as a result of a chance meeting with a tidy firm from one of the smaller clubs. Even then, if you could get thirty seconds of toe-to-toe fighting in before plod turned up, it was a major event. That was fucking tragic.

It was why so many lads he knew followed the national side. Travelling abroad with England was different, almost like the old days. The local coppers were invariably crap and the natives shitting it at the thought of all these hooligans coming to their town. Each trip was like a little war. But even then, you had to cope with the British filth. The bastards tracked you all over. And even now that the National Football Intelligence Unit had been disbanded, it didn't look like getting any easier.

He scratched the back of his head and smiled to himself at the irony of the situation. Here he was, the person almost solely responsible for getting the NFIU disbanded, moaning about how good the police were getting. Silly sod.

But tonight was different. He felt the buzz again; the tingling in his stomach and the thumping of his heartbeat in his ears; pumping him up, getting him ready. That sense of excitement: part fear, part hope. They were like old friends. It was good to see them again. He pushed open the door and walked inside.

'What the fuck are you smiling at?' He looked up to see Hawkins, Stretch and PJ standing at the bar. A glance around showed the place was more popular than last week. But then it would be. Most of the people there had been specially invited.

'Nothing. Just remembering the good old days, that's all.'

'What, like Saturday?' said PJ sarcastically. 'It's a bloody piss-poor state of affairs when you can't even have a decent tear-up with Chelsea.'

'They're fuck-all these days. Too old. You see the state of some of 'em? Shit, in a couple of years they won't be running away, they'll be shuffling!'

'No new blood coming through, that's their trouble,' said Stretch. 'Same with most mobs now.'

'Not us,' said Hawkins excitedly. 'I heard some of our under-fives had a tidy tear-up with some Huddersfield kids at King's Cross on Saturday night. The future's bright lads, the future's claret.'

Billy smiled and then gave a discreet nod up the bar as Sal came wandering over, the ever-present smile as beaming as always. 'Hello, Billy. Pint?' She started pouring it even before he could answer.

Billy looked at her. She knew exactly why they were here and what was almost certainly going to happen; yet he couldn't detect anything in her voice or expression that showed any kind of fear or concern. She had totally blanked everything. Well if that's what she wanted, that was fine with him. 'Steve around, Sal?' he asked.

'Out back. Pop through if you want.'

He nodded and made his way through to the back kitchen where Steve was busily loading some glasses into a dishwasher. 'All right, Billy. How's things?'

'Good.' Billy paused, uncertain of how to proceed.

'It's OK,' said Steve, looking up but continuing to load the machine as he spoke. 'Sal told me all about it. Just be careful, that's all. I don't mind a bit of damage but I don't want the Old Bill coming round.'

Billy nodded. 'Don't worry, nothing'll happen. This is just for show. That's all. These two won't want to have a pop; it's not their style.'

'Just out of interest,' asked Steve, slamming the door of the washer shut and drying his hands on a beer towel, 'what are you going to do for the rest of the week? I mean, you know they'll be back. If not tomorrow, the next night or the next. And this time, they'll come mobbed-up and ready to make a point. If not with you, with me and this place.'

'Just leave that to me,' replied Billy calmly. 'It'll be sorted long before anything like that happens.' He paused for a second and then went on. 'I need you to do something for me, Steve. When they turn up, I don't want anything to happen in the bar. So can you take your man upstairs? I'll have my chat with him up there.'

Steve nodded slowly. 'Shouldn't be difficult. I'll tell him the money's up there. You best get set up though. Time and all that.' He nodded in the direction of the clock above the door and Billy turned to see that it was almost twenty-five past. Time to move.

Twenty minutes later, PJ leant against a cold concrete wall cloaked in shadow and smiled to himself as the door of the St George swung shut behind the two men. He'd begun to wonder if he'd have trouble recognising them but, as soon as he saw the black jackets and arrogance, he'd known. 'Smug fuckers,' he thought, 'wouldn't last a second in a half-decent rumble.'

He reached into his pocket and pulled out his mobile, hitting the redial button without even looking at it. The small but brightly lit screen cast an odd, almost eerie green glow on his face as he waited for it to connect. First ring. 'They're inside,' was all he said before killing the call. 'One down, one to go,' he whispered to himself as he flicked through the programmed numbers. Fourth number in; call. Again, first ring. 'All systems go, boys. Let's have you round here pronto.'

Upstairs, Billy stood in the middle of the dimly lit room staring at the door, an unlit cigarette hanging from his mouth ready to light as soon as Steve delivered his man into the room.

'This is all a bit *Lock, Stock and Two Smoking Barrels,* ain't it?' whispered Geoff. 'Why don't we just kick fuck out of these two bods and send 'em on their way?'

Billy smiled, his gaze still fixed on the door. He was right of course. The whole setting was one big cliché but that was exactly what he'd wanted. He'd even asked PJ to make sure that the lads outside were leaning against the wall on the other side of the street when the two men left. Just like a scene from *The Warriors.* 'Because if we do that, Geoff, they'll just come back mobbed up and trash the place when we're not here. This way, tonight we prove a point and then tomorrow it becomes business.'

'Business my arse, this is bollocks. That's what it is. If it was down to me ...' He stopped as the sound of heavy footsteps on the wooden stairs interrupted his train of thought.

Billy flicked his lighter, lit his cigarette and glanced around the room. He had six lads in there with him, including Geoff and Hawk. Stretch was downstairs in the bar with another ten while PJ was outside with ten more. 'Heads up, boys, it's show time.'

The door flew open and Steve walked into the room, closely followed by Barry, the dark-eyed man from last week. As soon as he saw Billy, he stopped and looked around. 'What the fuck is this?'

Billy drew heavily on his cigarette and stared at him as Steve shrunk into the shadows. 'Listen ... Barry. I want you to give a message to Mickey. Tell him that the St George is now the official residence of the CSS. And as such, I'm terminating the contract with him because although the security cover he provides is, I'm sure, nothing less than comprehensive, the simple fact of the matter is that we prefer to do our own.' He paused and took in another lungful of smoke and then exhaled it. 'That's it. You can go now.'

Barry looked at him and then the others before bursting out laughing. 'Are you taking the piss or what?'

'No,' replied Billy, the tone of his voice businesslike but bordering on sarcastic, 'I wouldn't say that at all. In fact, I'd say I was being deadly serious. This is our pub now. And like I said, you can go.'

A silence fell over the room, punctuated only by the regular thumping from the music downstairs. A heartbeat to their confrontation. 'Who the fuck do you think you are? The CSS ... shit. D'you really think I give a toss about a few thick yobs who go to football? I've a good mind to tear your fucking head off and then blitz this shit hole.'

Billy smiled, took a last drag from his dog-end and dropped it on the floor before crushing it into the wood with his heel. 'Come on, Barry, you're a bright bloke. You know that's not going to happen. Now, run along and tell Mickey what I told you. There's a good lad.'

'Don't patronise me, you cunt.' He suddenly leant forward slightly, peering through the semi-darkness. 'Hang on a minute ... you're the geezer from last week. Downstairs. The one involved with the copper. Well, fuck me. Bit braver with your mates behind you aren't you, son?'

'Listen, Barry, why don't you stick to what you do best and that's running errands, not using your brains. Now, I'm getting bored with saying the same thing over and over, so why don't you run along to Mickey and give him the message. And you can tell him I'll be in touch real soon.'

Barry laughed out loud. 'Oh I'll tell him, old son. But I hope you realise what you're getting yourself into.' He turned to leave but caught sight of Steve in the corner. 'Shame. I had a soft spot for this place.'

As soon as he had left, the room settled into an uneasy silence. Billy could hear the heavy footsteps storming down the stairs and knew that within seconds of leaving the pub, a mobile phone would be relaying details of what had taken place. One thing about modern technology, news certainly travelled fast. 'Fuck me,' said Geoff, breaking the tension. 'He was an evil-looking bastard. We could do with a few of him in The Squad.'

Hawkins walked over and put his hand on Billy's shoulder. 'Loose fuckin' cannons, lads like that. It's all them steroids. Fucks the brain and shrinks the knob. You all right, Billy boy?'

Billy smiled and nodded. But his mind was racing. He'd made the first move but, to avoid getting dragged into any kind of war, he had to make sure that the timing of the next was perfect. One thing he was sure of though, they wouldn't be back tonight. Not with a pub full of lads. Even Mickey James knew better than that. 'Yeah, no problem. I could do with a beer though.'

As they made their way down the stairs and into the bar, it was clear that the lads from outside had also come in out of the cold. Billy called out to Stretch and PJ and motioned them over. 'What happened?'

'Got a bit hairy down here. I reckon your boy twigged something was going on. Especially when Darren decided to wind him up a bit.'

Billy cursed and glared along the bar at him. 'What did he do?'

'You know what he's like. Walked over and just leant on the bar staring at the bloke. When he started to get a bit narked, Darren asked him if he knew George Michael.'

'You what?'

'Funny, that's what *he* said. So Darren told him he thought he looked like one of the geezers in the George Michael video. The one with all the faggots in it.'

'What did he say to that?' asked PJ, barely able to stop from laughing.

'He told Darren that if he ever wanted something stuck up his arse, he was quite happy to put his right foot up there. And indeed, would do if Darren didn't fuck off sharpish. That's when the other one appeared and they did the off.'

Billy shook his head. 'Darren's a fucking idiot. What about you, PJ?'

He smiled. 'They near shit themselves when they came out and saw us leaning against that wall. Gave 'em something to think about though, that's for sure.'

Billy nodded and looked around. There were about forty people in there - twenty-six of them serious hand-picked lads - most of whom were starting to get a bit lively now that business had seemingly been concluded. Stories of former glories were already flying about and the three of them listened as Hawk described how he'd slipped over on some horseshit as they had tried to charge a group of Man United fans in Plaistow the previous December. The whole tear-up had fallen apart as both sets of lads, and a few of the coppers, had stopped what they were doing and started taking the piss instead. 'If they ever want to stop hooliganism, that's all they have to do. Spray all the roads with crap. It worked for me.' Despite the fact that they had all been there, and seen it for themselves, they all roared with laughter.

The smile stayed on Billy's face and, for the first time that evening, he started to relax. He had enjoyed that upstairs. A bit dramatic, but it had certainly had the desired effect and things had gone as well, if not better, than he had hoped. And although he had some work to do to pull it off, at least things had started moving. More importantly, an idea had started to gel together - a bloody good idea.

He walked over to the bar, grabbed the bell and gave it three loud rings. When everything fell quiet and he had everyone's attention, he climbed up on a bench and after surveying the scene, said, 'Boys and girls, welcome to the new and official home of the CSS. The beers are on me.'

The buzzing of the alarm clock snapped Billy from his sleep and threw him back into the real world. For a second, he lay there staring at the ceiling, unsure if the events of last night had actually happened or if he had dreamt everything.

He was still pondering this when a creak from the bedroom door made him turn his head, just in time to see a tiny dark-haired body come flying across the room towards him. Instinctively, his hands shot towards his testicles but it was too late. A bony knee struck home, forcing him to yell out in agony. A second body appeared. This time, a fist crashed into the bridge of his nose before it grabbed a pillow and began battering him around the head as he struggled to suck in oxygen. He let the blows rain down on him for a few seconds and then, when he'd managed to compose himself, yelled, 'Right you little bleeders. That's it!'

Billy shot his arms out to his side and then swept them upwards, trapping the two boys and smothering them in the duvet. Within seconds, he had rolled on top of them. Their young voices were screaming: half shock, half laughter.

'Will you three give it a rest. Come on, Billy, I've got to get them to school.' He looked up to see his wife standing in the doorway. She was wearing a grey trouser suit, with her blonde hair beautifully styled and make-up perfect. Even with a plate of toast in one hand and a mug of tea in the other, she looked stunning.

'But Sam, they must be punished,' he joked, and rolled them about a bit more before pulling the duvet down and exposing their heads. 'If you two aren't careful, I'll take you to see Orient again!' He held them down for a second more and listened to their laughter before letting them go; sending them off in the direction of the bathroom and telling them to get ready or else.

Sam handed him his toast and placed the mug down beside the bed. 'You should take them to football. You know they'd love it.'

'Yeah, I know. But you know how it is.'

'I know how you are.'

He looked up at her. 'You're gorgeous, do you know that?'

'Oh, is that right?' she replied, her smile sending shivers up his spine. 'I always thought I was your second-string bird.'

Billy reached up and pulled her down on to the bed. He was pleased to notice that, even after all this time, she didn't resist. 'No. You're strictly number one and you always will be. I'd do anything for you. You know that.'

She kissed his forehead. 'Would you? Would you really?'

He smiled at her and reached out, pulling her towards him so that he could feel her breasts pushing against his chest. The faint smell of her perfume caused an instant reaction in his groin. 'Anything.'

She reached out and lovingly stroked the side of his head. 'Then drop the kids off at school will you? I said I'd try and get into work early this morning.'

Billy looked at her for a second and smiled. 'Make it worth my while and I might.'

'Is that right, you cheeky sod? So what's it going to cost me then?' She slid her hand under the duvet and slowly ran it down his body towards his rapidly hardening penis, the first touch making him gasp. The second made him groan.

Hawkins was standing outside his house when Billy turned the Range Rover into his road. He didn't look best pleased. 'Where the fuck have you been? If I'd have known you were gonna be late, I'd have had something to eat. I'm bloody starving.'

'Keep your bastard hair on. And don't slam the fucking door like that. This ain't off the car lot, this is my fucker.'

'Well?'

'Well what?' Billy glanced at him as he accelerated the car away from the kerb and off in the direction of Forest Gate. He looked like shit.

'Last night you told me you wanted a hand doing some stuff this morning and you'd pick me up at half-nine. It's now ten to ten. So are you gonna give me some kind of reason why I've been standing outside in the cold for twenty fucking minutes?'

Billy smiled. 'Sam had to get to work early and I had to drop the kids at school but the traffic's shite. Don't worry, we got plenty of time.' He stole another look at Hawkins, only to find him staring back.

'You lying fucker.'

'What?'

'Don't fucking "what" me. You were still in bed, you bastard. I can see it on your lying shit-head face.'

Billy looked at him again, pleased to see that this time he was smiling. 'On my mother's eyes, I dropped the kids at school.'

'Yeah, afterwards maybe. And I bet the poor little sods were late as well. Here, pull in at McDonald's for fuck's sake. I got to eat something.' Billy turned into the drive-thru. Within a few minutes, they were off again.

'Why didn't you go in?' Billy asked Hawkins as they sat at some traffic lights.

'Well that's why they have drive-thrus. So you don't have to go in.'

'No, you prick. When I was late, why didn't you go indoors?'

Hawkins swallowed down the last of his burger and then reached for the second. 'Locked myself out ain't I? And Julie's gone to work.'

Billy laughed out loud. 'So I get the earache 'cause you're a thick fucker.'

'That's about the size of it.' The car settled into silence as they approached Forest Gate. They had work to do. Serious work.

When Billy had found the road he was looking for, he drove up and down it a couple of times and then, when he was sure, pulled the car into the kerb and turned off the engine. After staring back up the road for a second, he picked up his mobile, reached into his pocket for a crumpled piece of paper and slowly and deliberately dialled the number scrawled on it. The answer came in four rings. A short, almost brusque 'Yeah?'

'Is that Mickey?' Billy turned to face Hawk, who was staring back at him, his face a mixture of apathy and tomato sauce.

'Who wants to know?'

'I do. I bumped into some of your boys at the St George near Upton Park last night. I think you and I should have a meet.'

'And who exactly are you?' Billy smiled to himself. There was a definite edge to the voice even though it appeared relaxed. And there was a total absence of expletives.

'I'm a friend of the family. But like I say, we need to meet. Then you'll find out.' There was a long pause before the reply came.

'When?'

'How about right now?'

'Where?'

Billy left another pause. Hawk looked at him, the apathy replaced by bewilderment. 'I'm sitting in the black Range Rover just up the road from your mum's house. You got ten minutes.' He cancelled the call and threw the phone onto the dashboard.

Hawkins shook his head. 'You do know that's a mobile number. He could be absolutely fucking anywhere.'

Billy let out a laugh. 'I used to come here when I was a kid. Not often, but once in a while. Mickey was a bit of a wanker even back then, but his sister had the biggest pair of tits you ever did see. Fuckin' massive they were.' He pulled out a cigarette and threw it to Hawk, taking out a second one for himself and lighting it. 'She used to show 'em to us for a quid. Straight up. We used to have a whip round from our pocket money. First pair of tits I ever saw. See that house down there? Number forty-eight? That's where he lived.'

Hawkins sucked on his smoke - the first one of the day. It was all he could do to keep from coughing. 'So fucking what? That was years ago.'

'The old woman still lives there.'

45

'How the bloody hell d'you know that?'

Billy looked him and raised an eyebrow. 'What d'you take me for? Some kind of mug? I checked, you prick. www.192.com.'

'You what?'

'It's an Internet site. Lists the electoral register. I had a look last week and she was still listed as the occupant.'

Hawkins looked up the road and then back at Billy. 'They're well out of date, you nonce. She could have moved... or died even. Besides, even if she does still live there, that don't mean he does.'

'Listen,' said Billy, shaking his head, 'how fucking long have you known me, Hawk? Do you really think I haven't made sure?' He flashed a look across at the car and then back at the front of the house. 'See that white BMW up there? The one with the flat tyre covered in shite? That's Mickey's. I sold him the fucker just before he got sent down. Now, see that shop up on the corner? They deliver papers. I nipped up here on Monday and had a quiet word with the Paki bird behind the counter. She told me that every week, number forty-eight has the *Daily Mirror, What's On TV* and an *Autotrader*. So unless old mother James is getting into the car game, chances are, they're for Mickey. Is that all right now? Are you happy?'

Hawkins stuck out his bottom lip and nodded. 'Tell you what,' he said, pointing up the road, 'if that's him, I guess the answer is yes, I am.'

Billy turned to see Mickey James walking towards them. He looked stockier than Billy remembered, which certainly gave him the appearance of being a serious hard man; something reinforced by the look on his face. Clearly, here was a man not best pleased at his current situation. 'He's got something in his right hand,' said Hawkins, his voice suddenly deadly serious. 'Could be a blade or a spray. Maybe even a copper's baton.'

They both stared as the man approached. Billy knew he wouldn't be able to see them through the darkened windows so, when he was about thirty feet away, he opened the door and climbed out. 'Hello, Mickey. How's your sister?'

'Well fuck me!' he said, stopping dead in his tracks. 'Billy Evans!'

'The one and only,' replied Billy, not moving too far from behind the car door - just in case. 'We need to talk, Mickey.'

'Fuckin' right we do, old son. Who you got in the motor?'

Billy stepped out from behind the door and flicked his dog-end into the road. 'Just a face. We've got business elsewhere later.'

'Tell 'im to piss off for half an hour. There's a café up the top of the road.'

Billy turned his head as Hawk got out and, without a word, walked off in the direction of the café. Billy watched him go and then turned back. 'Shall we?' he said, climbing back into the driving seat and inviting Mickey to get in beside him.

Mickey walked around the front and got into the passenger seat, waving away the offer of a cigarette as he did so. 'I been hearin' a few things about you, Billy boy. The thing with the coppers in Italy... that was sweet. Earned you a lot of respect.'

Billy shrugged his shoulders, but not before noticing that whatever it was Mickey had been holding in his hand had gone - probably into a pocket. 'I do what I can. You know how it is. A bit here, a bit there.'

'I also heard a rumour you got into the import/export trade. That right?'

From the tone of his voice, he couldn't have been less interested, yet Billy knew full well what he was up to. When you lived on the wrong side of the law, information, however vague or apparently meaningless, was everything. It gave you leverage. And leverage was power. He lit himself a cigarette and inhaled deeply before lowering the window slightly and exhaling out into the fresh air. 'Depends what you heard.'

Mickey sniffed. 'Just rumours, that's all. You know how it is.' He paused for a while and then, when he was sure Billy wasn't going to let him have anything worthwhile, jumped in with both feet. 'So why you still pissin' about with this football thing then? Fucking kids' stuff.'

Billy laughed. 'It's what I do, Mickey. Always have and always will. Call it a weakness if you like.'

'What a waste,' replied Mickey with a slow shake of his head. He paused for a second and then went on. 'We've known each other a long time, Billy, but you know I can't let you get away with taking liberties like last night. I mean, you can give it the large one all you like down at Upton Park, but you come treading on my toes ... well, that's disrespectful. I've got a reputation to consider.'

'So have I, Mickey, and so have The Squad. And the fact is, as from last night, that's our pub. How would it look if word got out that we were paying for security? We'd be a joke. Besides, if money's going to change hands in there, it's coming to us. No more is coming your way, that's for sure.'

Mickey smiled. 'Looks like you've got a bit of a problem then, Billy boy.'

'No, Mickey. Not me, *we. We've* got a problem.'

'Is that right?' said Mickey sitting up and turning to face Billy, a slight trace of a sneer on his lips. 'So how'd you make that one out then?'

Billy stared at him. His expression becoming deadly serious. 'Your boys start bringing grief to the St George, the next Saturday night, two of your pubs or clubs will get a visit. And not from one or two hangers-on either. These'll be A-list main firm lads. A minimum of fifty and maybe even three times that if I'm in a bad mood. You reckon you could stay in business once word gets out that pubs you're supposed to be looking after are getting trashed on a regular basis?'

Mickey looked at him and smiled, his face a picture of calm but his eyes blazing. 'Is that a threat?'

Billy laughed. 'Just laying my cards on the table Mickey. That's all. Making sure that we're both in possession of all the facts, so that there are no doubts. But I don't want no war. It wouldn't do either of us any favours.'

'So what *do* you want?'

'I told you. I want the St George. No more, no less.'

Mickey turned his head and stared out the window for a moment. Although he might not be into football, he had still grown up with the CSS. They were as much a part of local folklore as the Blitz, and Mickey knew full well that they could total a pub in thirty seconds and then vanish. He'd seen it happen. More importantly, he knew that if Billy was the main man, he had a huge amount of manpower at his disposal and once they'd trashed the first pub, there would be no going back. And he had too many other things going on to get sucked into something he knew he could never win.

And that was a fact. He could never win. Billy might not know it, but he had him by the bollocks. Even on a good day, the best he could muster was four or five lads. Hard bastards true enough, but against the numbers Billy could pull together with one well-chosen word, they might as well piss in the wind. The only thing Mickey could do now was to save face. 'A little bird tells me that you're well connected when it comes to importing little blue tablets.'

'I have my sources,' replied Billy thoughtfully, slightly surprised at the sudden change of direction. 'But to be honest, I only dabble once in a while. They're too much hassle.'

Mickey turned round and smiled. 'I think you and me have some business to do, Billy boy.'

Billy sat drumming his fingers on the steering wheel as he waited for the lights to change. He was buzzing. He'd gone to front up Mickey James not knowing what to expect, but this ... this was something else.

He glanced across at Hawkins, who sat silently staring out of the window. He hadn't said a word since he'd told him what had happened and Billy was unsure if the full impact of it had actually sunk in or not. He was still considering this when the blast of a car horn interrupted his train of thought and after giving the driver behind an appropriate, if less than complimentary, gesture, Billy gunned the Range Rover's engine and blasted it away from the junction. Within seconds, they had caught up with the traffic taking them back along the A12 to Romford. He couldn't take it any longer. 'Well?'

'Well what?'

'Well... what do you think?'

Hawkins stuck out his bottom lip and shrugged his shoulders. 'Fuck knows.'

Billy stole another look at him. 'What does that mean? Fuck knows?'

'Fuck knows,' Hawkins replied, his voice carrying a slight trace of irritation. 'That's what it means. Fuck knows.'

Despite the grey March morning, the immaculately whitewashed walls of the two-storey car showroom gave off a healthy, almost saintly glow; an effect enhanced by the reflected light glistening on the highly polished paintwork of the various BMW and Mercedes saloons spread across the forecourt in front of it. There was no doubt about it, W. Evans Executive Motors Ltd had the air of a successful and profitable concern, which is exactly what it was. And Billy Evans, sole proprietor, never failed to smile when he saw it.

He was still smiling when a dark blue Transit van flashed its headlights at him and, after a brief thumbs-up, Billy drove the Range Rover across the traffic flow and pulled up in front of the showroom windows, turning off the engine even before it had rolled to a halt. He sat there for a moment and then twisted towards his passenger, studying his face in an effort to try to work out what was going on inside his head. Billy had known Hawkins almost all his life but he'd never seen him in this kind of mood before and he was finding it a bit weird. 'Look, if you ain't interested, all you've got do is say so. It'll be sweet.'

More silence. And then, without looking round, and in a voice that sounded almost apologetic, Hawkins spoke. 'Look, it's not that I'm not interested, Billy. Honestly. But this ... well, this is all new to me. I mean, we play up a bit at football sure, and we've been in some serious shit over the years. But I ain't never broke the law before. Well, not the proper law anyway. And that's what you're asking me to do.' He paused for a moment, hoping for an interruption. But when none came, he turned to face Billy and continued. 'You might be used to bending the rules, but I ain't. And I gotta think about Julie. She might not be much of a wife, but she's the only one I've got. And you know what she thinks about you.'

Billy waited for a moment and then reached into his pocket for his cigarettes, lighting one for himself before passing the packet across the car. He did indeed know what Julie thought of him. And it wasn't good. When Billy had arranged the trip to Rome earlier that year, one thing he hadn't expected was that his best mate would end up spending a week in an Italian nick before getting deported. But to make matters even worse, when Hawkins had finally arrived home, he'd found a letter from his employers telling him that they were less than impressed to discover that one of their managers was involved with football hooliganism. As a result, he'd been sacked. Julie had gone ballistic. And when rumours about Billy's involvement with a stolen car ring began to circulate, she freaked, accusing him of setting her old man up to take the fall for him.

Although Hawkins had told him that he didn't see it like that, the truth was that to a certain extent, Billy did. When he'd been putting the trip together, he hadn't fully considered the implications for his friend and had felt guilty about what had happened to him ever since - especially as Hawk hadn't been able to find another job. And, after almost five months, Billy suspected that money was getting tight. He owed him. And he knew it.

'Look, Hawk, I understand what you're saying. Honest I do. And like I say, if you don't want in, then that's fine. I just thought you'd fancy getting back to work, that's all.'

Hawkins laughed, his voice loaded with irony. 'Ain't that the fuckin' truth. But this, Billy, this is a whole new ball game - not just for me, for all of us.'

Billy was about to reply when a slim, middle-aged woman suddenly appeared in front of the car, her dyed red hair perfectly suited to the expression of displeasure on her face. Billy looked at her for a second before winding down the window and sticking his head out. 'I'll be two minutes, Jill. OK?' With a final glare, she vanished back into the showroom. 'Jesus wept,' he said, as the electric motor pushed the window up, 'you'd think I worked for her, not the other way round.' He paused for a second and then returned his attention to his passenger. 'Look, Hawk, take a look around you. I'm thirty-three years old and I built all this from fuck all. D'you really think I could have done that without bending a few rules? No fucking chance. It's the way of the world, mate. The secret is knowing which rules to bend and how far to bend them without getting caught. And I know, Hawk. You know that better than anyone.'

'So why d'you need any more? This place must turn over a fucking fortune.'

Billy sniffed and returned his gaze to the rows of cars. 'Because I'm a greedy bastard, that's why. The day won't ever arrive when I look at my bank balance and think I've got enough. You can't have enough. Besides,' he twisted around in his seat, his voice suddenly excited, 'this ain't just for me. It's about all of us. The whole squad.'

Hawkins was about to speak when the red-haired woman appeared again and tapped on the bonnet. If anything, she looked even more irritated than before. 'I think you better sort her out before she kills us both.'

'All right. But take the motor and meet me back here in a couple of hours.' Billy pushed open the car door but, before he had both feet on the ground, he stopped and leaned back in. 'One way or another, we gotta do this, Hawk. It's much too good an opportunity.'

Hawkins leant back in his chair and rubbed his hands over his face. He felt incredibly tired all of a sudden and, coming on top of events this morning, sitting in the bright light and excessive heat of Billy Evans' office was not helping. 'So let me get this straight. You're *not* offering me a job.'

'No, Hawk,' said Billy with a shake of his head. 'Not a job. Like I said, I'm offering you a partnership. You and me, equal partners.'

'In the protection game?'

A sly grin spread across Billy's face. 'Not protection, Hawk. Security.'

Hawkins stood up, walked over to the large window that made up one side of the office and stared out over the rows of used cars. 'Security my arsehole. It's fucking extortion, Billy. That's what it is, extortion.'

Billy stared at the back of his head. 'Not the way I see it. We'd be a legit company offering a legit service.'

Hawkins spun round angrily and looked at Billy for a moment. He was beginning to wonder if he really knew him at all. 'Are you listening to yourself? You sound like you should be in some shite movie.'

A thin smile appeared on Billy's face as he stood up and walked over to a small fridge in the corner. Reaching in, he pulled out two chilled bottles of Budweiser and, after flicking the cap off one, returned to his seat and held the open bottle out across the desk.

'And besides,' continued Hawkins without moving away from the window, 'do you seriously think this Mickey James geezer is going to roll over and back down just because you fronted him up?'

'I told you all this,' responded Billy calmly. 'He's not backing down. It's a trade. Business.' He waved the bottle around, motioning for Hawkins to take it off him. 'Will you sit down and have a beer for fuck's sake. You're driving me up the bloody wall.' Hawkins sighed and returned to his seat. He took the bottle and gulped it noisily as Billy continued. 'Anyway, it's not the whole thing he's handing over, just the pubs.'

Hawkins pulled the bottle away from his mouth and let out an ironic laugh. 'Oh that's all right then.'

'Look,' said Billy, leaning forward on his elbows, his voice suddenly lower and more serious. 'Mickey James is many things, but he ain't stupid. Since he got out the nick, he's been pulling together a tidy little empire of back street pubs and small clubs all over the East End. Nothing major, just places that the big boys can't be arsed with. But he always knew that sooner or later he was going to tread on someone's toes and they'd come after him. What he didn't expect was that it would be us.'

Hawkins put down his bottle and folded his arms across his chest. 'Not us, Billy, you. Let's get that straight from the off.'

'Me, us, you, what the fuck does it matter? The point is that Mickey also knows that once you've got a foothold in a club the real money comes from selling stuff to the punters. If you're the one bringing it into the country as well, it's double bubble.'

Hawkins shook his head as he looked across at Billy. Ten minutes ago, when his best mate had let slip that he'd been importing pills on and off for the past two years, he'd been stunned. Now he just felt sick. For although he was well aware that a few of the lads took stuff when they were at games, the truth was that Hawkins despised drugs and the whole sad culture that went with it. He hated what it did to people and he hated what it was doing to his country. 'I gotta say, Billy, I've known you pull some stunts over the years, but you're bang out of order with this drugs shit. You know what I think about all that bollocks.'

'Yeah, OK. I know,' said Billy, holding up his hands. 'But that's the point, Hawk. Pills and dope are nothing but a shit load of trouble. If it ain't the Old Bill on your case, it's some other cunt. The bloody sooties, the chinks - shit, even the fucking Pakis are getting in on it now.'

'So if it's so much bloody grief, why not just stop?' said Hawk dryly.

Billy stood up and walked out from behind the desk. 'Because aside from the fact that it's a tidy earner, the contacts and routes I've got are a commodity, that's why. But gospel, Hawk, I've been looking to off-load them for a while. So if Mickey wants them, he can have them with my blessing.'

Hawkins picked up his bottle and finished it off. 'And you get what? The chance to run your own little protection racket?'

'Will you give all this *you* shit a rest? It's *us,* Hawk, us.' He took two cigarettes from a packet and, after lighting both, handed one to Hawkins. 'Look, the point is that we've got a chance here to do something that no other firm has ever done before. At least not properly. If we play it right, we'll be able to fund the tickets, the travel, the fucking lot. Shit, we'll even be able to do the beer-ups.' Billy paused for a second, an expression of excitement spreading across his face. 'CSS Security Ltd! It's fucking brilliant!'

Hawkins couldn't help but smile. They had talked about doing something like this for years, more often than not in the back of a van on the way back from some northern shit-hole. He glanced up at Billy, who was now standing over him. From the look on his face, you'd have thought he'd just won the lottery. 'This could work, Hawk. You know it could. And it could be the start of something fucking massive.'

After staring at him for a second, Hawkins took a long drag on his cigarette, stood up and walked back over to the window. He looked out across the cars for a moment and then turned round. 'I ain't saying I want anything to do with this. But, just out of curiosity. How?'

Billy laughed out loud and rubbed his hands together as he sat down at his desk. He knew his mate would see sense. 'Right,' he began, 'here's how I see it. In exchange for - well what I've got - Mickey has offered to hand over control of all the pubs he's got a hold over, but not the clubs. That's fair enough as far as I'm concerned 'cause it means we've haven't got to worry about doormen and any of that bollocks. Yes...?'

Hawkins nodded and drew on his smoke. 'You finish describing your grand plan first. Then I'll say my bit.'

'OK then. Well, he reckons he's got seventeen pubs so ...' He grabbed a calculator and began tapping in the numbers. 'Seventeen pubs at a hundred and fifty quid a pop, which is what he's taking out the St George, that's just over two and a half grand a week and ...' He stopped for a moment and looked up at Hawkins, his eyebrows raised in surprise. 'Fuck me! That's over a hundred and thirty-two thou a year!'

The two of them sat there in silence for a moment, each wrapped up in their own thoughts. 'Well?' said Billy, as he suddenly dived for the fridge and retrieved two more bottles. 'What d'you reckon?'

'Sounds easy when you say it quick,' said Hawk, taking his beer and flicking off the cap. 'Walk in, collect the money and walk out.'

'It *is* easy, Hawk. Everything's already in place. That's the beauty of it. All we gotta do is walk in and take it over. It's money for old rope.'

Hawkins took a mouthful of beer and after stubbing out what was left of his cigarette, shook his head. 'Call me naive, but aren't there one or two things you've overlooked here?'

'Such as?'

'Well, let's see...' He leant back in his chair and counted the points off on his fingers. 'Who's going to do the collecting? What happens to all the money? What happens if someone gets the arsehole and refuses to pay up? What happens if there's trouble in a pub and they want us to sort it out? What happens if the Old Bill come sniffing?' He leant forward. 'What, what, what. Do you really need me to go on?'

Billy looked at him for a moment and smiled. 'You're warming to this, aren't you? Come on, you twat, admit it. You're starting to think that this is a fucking blinding idea.'

'It has potential, I have to admit,' said Hawkins smarmily. 'But that ain't to say it could ever work. Or that I'd want to be a part of it.'

'OK then,' said Billy. 'Let's stop pissing around and give this some serious thought.' He stood up and began pacing up and down the room, his hands moving continuously as he spoke, adding visual substance to his words. 'First off, if we're gonna do it, there's no point pissing about and treating it as some kind of hobby. If we do that, pretty soon people would start taking us for mugs and we'd get trouble. No, we have to do it properly right from the off.'

'So how do we do that then?' asked Hawkins, not even attempting to hide the sarcasm in his voice.

Billy lifted his bottle from the desk and took a mouthful. 'We set up a proper and totally legit limited company as a front.' He turned and looked at Hawkins, a huge grin on his face.

'Fuck off! You wouldn't.'

'I fucking would, CSS Security Ltd. I told you, it's perfect.' They both burst out laughing at the idea of it. When they had calmed down, Billy took a mouthful of beer and continued, his voice increasingly excited. 'Two directors, you and me, with a few of the less law-abiding lads on part-time wages to do the collecting. After taking out the wages and expenses, the rest of the money goes straight back into the pot to fund the erm... social club. Yeah, I like that idea. That can be one of your jobs.'

'Oh, is that right?' said Hawkins with a sneer, leaning back in his chair. 'And how much would I be paid for all this work?'

Billy walked over and sat on the desk in front of him. Without a second's hesitation, he said 'Thirty thou a year. And I'll even lob in a decent motor. You might have noticed, I've got a few outside.'

Hawkins fell forward so that all four legs of his chair were firmly on the floor and looked at him in amazement. Not for the first time that day, he was stunned. 'You're fucking serious, aren't you?'

'I am, Hawk,' replied Billy. 'I'm deadly serious. This is just what we've been waiting for.'

The ringing of a telephone broke into their conversation and, after leaving it for what seemed an eternity to Hawkins, Billy cursed and picked it up. He listened for a few seconds, moved round to the back of his desk and, after pulling some papers from one of the drawers, began reeling off details of a Jaguar XK8.

Hawkins watched him for a second before standing up and moving back to the window. He had suddenly begun to realise that this was a lot more than one of Billy's pie-in-the-sky fantasies. He was actually deadly serious - and he couldn't get his head around any of it: the idea, the money, anything. It was all too much.

He grabbed his jacket from the chair and, without a word, walked out. Before Billy could catch him, Hawkins had vanished.

CHAPTER 5
Friday 24 March 2000
17.15

Graham Hawkins stepped out from the semi-darkness of the tube station and wasn't the least bit surprised to see a black Range Rover parked on double yellow lines opposite. The instant he saw it, the driver's door opened and Billy Evans stepped out. For once, the brash mannerisms and cocky smile were absent, replaced by an expression which could have been either embarrassment or concern.

After staring at him for a second, Hawkins gave up trying to work out which it was, lit himself a cigarette and crossed the road, climbing into the passenger seat without a word.

'How long you been waiting here, then?' he asked casually as Billy climbed into the driver's seat beside him.

'An hour or so. I had nothing better to do anyway,' he lied. 'Just thought I'd track you down and make sure you hadn't lost the plot.'

'Lucky guess, weren't it?' said Hawkins. 'I could have been anywhere.'

'You live round the fucking corner, Hawk. And you're skint.' He cringed even as he said it. 'Sorry. I didn't mean ...'

Hawkins sucked in a mouthful of smoke and let it drift slowly from his nostrils. When he spoke, his words were measured and almost monotone. 'Fair point, mate. And yeah, you're right. I'm skint. We're havin' to live on Jules' wages until my appeal and you know what nurses earn. Fuck all.'

Billy could have died. 'I didn't think, mate. Sorry. But you know, if you need anything to tide you over, you've only gotta say.'

'That'd be right.' He replied with an ironic laugh. 'Can you imagine what Jules would say if she found out I'd even told you about this? She'd go fucking mental.'

The car settled into silence as Hawkins slowly finished his cigarette. When Billy spoke, it was only to break his own feelings of unease. 'Listen,' he began nervously, 'sorry if I was a bit... intense back at the office.'

'Forget it, Billy,' interrupted Hawkins. 'You just freaked me a bit. I got all kinds of shit going on at home at the moment and you coming out with all that ... well, you know.'

Billy nodded. 'It was just a stupid idea, Hawk, that's all. You know what I'm like. All talk.'

'No, Billy, it wasn't a stupid idea. It's a fucking good idea.'

To say Billy was shocked was an understatement. 'You've changed your tune son. What's happened?'

'No I haven't, Billy. Like I say, it's a good idea. But not for me. I could never get involved in anything like that.' He wound the window down and flicked the butt of his cigarette out, watching it bounce around among the commuters before winding the window back up and staring out through the windscreen. 'It's funny, if you asked me to walk into a pub full of Millwall and front them up, I'd do it without a second thought. Shit, I've done it. But the idea of walking into an empty pub and asking the landlord for money - I'd shit myself. It's a whole different game, Billy. And you might understand it, but I don't. I could never square it with myself.'

Billy looked at him for a second. 'It doesn't have to be like that, mate. Not for you anyway.'

'You what?' asked Hawkins quietly.

'I've been thinking about it while I've been sat here,' Billy replied casually, careful not to get carried away again. 'Like I said earlier, there isn't any reason why we can't set this up as a fully legit, tax-paying company.'

Hawkins laughed. 'The business plan would certainly be worth looking at.'

'Look, it's complicated, but it would work, so just hear me out, OK?'

Without taking his eyes away from the windscreen, Hawkins nodded. So Billy continued. 'Right, the fact is that we have a chance to take over a business which has a guaranteed turnover of over a hundred and thirty-two grand. As I see it, at the moment overheads are negligible, all the profit goes into one man's pocket and the taxman gets zero. OK so far?' He

60

waited for a reaction but none came, so he carried on. 'Now, for a variety of reasons, we would prefer to run the business as a legit concern and put over half the profit into what we'll call a social fund.' He paused for a second and took a deep breath. 'There is, however, one small problem; one hundred per cent of the income will derive from what could be thought of as an "illegal" occupation. So, the key, from a purely business sense, is how to get over that problem and give the company a more erm ... traditional function.'

Hawkins nodded slowly. 'So how do we do that then? Just out of interest.'

'We don't,' said Billy, grabbing his smokes and lighting up. 'We disguise it.'

'We what?'

'We disguise it. Hide the true nature of the business behind a front. In this case, providing twenty-four-hour security for garage forecourts.'

Hawkins looked at him. 'At the risk of sounding a bit repetitive ... what?'

'Listen, Hawk, I've got contacts in the motor trade all over Essex and east London. Believe me, obtaining an iffy invoice for anything isn't a problem, especially when it's for a service that's tax deductible.'

The car fell into silence again. Hawkins remained staring out of the window, but Billy could sense he was thinking things through. Working out the possibilities and, also, the potential pitfalls. 'So let me get this straight,' he said thoughtfully, 'you walk into a pub, take a hundred and fifty off the landlord and then, to keep the books straight, invoice some dodgy garage in Southend. He then submits that invoice to his accountant as a legitimate expense, saving himself a hundred and fifty pounds on his tax bill.'

Billy smiled at him. 'In a nutshell, yeah. Clever or what?'

Hawkins shook his head and returned his gaze to the passing commuters. 'OK, let's assume for one second that it would work.'

'It would work,' interrupted Billy, smugly.

'But let's assume it for a minute, shall we. What about the pubs? Who's gonna collect the money? And you'd still have to provide a service of some sort or another. If people start kicking things off in places you were supposed to be looking after, sooner or later someone's gonna get pissed off.'

'Not a problem. As I said earlier, we'll use some of the lads on part-time wages to collect the money and everything else will be sweet. It'll look after itself.'

'How the fuck d'you make that out?'

'Look, Hawk, I checked it out with Mickey. All the pubs are within three miles of the Boleyn, which means that every fucker around there is West Ham anyway. And you know as well as I do, chances are, any lads likely to kick things off on a Friday night in any of those pubs are probably part of our lot. So once we put the word out, they're hardly likely to shit on their own doorstep are they? Not unless they want me on their case. In fact, I'd say it'd be quite the opposite. And even if they're not West Ham, they'll sure as shit know who we are. And would you want us on your case? No fucking chance.'

'But what if—'

'*If* someone steps out of line, they'll deserve what they get. And there are plenty of lads in The Squad who'll happily dish out a kicking should the opportunity present itself. It might have escaped your notice over the years, but not everyone among our happy band is as sensitive and caring as you and me.'

Hawkins sighed. Sitting in a Range Rover on double yellow lines, it was hard to find much of a flaw in Billy's plan. Although how much of that was down to his friend's enthusiasm and how much down to his own stress level was hard to work out. The truth was, he was desperate to get back to work and ease the financial burden at home. What little he and Julie had saved had all but gone, and although the dole was helping, they were beginning to worry about the mortgage. He'd even told his wife that he was going to stop going to away games but she'd told him that she wasn't having it, mostly, he suspected, because she knew what a negative effect it would have had on him. He smiled to himself as he thought of it, but the reality was that each time he walked out the door he was on a guilt trip because he knew she was counting every penny. Well, if this was a way to ease the strain on her, then so be it. Although Christ knows how she was going to react when he got home and told her Billy had offered him a job, especially a dodgy job. She'd got the arsehole this morning when he'd told her that he was off out with him today.

Hawkins leant back in his seat and rubbed his eyes. There was no choice. The problem of his wife and her opinion of Billy would have to be dealt with later. He sat up and looked across the car. 'So where do I come in then?'

Billy sat up and looked across the car with a huge grin. 'At the top, mate,' he replied, not even trying to conceal his excitement. 'Partners, remember?'

'Yeah, that's great, Billy. But what am I actually going to do?'

'It's simple, Hawk. Once I've sorted things out with Mickey, we set up the legit side of the business and you run it. The wages, invoices, everything will be down to you. Most important thing is the social club. You'll be like The Squad's official ticket agency and travel agent all rolled into one.' He stopped for a moment and then added, 'Anything dodgy, just leave it to me. OK?' He held out his hand, his eyes gleaming with the thrill of anticipation. 'It'll be the bollocks, Hawk. It really will.'

Graham Hawkins looked at him and, after a day of unease and anxiety, finally allowed a smile to spread across his face.

'What the fuck!' he said, before reaching across and grasping his friend's hand.

Julie Hawkins sat on the sofa and stared at her husband; hardly able to comprehend what she was hearing. 'Let me get this straight,' she began. 'Billy's offering you a job?'

Hawkins nodded. 'No, Jules, not a job. He wants us to be partners. Like I said, he puts up the capital; I manage the business.'

'But, a security company? Graham, you don't know anything about security.'

'Maybe, but I know about business. In case you'd forgotten, I did do two years' worth of business studies at college and I was running a senior department in a major corporation before they gave me the elbow.'

Julie took a sharp breath. 'And we all know who was to blame for that, don't we!'

Hawkins stood up and began pacing the room. 'Don't start all that shit again, Jules. I am a bloody grown-up you know. I can take responsibility for myself.'

She watched him for a few minutes and shook her head. Five years they had been married, and she had lived with his addiction to West Ham from day one. Not shared it; lived with it. It was the one part of his life that he kept totally secret from her. What happened at football, stayed at football, he had always said. And the truth was that she was more than happy with that. She knew full well what he was up to of course; she wasn't stupid. But this way was easier. Because if he didn't tell her, she didn't have to deal with it.

He stopped pacing and sat down beside her, taking her hands and staring into her eyes. 'Look, Jules, I've known Billy ever since I was a kid. He was best man at our wedding and I'd trust him with my life. For years we've talked about working together, and now we've got that chance. We'd be partners in our own business and with a decent salary as well. I know you're pissed off with him love, but we'd be mad to turn this down. Besides, you might not have noticed, but I haven't exactly got the job offers piled up.' He paused for a second before adding quietly, 'And I need to get back to work.' Julie Hawkins could hear the desperation sneaking into her husband's voice and felt a tear come into her eye. Over the past few weeks she'd begun to notice a change in him - a bad change. She was certain that depression was setting in, and, the longer he was out of work, the worse it was going to get. She lifted up his hands and kissed them. 'Just promise me one thing. This business you're setting up, it is...'

'Legit?' he offered. 'Yes, Jules, it's totally legit. D'you think I'd want to be involved if it wasn't? Christ, you know what I'm like. I panic if I'm double parked.'

She reached out and grabbed hold of him, pulling him close and squeezing him as hard as she could. Then, after a few seconds and without letting go, she said, 'OK, if you're happy, I'm happy. I'll even be nice to Billy for you.'

And, for the first time in months, she heard him laugh, and felt him relax.

CHAPTER 6
Sunday 26 March 2000
11.10

Julie Hawkins looked up from the newspaper and stared at her husband. He was in his typical Sunday morning pose; spread across the sofa with a cup of tea in one hand, a cigarette in the other and his eyes glued to *Soccer Extra*. The only difference between this and any other Sunday was that for once, unlike her, he was actually dressed, although, sadly, it wasn't for her benefit. She glanced towards the hall as the doorbell chimed for a second time.

'Will you get that?' she asked. 'I'm not dressed yet.'

'Jules,' he replied, gesturing at the television. 'It's Joe Cole...'

She looked at him for a second and shook her head before folding her paper and standing up. 'Bloody amazing,' she hissed as she walked along the hall, tightening the cord of her dressing gown as she pulled open the front door.

'Hello, Julie.'

She froze for a moment and then folded her arms across her chest. 'Well, well. You're early, aren't you? I thought you weren't picking him up till noon.'

Billy smiled nervously. It wasn't hard to work out that he had some bridges to build. 'I've got something for you. Well, it's for Hawk really but, well, you know...'

'You best come in then,' she said, moving to one side.

'No. Not yet. You need to come out here. And bring the old man with you.'

'I'm in my dressing gown - just in case you hadn't noticed. And it's bloody cold.'

'Please. It's important to me. Besides, you look all right.'

'Cut the flannel, Billy. It doesn't work on me.' She looked at him for a moment, struggling to work him out. 'What are you up to now? Is it going to mean more trouble for my old man?'

He looked genuinely embarrassed, and for a second she felt almost sorry for what she'd said.

'Look, if you want me to say sorry for what's happened, then fine. I'm sorry. OK? I know he's had a hard time, Julie, and I'm trying to make amends. Do you have to make it harder than it already is?'

'Who is it, Jules?'

She half-turned her head towards the living room, her eyes remaining fixed on the man standing on her doorstep. 'It's Billy. He wants to see us out here.'

Her husband wrenched himself away from the television and walked out into the hall. 'You're early. What's up? Sam thrown you out?'

Billy smiled and gestured at them to follow him as he walked back up the path. At the end, he stopped and turned. 'There you go!' he said triumphantly. 'Mercedes CI80, 1998, twenty thousand on the clock.' He rubbed his hands together, the archetypal car salesman. 'I've got to say it. This is a quality motor.'

Hawkins walked forward and stroked his hand along the bright red paintwork of the front bonnet, his hand instinctively drawn to the round badge sticking up from the front grille. He looked at Billy, then at his wife; an expression of shock on his face. 'I can't take this. How the bloody hell am I gonna afford it?'

Billy laughed and threw the keys to him. 'You don't have to, you daft prat. It's a company car. Well,' he added, glancing round at Julie, 'I'm not having my partner coming to work on the tube, am I?' He waited for a second and then walked forward, putting his arm around his friend's shoulders. 'Everything's down to the company, mate. There's even an account card for the juice in the glove box. Just remember to stick unleaded in it, OK?'

Hawkins turned round and looked first at his wife and then at Billy. His face was a picture of amazement. 'I don't know what to say ... I'm ...'

Billy thumped him on the shoulder. 'You haven't got to say anything. Just take Julie indoors for Christ's sake; she looks bloody freezing.'

Julie lay in the bath and stared at the ceiling. This time last week, her husband was out of work and she was having sleepless nights worrying about how they were going to pay the mortgage. Now, he was a partner in a new business and they had a Mercedes parked outside. So why wasn't she thrilled to bits? It hadn't taken her long to work it out. Because no matter what questions she asked, the answer was always the same: Billy.

The stupid thing was, from the moment she'd first met him and Samantha, she'd really liked them both and they'd got on really well ever since. Although it had always been pretty clear, even to her, that he was a bit dodgy. At his age, you didn't get what they had through hard work alone. But there was something about his cheek which made everyone he met warm to him. She had seen it a hundred times when the four of them had gone out together. And in truth, she had been no exception.

Yet while she had been happy to turn a blind eye to what he did for a living, as well as to what the two of them might or might not get up to at football, she had always been secretly relieved that her husband's occupation was entirely unrelated to him. Because that way, if anything had happened, she had been safe in the knowledge that it would have no real impact on either her husband, or her.

But then her worst fears had been realised in Rome and now, against her better judgement, the two of them were going to be working together. And although pleased for Graham, and delighted that they'd have a decent amount of money coming in, she couldn't really work out how she felt about it. It was as if she was walking a tightrope and someone had taken away the safety net.

Maybe she was wrong, and, as Graham had told her, this really was the start of something brilliant in their lives. She certainly hoped so. But what if she wasn't? What if what had happened in Italy was a foretaste of what being involved with Billy Evans was to bring?

She let out a loud groan and allowed herself to slide under the water. Either way, at this time on a Sunday morning, it was all too much to think about.

Graham Hawkins steered the Mercedes on to the A12 and put his foot down. He was in love. 'This is the dog's bollocks, Billy.'

'Forget it, mate,' he replied, with a wry smile. 'I'm happy to do it, honest. Besides, it'll make a change for you to drive to bloody games. It was gettin' on my tits ferrying you around. And don't forget, it's sunny Old Trafford next week.' He looked out of the window for a second and without turning round, asked, 'How much did you tell Jules?'

'Not much. Nothing about the pubs anyway. She'd fucking freak. As far as she's concerned, we're specialising in garages and car parks, that kind of thing.'

'Good.'

'What d'you tell Sam?'

'Sam!' exclaimed Billy, almost laughing as he spoke. 'Sam knows fuck-all, mate. Not about work or football. And that's the way I want it kept, thanks.'

The car settled into silence for a while, both men thinking about how their respective wives would react if they ever found out the truth about their husbands.

Billy broke the quiet. 'We need to get this whole thing moving today. Start picking out which lads we want to bring on board. I reckon, to start off, we only really need three. What d'you think?'

Hawkins nodded in agreement although he immediately felt uncomfortable. Try as he might to put it to one side, he knew full well that the legality of the whole operation was going to cause him problems in the weeks to come. In some ways, he hoped it always would. 'I've been thinking about it already,' he said. 'Most of the lads wouldn't want to know anyway. Jobs, morals, annoying stuff like that.'

'So? Who d'you think?' asked Billy.

'PJ for one. He's a clever bleeder and doesn't give a shit what he does as long as he earns. Stretch is pretty much the same, and Geoff. Nothing fazes him, so he'd be perfect.'

A slight smile appeared on Billy's face. 'I thought the same. But would Geoff do it? You know him better than me.'

'I reckon so,' replied Hawk, flicking his eyes from mirror to mirror as he tried to avoid a Renault pulling up on his inside. 'Look at this daft cunt!'

Billy turned to his left to look at the car alongside them. Despite the fact that there was only the driver inside, claret and blue scarves hung from each of the back windows as symbols of the driver's affection. Billy watched him for a moment and shook his head. 'Fucking scarfers. They should never have scrapped care in the community.'

'Fucking good job they did, I reckon. Who else would watch Millwall?'

Billy laughed and, after a final shake of his head, turned back to face Hawkins. 'So, what about Geoff, then?'

'Well, I know he's done a fair bit of doorman stuff, although I don't know what he's up to now. Best thing to do is ask him.'

'OK,' said Billy. 'We'll sound them out today. After the game.'

'What about Mickey?'

'Deal's done, mate. Spoke to him yesterday. His lads'll do the rounds this week and then, the week after that, they'll take one of ours round and er ... introduce them.'

'Who? You?' asked Hawkins, desperately hoping his name wasn't in the frame.

Billy looked at him for a second and then leant across and punched him in the arm. 'Don't worry, you twat. I'm not gonna ask you. Leave it to me. I'll sort that out.' He paused for a second, seemingly embarrassed to carry on. 'Listen Hawk, I know it's stating the obvious, but it's best said. Softly, softly with, this, OK? The less people who know about it the better. At least at the start.'

Hawkins nodded but didn't reply. He couldn't have put it better himself.

Billy and Hawkins stood in silence and smiled as they surveyed the front of the St George some thirty metres along the street. It was clearly rammed solid. Not only were there a dozen or so lads leaning against the wall outside, but the noise pouring from the double doors, propped open to provide an escape route for the cigarette smoke, was ridiculous, echoing off the high walls and filling the street. It was a combination of shouting, singing, laughter and jukebox: the theme song of the match-day pub. 'Word obviously got around, then,' said Billy, with a laugh.

'I guess you could say that,' replied Hawkins, glancing back up the street in the direction they had just come. He caught the eye of one of the two young lads standing at the end, and lifted a hand in acknowledgement. He'd done his share of spotting in the past; so had Billy, standing there for hours on end, keeping an eye out for any unwelcome visitors. And it wasn't much fun. But at that age, it was a way to become involved and to get your face known. 'You know it'd be almost impossible for anyone to hit this place, don't you?' he said. 'They'd be seen before they got anywhere near it.'

Billy nodded. It was indeed a perfect setting. The street was quite narrow and about a hundred metres long in total, with a ninety-degree bend about two-thirds of the way along. The shorter of the stretches joined on to a residential street, while the longer one fed out on to the main road. It also had a slight kink in it, which had the effect of keeping it hidden from prying and unwelcome eyes. More importantly, almost one entire side was taken up by the rear of a large warehouse, while the other comprised a mixture of old houses converted to flats and offices. The only other building was the pub, about halfway along the longer stretch. If anyone wanted to have a go, no matter what direction they came from, they would have a fifty-yard dash first; plenty of time to get out of the pub and at them.

Like Hawkins, Billy had been pleased to see the two lads as he'd walked into the street. Not that it was really necessary against a club like Wimbledon, but it showed that someone was thinking. Sunday games were always dodgy. You never know who might have a pop. And even if they didn't, it was good practice. 'Notice one other thing?'

Hawkins laughed. 'Yeah, no fucking Old Bill. I bet they're all at the Boleyn, wondering where we've got to.'

Billy smiled and thumped his friend on the back. 'I bet Pat is a bit pissed off as well. His profits'll be through the bloody floor. Come on, I need a beer.'

The two of them made their way over to the pub and forced their way into the throng. It was manic inside, the noise level almost constituting an assault. At one end of the room, a group of men were shouting abuse at the television as Sky Sports delivered the early Nationwide game, while at the bar another crowd were talking loudly about plans for the trip to Old Trafford the next week. Billy shook his head and smiled to himself. He loved pre-match pubs: the banter, the laughs, the atmosphere; there was nothing like it anywhere else.

A shout from the far corner somehow managed to penetrate the chaos and they turned to see both PJ and Stretch standing on a table and motioning them over. Billy raised his hand to show that they'd heard and changed direction to head towards them. It took an age, for not only did the two of them know everyone, everyone knew them.

They had just about made it halfway when another shout caught Billy's attention and he turned to see Sal standing at the bar. After telling Hawk to go on, he changed direction again and headed towards her. 'All right, gorgeous. How's tricks?'

She smiled at him and leant forward to speak, almost having to shout to be heard. 'Busy. You might have noticed.'

He stood back and held out his hands. 'See, I told you I'd look after you.'

'Yeah, I need to talk to you about that,' she said. 'You got a minute?'

'What? Now?'

She raised an eyebrow, reached forward and lifted up the hatch in the counter. Billy shrugged his shoulders and walked through to the kitchen. 'Now it is then,' he said out loud to himself.

Once they were out of the noise, he stopped and turned to face her. 'Well?'

She looked around nervously and then said, 'What's happening with Mickey James?'

He looked at her for a moment before reaching forward and putting his arm on her shoulder. 'Don't worry, Sal. It's sorted. Honestly.'

'No, Billy, that's not good enough,' she replied angrily. 'I need to know what's happened. We've been shitting a brick since Thursday night, wondering if his lads are going to walk through the door at any minute and turn the place over. You put us in that position, so now you bloody well tell me what's going on.'

Billy pulled his arm away and reached into his pocket for his cigarettes. He offered one to her and then lit them both. 'You've got nothing to worry about, Sal. Honestly. I've taken over.'

She took the cigarette out of her mouth and looked at him, her expression one of total surprise. 'You what?'

'Mickey and me did a deal. He keeps his clubs; I take the pubs.'

'Just like that?' she said.

'Pretty much,' replied Billy calmly.

She put her cigarette in her mouth and left it hanging there while she ran her fingers through her hair. 'So what you're sayin' is that, instead of having his hands in my till, now I've got yours.'

Billy looked at her, stung by the insinuation. 'D'you really think I would do that to you, Sal? After all this time?'

She turned to face the bar as the noise suddenly increased.

Someone on Sky Sports had obviously just scored. 'Billy, I don't know what to think. Honestly I don't.'

He took a deep breath and smiled at her. 'Look, Sal, I've known you and Steve for more years than I care to remember and the two of you are some of my mum and dad's oldest mates. If I'd have let that bastard carry on ripping you off, I'd never have been able to look the old man in the eye again, so that's why I stepped in and put the block on it. I'm certainly not about to start doing it myself.'

'So why take over all the others then?'

'It was just easier to do that than get in a war I didn't want and didn't need. Besides, you'd have been in the firing line. And I couldn't do that to you.'

She took the cigarette from her lips and smiled at him. But the smile was somehow more genuine than usual. 'Thanks, Billy. I needed you to tell me that. But do one thing for me, will you?'

'Anything, Sal. You know that.'

'Just be careful, that's all. There's some nasty bastards out there and this isn't football or dodgy motors you're pissing about with. This is serious. I don't want you gettin' hurt.'

Billy looked at her for a second and then gave her a broad wink. 'Don't worry about me, Sal. I can look after myself. And besides,' he took a final draw on his cigarette, 'if I have any hassle, I've got a few lads to help me out. You might have noticed, they seem to have taken over your pub.'

The archetypal match-day smell of burnt onions mixed with warm diesel fumes filled the air as Billy and the others wandered along in the direction of the ground. Purposely late to make their customary and inevitably conspicuous entrance, they were in a particularly jovial mood - thanks in no small part to the quality, not to mention quantity, of the beer in the St George.

'Hang on,' said PJ, as he stopped by a hot-dog stall. 'I've gotta eat something or I'll puke.'

'Fuck me, PJ,' moaned Geoff. 'Now you've started me off. Get me one, will ya. I'll give you the money at the ground.'

'Make that three,' added Hawk.

Billy wandered over and after taking a long, loud sniff added: 'Four. No onions on mine, though.'

Stretch stopped and shook his head. 'Jesus wept,' he said irritably. 'Check out the time lads. Bloody kick-off's in ten minutes.'

'Yeah,' interrupted Darren. 'Stretch wants to see if he can get on telly today. His mum's watching, ain't she boy!'

'Bloody hell...' laughed Geoff. 'You should have said. If your old mum wants to see her little boy on the box I'll show her that CCTV film we got from Filbert Street. She'd ...' He paused in mid-sentence and stared out across the road. 'Heads up. What've we got here?'

They all turned round and stared through the traffic, instantly spotting three casually dressed lads nervously trying to work their way through the crowd on the opposite pavement. 'Fuck me,' laughed Geoff. 'It's Wimbledon's firm!'

'Hang on,' said PJ, the serious tone in his voice and concerned expression on his face instantly stopping the others short. 'We need to be careful. They might be some of those nasty Saints lads come back for Billy.' Before anyone could react, he stepped forward and put his arm round their main man. 'Don't worry son,' he added, all the while maintaining his false concern as the others burst out laughing. 'We'll look after you.'

'Why don't you just fuck off and die!' replied Billy as he pushed him off and grinned. 'Christ, if I had a quid for every time I've saved your arse, I'd never have to work again.'

Hawk shook his head. 'You don't anyway, you ponce.'

'Here, watch this! I'll put the shits up these gimps!' laughed Darren, grabbing PJ's hot-dog before running off across the road and melting into the crowd behind them.

'He's such a bloody idiot,' laughed Hawk. 'Come on.'

The five of them began moving, keeping pace with Darren as he hurried to catch up with his prey. Suddenly, he broke into a trot until he was alongside the Wimbledon fans.

Beaming widely at them, he pointed out the others across the road; their anxious glances were returned by Billy and the others. Only when they sprinted away from him did Darren stop talking and burst out laughing. The three lads slowed down only when they were within arm's length of a Transit van full of the Met's finest.

'Did you see them boys run?' he laughed as he rejoined the others. 'Is there anything funnier than the sight of some South London chancers shitting it? I don't think so.'

Billy shook his head and carried on walking. The six of them continued to laugh and joke until they arrived at the main gates. He was searching for his ticket when a familiar voice stopped him in his tracks and he looked up to see a heavily built policeman standing in front of them, his black hair and thick moustache giving him an uncanny resemblance to David Seaman, the Arsenal goalkeeper. If it wasn't for the uniform and an extra three stone, they could almost have been twins.

'Well, well. If it ain't Mr Roberts,' said Darren. 'Hang on, I thought the Gooners had Leicester today - you've not been dropped again, have you Dave?'

'Bit late today, ain't we lads?' asked the policeman, ignoring Darren's remark.

'Well,' said Billy, as he moved towards the front of the group. 'We like to keep our favourite liaison officer on his toes. How is the grassing business these days?'

Roberts nodded slowly as a slight smile appeared on his face. 'Not too bad, as it goes. I hear you've moved pubs.'

'Bloody hell!' exclaimed Billy. 'The old taxpayers get value for money out of you, don't they! How much did that little snippet cost?' A muffled roar went up from the stadium, signifying that the teams had come out, and the others instinctively began to move towards the turnstiles, leaving Billy and Roberts staring at each other.

'One day Evans,' muttered the policeman after a pause. 'You'll push your luck too far and I'll have you.'

Billy looked him up and down and shook his head. 'Better men than you have tried, Gary old mate, much better. And yet after all this time I'm just about to walk into Upton Park without a stain on my record and they're ... well, fuck knows where they are. So what does that tell you?'

'About them?' asked Roberts. 'Or about you?'

'Take your pick,' laughed Billy as he began to walk away. 'Either way, I don't really give a toss.'

Hawkins pulled the Mercedes into Billy's gravel drive and turned off the engine. It was getting late and every light in the house was blazing. 'Look at that. It's like bloody Southend sea front.'

'Stop moaning, you tight arse. You can afford it.'

Billy nodded. 'Fair enough.' He rubbed his eyes and then looked at Hawk. 'So, we all set for the morning then?'

'Yeah, I reckon so. I spoke to the lads and asked them if they fancied doing a bit of debt collecting and they're up for it. They're coming over to the car lot in the morning, so we can talk things through properly. Once they're happy, I guess we can start work on sorting out the rest.'

'Well then, partner,' said Billy as he pushed the door open, 'I'll see you at nine o'clock sharp. We've got money to make, my son. Lots of money.'

CHAPTER 7
Monday 27 March 2000
09.00

Billy pushed open the door and walked into his secretary's office to find Hawkins sitting quietly by the window waiting for him.

'What you out here for?' he laughed. 'And what's with the suit? You in court later?'

Hawkins felt himself blushing and coughed to cover his embarrassment. 'Well... I wasn't sure ... and ... you know.' He nodded in the direction of the woman sitting behind the desk working her way through the mail.

Billy raised a hand in silent apology and turned to his secretary. 'Mornin', Jill. Put the kettle on and come through, will you? There's something I need to talk to you about.'

'The kettle's always on,' she said, her voice a mixture of arrogance and sarcasm. 'Would your friend like a drink?'

'Er, no thanks,' Hawk replied nervously. 'I'm fine ... honestly.'

'Come through then, Hawk,' said Billy, walking through into the office and dumping a briefcase on the floor. 'And shut the door behind you, will you?'

Hawkins followed him into the office and looked around. The cleaners had obviously been busy because it was spotless. But it wouldn't stay like that for long. It never did. 'Jesus, she scares the shit out of me.'

'Me too, mate,' whispered Billy. 'But she's the best secretary I've ever had. And she knows the score. I tell you what, if the Old Bill ever got her talking, I'd be fucked.'

'They wouldn't dare, would they?'

Billy laughed, and lowered his voice even further. 'First two weeks she was working for me, I thought she had PMT. It was only when she actually got it that I realised what a stroppy cow she is!'

A knock on the door interrupted them, and Jill walked in with a West Ham mug full of hot coffee in one hand and a pile of letters in the other. She dumped both on the desk and stood there, waiting.

'Jill, this is Hawki... I mean, Graham Hawkins. Me and him are going into business together.'

Hawkins stood up and held out his hand. She looked at him for a second and then reached out and lightly shook it.

'What kind of business?' she asked, turning back to Billy. 'And what will it have to do with me?'

'We're setting up a company called CSS Security Ltd. Graham here will be doing most of the work and will be using the back office once I sling David out. The only impact it will have on you is that for the first few weeks, I'll be a bit scarce.'

She nodded and then smiled. 'That's fine then. If you need anything, stationery, information ...' she said, turning to Hawkins, 'just ask and I'll see what I can do.'

'Thanks, I appreciate that,' he replied, well aware from the tone of her voice that he was pretty much on his own. 'But I'll try not to bother you too much. I'm sure you've got more than enough to do without having to help me out.'

Billy looked at them and shook his head. 'Thanks, Jill. Give David a shout, will you? I'd best break the news to him that he's moving back downstairs.'

When she had left, Billy took out his cigarettes and threw one to Hawk. 'OK, what's the plan?'

Hawkins walked over to the desk and sat down. 'Who's David?'

'He looks after the servicing side of things. Nice bloke actually, sits in the Bobby Moore stand. He's been using the back office while his was being decorated. Trouble is, *he* was supposed to be doing the decorating, and, all the time he's been up here he hasn't bothered. Six months the bastard's got away with it, so he can't really complain.' He lit his cigarette and blew out a lungful of smoke. 'So ...'

'Well, the lads are coming in later. So we'll need to talk to them and work out hours and wages, shit like that. I'll sort out some stationery this morning and we'll need some phones. I reckon we best use one landline for the office and stick to the old "pay-as-you-talk" stuff for the rest. That way, if anything happens, no one can trace them back to us. I also think we should have a pager.'

'What for?' asked Billy, leaning forward and taking a mouthful of coffee.

'Well, I reckon that if someone at one of the pubs needs to get hold of us in a hurry, a pager is better than a phone. It's also easier to carry and a bit more discreet.'

'Good thinking,' replied Billy with a nod.

'I'll sort all that anyway. I know a few lads in the game so we should be able to get hold of a pager with an untraceable number. And I'll go and see Paul at the ground as well; pick up the tickets for Saturday.'

Billy finished his coffee and stubbed out his cigarette. Paul was probably one of the most important people either of them knew, for he was their sole contact inside the club; the man who made sure that they got tickets for every single away game. It was a risky business for him, as every time he supplied stuff to them, he was putting his job on the line. But he was happy to take that risk. And even though he'd never thrown a punch in his life, Billy and the others still thought of him as being one of The Squad. He knew that; that's how he got his particular buzz.

'OK, I'll have a chat with my accountant this morning and get him to set up the company. And I'll sort out a list of garages to contact. We'll start working through them tomorrow, but that won't be a problem. Anything else we ain't thought of yet?'

Hawkins shifted uneasily in his chair for a moment. 'Yeah, there is one thing. We need to discuss the practicalities of this.'

'The what?'

'We need to know what we do if one of the pubs has something they want sorting. Who do we use and how do we do it?'

Billy leant back in his chair. 'I spoke to Mickey about that. He reckons that he just leaves most stuff to the Old Bill.

Remember, these are just small boozers not big pubs, so most things happen on a Friday or Saturday night. The only stuff he has problems with are the odd mouthy cunt and a few dealers who don't know when they've outstayed their welcome. If the landlords ever complained, Mickey used to send a couple of lads round to sort them out. But don't worry about all that. You just get this end moving and leave the rest to me.'

Hawkins relaxed a little. He was still very uneasy about that side of things. 'When you gonna tell the others?'

'Wednesday, at the St George. That's when I'll tell The Cabinet. They're the only ones who need to know for now. Once things get established, then we'll start to filter things out. But like I say, the fewer people who know, the better.'

The three men sat and stared across the office at Billy and Hawkins, their expressions ranging from mild amusement through to total apathy. 'So ...?' asked Billy. 'What d'you reckon then?'

Stretch scratched the back of his head and looked around the room. 'Seems sound to me, Billy. What's the wages like?'

'Well, I reckon that we're looking at no more than two afternoons a week, Wednesday and Thursday probably, at a hundred and fifty quid each a day. That's for just two of you. Anything else is over and above that.'

'Like what?' asked Stretch.

'Nothing, we hope,' said Hawkins. 'But if anyone's causing grief for the er ... clients, it'll have to be sorted.'

PJ laughed. 'Clients my arse.'

'No.' Billy snapped. 'That's exactly what they are, PJ. And don't forget that. As far as anyone is concerned, this is a business. It's not a fucking scam.'

'OK,' replied PJ, holding up his hands. 'I was just saying, that's all.'

Geoff leant forward and took a cigarette from a packet on the desk. 'So, what happens to the rest of the money?'

Hawkins looked at him and smiled. He had placed a silent bet with himself that Geoff would be the one to ask that. Behind that dumb exterior, he always had been a shrewd bastard. 'Billy and me are taking a wage. Billy set it up, after all, and I'll be running the business side. As for the rest, after your wages, we'll be using that to fund The Squad.' He waited for a reaction, which wasn't long in coming. And again, it came from Geoff.

'You what?'

'It's simple. All the profit from this will go back into providing tickets for The Squad. I haven't worked out all the detail yet, but we reckon that the income will pay for twenty season tickets as well as twenty tickets for every away game.'

'And who'll get them then?' asked Stretch.

'The Cabinet will all get free ones,' interrupted Billy. 'And the rest will be sold cheap to close mates or given to observers from other mobs.'

The room fell into silence for a moment. 'What that means is that we'll each save over twelve hundred quid a season on tickets alone. Any spare cash after that will go towards travel expenses,' added Hawkins for effect.

'Fuck me!' said PJ. 'You have been busy boys this week, ain't you.' He paused for a moment and then smiled. 'Well, I can't speak for these two, but you can count me in.'

Billy pushed open the door of the back office to find Hawkins in his shirtsleeves, moving the furniture around in an effort to release a bit of space and make the place feel a bit more comfortable. To call it cramped would have been an understatement. 'Very domestic. I'm quite touched. Did David say anything?'

'In between the grunts,' replied Hawkins, standing up and wiping the sweat from his brow with a piece of blue tissue. 'I kind of got the impression that he wasn't best pleased.'

'He'll get over it,' said Billy. 'Listen, just leave all that shit. I'll bung the cleaners a few quid to sort it out tonight.'

'Now you fucking tell me!' he gasped. Sitting down on the desk with a thump. He reached over and picked up a can of Coke, draining what was left inside in a single gulp. 'Listen, I called my mate. He says we can have whatever we need phonewise. And BT will be putting in a new line on Wednesday. That all right?'

'Hawk,' said Billy, walking in and closing the door behind him, 'I'm not your boss. I'm your partner. You don't have to report to me. Just do what you've got to do.'

'Sorry, mate,' said Hawkins sheepishly. 'I'm just not used to it... you know.'

Billy walked forward and patted him on the arm. 'Get used to it. It'll be sound, mate. Honestly. Now, I'm off to see the accountant, OK?'

Hawkins nodded. 'Yeah, I'd best get up the ground before Paul pisses off.'

Billy reached into his pocket and pulled out an envelope. 'There's a couple of grand in there,' he said, tossing it on to the desk. 'Start-up money. Get whatever you need and sling the receipts in a box somewhere. I'll see you back here at about four o'clock, OK? We'll go for a quick beer before we knock off.'

He was almost out the door. Hawkins called him back. 'Er... haven't you forgotten something?'

Billy looked at him for a second. 'Oh, shit,' he said, reaching into his pocket and pulling out his wallet. 'Thirty pounds to watch football. It's a fucking disgrace.'

Hawkins climbed into the Mercedes and gently pulled the door behind him, failing, for the first time since he'd had the car, to acknowledge the satisfying 'thunk' as it shut. Instead, he stared out of the windscreen for a moment and then pulled out his mobile. 'Fucking answerphones,' he cursed.

After what seemed an age, the bleep sounded. 'Billy, the second you get this, call me. You're not gonna believe what I've just found out!'

He threw the phone onto the passenger seat and, with a final glance at Upton Park, started the Mercedes and headed back towards Romford.

Hawkins jumped up as Billy walked into the office. 'Where the fuck have you been? Didn't you get my message?'

Billy looked at him in surprise. 'What message?'

'The one I left on your fucking phone!'

'Oh bollocks!' He pulled his phone from his pocket and held it up. 'Sorry, mate. Forgot to turn it on after the accountants. He's sorting us out by the way. Reckons it'll take a week or so.'

'Look, fuck that,' Hawkins said, barely able to contain his excitement. 'Sit down and listen to this.'

Billy walked in and closed the door. But even before he could make it across the room, Hawkins had started. 'I was with Paul at the ground, getting the tickets for Saturday, and on the desk in his office is this memo, right...?'

'Whoa, slow down a minute. What were you doin' in Paul's office? I thought he always brought the tickets out, just in case anyone recognised you.'

Hawk threw out his arms in exasperation. 'I don't bloody know! I called him when I was outside as usual and he told me to come in. Jesus wept, does it matter?'

'Obviously not,' replied Billy.

'Look, just shut up and listen,' said Hawkins bluntly. He paused for a moment and then began pacing around the room, all the time keeping his eyes firmly fixed on Billy. 'This memo, it's only about security at Upton Park.'

'So ... what about it?' asked Billy.

Hawkins stopped pacing and leant forward with his hands on the desk. He could barely contain himself. 'So... the contract's up for renewal!'

'What contract?'

'The whole fucking thing, mate. Stewarding, car parks, VIP shit, the lot.' He stood up and lit himself a cigarette. A huge smile spread across his face. 'They've been inviting companies to bid for it for the past three months.'

Billy put his hand to his mouth and stared into space for a few seconds, deep in thought. 'What did Paul say?'

'Nothing. He didn't have to. Not after he'd copied this lot for me anyway.' Hawkins reached into a drawer, pulled out an A4-sized envelope and slid it across the desk.

'What is it?' asked Billy, picking it up but not bothering to look inside.

'That, my son, is a copy of the document giving full details of the current contract, including the finances, as well as information on how to tender for the next one. It's all there. Everything we need. Paul copied it for us.'

Billy dropped the envelope on the desk and stood up. For once, he was completely on the back foot and almost at a loss for words. 'You can't be fucking serious! Put in a bid for West Ham's security?'

'Why not?' asked Hawkins smugly. 'We're a legitimate security company, ain't we?'

'Who, in case you've forgotten, haven't even been in business one day yet.'

Hawkins looked at him for a second, surprised at his response. 'What's that got to do with it?'

'Because it'd be...' He stopped, took a deep breath and shook his head. 'I can't think straight in here. Come on.'

By the time they had walked through the building to his office, Billy had begun to get his head around the enormity of what Hawkins had given him. If they could pull it off, it would be the ultimate irony: the local hooligans in charge of their own club's security. He grabbed two beers from the fridge and, after handing one to Hawkins, lit himself a cigarette.

'OK, let me have a look through that.'

When he had finished, Billy put the papers back into the envelope and pushed it to one side before picking up the notepad on which he had written a list of points. He looked through it, thought for a moment, and then wrote a few more down. Hawkins watched impassively. He had seen him do stuff like this before and it never failed to impress. Billy had the capacity to absorb information like a sponge but, more importantly, he could spot every single flaw or possible problem; be it in a business document or a hastily constructed plan in the back streets of north London. It's what made him such a good businessman and a great mob leader.

He finally stopped writing and dropped the pad on the desk before taking a drink from his bottle and lighting up.

'OK,' he said, reaching forward and lifting his pad again. 'Let's leave the obvious problems until the end and go over the business ones first. Bids have got to be in by this Friday. Could we do it in time?'

'No problem,' replied Hawkins confidently.

'How many others are tendering?'

'According to Paul, they've only had two so far. One from Mirren Events Ltd, who are the outfit in at the moment, and the other from a company based in north London. But Paul reckons that their tender is too high and everyone expects the existing company to retain the contract even though their costs have risen.'

'How come?'

'Minimum wage. They have to pay people a bit more, that's all.'

Billy laughed. 'No, you tosser. How come they're expected to keep it?'

'Oh, I don't really know. Paul kind of hinted that the club have been happy, so why would they want to change? But I didn't really push it, in case he got too twitchy. It was hard enough convincing him to give us what he has.'

'Bloody cheek. We behave ourselves and some other bastard gets rich. So who are Mirren Events then?'

'I don't know much more than what's in there really,' said Hawkins, pointing to the envelope. 'They've held it for the Last two years and are based in Walthamstow. Like I say, I didn't push it with Paul.'

'Best find out then,' said Billy. 'So ... any chance any other bids are going to turn up?'

Hawkins shook his head. 'Doesn't look like it. It wasn't exactly publicised that much.'

'OK, say we did go for it, and won it, how would we manage?'

'Well, I can't see how they could suddenly find other jobs for all those people if they lost the contract. So I reckon we'd get away with re-hiring the people already working there.'

'What about all the CCTV stuff we'd need?' asked Billy, impressed that his friend was able to answer all these questions off pat.

'According to Paul, it all belongs to the club anyway. We'd just need people to operate it.'

'The people already doing it, I suppose,' said Billy with a grin.

'Exactly.'

Billy stood up and walked over to the window. He looked out over the car lot for a second and without turning round, started again. 'OK, the two big obstacles: the club and the Old Bill. They're not stupid. If a bid landed on their desk and they thought we were involved in any way, they'd sling it in the bin without a second's hesitation.'

Hawkins shrugged his shoulders. 'Well, CSS Security is a give-away for a start. Maybe the first thing we should do is change that.'

'Shit! I liked that idea. But you're right, I guess,' said Billy. 'It would spike it from the off. How about,' he paused for a second, 'St George Security?'

Hawkins laughed. 'Why not? It'd keep the right-wingers happy if nothing else. But that still don't solve the problem of us, mate. In case you'd forgotten, you're not exactly a favourite son down at Scotland Yard. I don't suppose I am either.'

Billy walked over to his desk and lit another cigarette. 'So, what do we do?'

'Maybe it's worth having a chat with Roberts.'

'What! The football liaison copper? What the fuck for?'

'Sound him out.'

'About what?'

'What if,' said Hawkins thoughtfully, 'we went to him and told him that we'd had enough, and wanted to wipe the slate clean.'

'Yeah,' said Billy sarcastically. 'I can see him swallowing that one.'

'No, I'm serious. If we can convince him that we're genuine, and that us winning this contract would solve all the security problems at a stroke, and permanently, I reckon he'd listen. After all, he knows better than anyone that the old days are gone now. And we're hardly gonna shit on our own doorstep are we?'

Billy looked at him and shook his head. 'Hawk, he's a cunt. He hates us as much as we hate him. And if he can shaft us, he'd do it without a second's hesitation.' He turned back to the window and stared out. 'No, what we've got to do is give this some thought, and fast. But if we don't get this bid in by Friday, we won't even be in the frame. So, you get on with that, and leave everything else to me.'

Once Hawkins had returned to his own office, Billy sat and reflected on what had been happening. Having an iffy security firm was one thing, but bidding to take over the contract at Upton Park was something else. He never usually liked to think that anything was beyond him, but in this instance, it might well be. Still, Hawk was happy and it would be a laugh to see how far they could get with it - if only for when he threw it out on to the hooligans' grapevine. It would certainly do wonders for their reputation. He'd never heard of anyone trying to pull a stunt like this before.

But what if they could pull it off? The figures Paul had given them showed that there was a lot of money involved but, equally, the possibilities for The Squad were major. He'd seen enough stewards in action in recent years to know that many of them were former lads who at some clubs were no more than an approved firm. The idea of having the law backing you up as you waded in was not unattractive - especially inside the ground. It'd be just like the good old days again.

He smiled at the thought of it and then, after hesitating for a moment, reached up on to his shelf and took down a copy of *Yellow Pages*. After flicking through it for a minute, he found what he was looking for and began dialling the number. 'Fuck it!' he said out loud. 'Let's give this a decent shot.'

'Hello ... is that Mirren Events? Oh good. My name's Evans, of W. Evans Executive Motors in Romford. I'm looking to change the security firm who cover my premises. Can you give me some information about your company, please?'

Ten minutes later, he picked up his mobile and made another call. 'Mickey. It's Billy. Listen, mate, I need a favour. Yeah, another one. You ever heard of a geezer called Ian Mirren?'

Billy sat in the upstairs room of the St George and waited for his words to sink in. Even Hawk looked a little shocked, although he'd known exactly what was going to be said.

'So let me get this straight,' said Stretch. 'You want us to go up to Old Trafford on Saturday, mobbed up, and put on a show. Then, in ten days time, when the Geordies come down, you want to start a war with them.'

'Yep,' said Billy smugly. 'That's exactly what I want.'

'Fucking respect!' replied Stretch, settling back in his seat and smiling. 'It's about fucking time.'

The room suddenly burst into excited noise as the others began to discuss this unexpected revelation. Billy let them get on with it for a few minutes and then calmed them down. 'OK, listen. Let's get a few things straight about Saturday, shall we? This is all about showing every mob in the country that we're still on the scene and, when we fancy it, we ain't afraid to take it to anyone, anywhere. So, I want as many lads up there as possible and I want them taking liberties. But the main thing is that we have to be seen to be trying to hit their main lads. If we can actually get to them, all the better.'

'Hit Wetherspoons,' said PJ matter-of-factly. 'The Salford lot are usually in there and they're the main faces at United these days. If we turn them over in their own pub, everyone'll sit up and take notice.'

'Never do it,' replied Stretch. 'Old Bill will be all over it like a fucking rash.'

Billy broke in. 'Well, let's get our heads around it. They're not gonna be expecting anything other than a normal show, so we've got that on our side. But I want it done properly. I don't want us corning out of this looking like some two-bob firm. That means no hits on places full of scarfers, and we'll have to avoid the Old Bill for as long as possible. Once they get on to us, it'll be game over. And, if either of those things happen, the Mancs will claim a result. That'll make me very unhappy. '

'Why now?' asked Geoff.

'We've been too quiet lately, that's why,' said Billy, with a sideways glance at Geoff. 'Sometimes I think the coppers have got us in their pocket the way they're all over us every bloody week. Well, bollocks to that. It's about time we rattled a few cages.'

'And on the subject of the Old Bill,' cut in Hawkins, 'we all know what cunts they are up there. But, with Euro 2000 coming up they'll be even worse. So nothing stupid, right?'

Billy nodded. 'That's right. I don't want none of you lot getting a tug up there. And no fucking blades either.' He paused for a second and looked around. 'So... ideas?'

'Who else are we likely to bump into on the way?' asked Geoff quietly.

'Oldham are at home. They've got some game lads, so it might be lively after,' said Hawkins. 'The only ones heading up the M6 are Watford going to Everton, so they're not worth bothering with. The Rent Boys are at Leeds, though, and Millwall are at Notts County. So you might bump into some of them if you go by road and stop on the M1. Unlikely, though.'

'Still, got the Cockney Reds on the train, though,' said PJ, rubbing his hands together. 'That'll be fun.'

'I hope to fuck you know what you're doing,' said Hawkins as he pulled up outside Billy's house, 'or you'll screw everything.'

Billy looked at him and winked. 'Have I ever called it wrong before?'

'No,' replied Hawkins. 'That's what worries me.'

CHAPTER 9
Thursday 30 March 2000
15.15

Billy walked into the office and sat down with a thump.

He waited a moment and then looked at Hawkins. He was surrounded by sheets of A4 paper and in front of him sat a black laptop computer, humming away.

'How'd it go then?' he asked, his fingers still poised over the keyboard.

Billy looked at him and frowned. 'This week gets weirder by the bloody minute,' he said wearily. 'I've been to eleven different garages today, all owned by mates in the trade, and d'you know what most of 'em said when I mentioned the twenty-four-hour coverage thing? "That's a fucking good idea".'

Hawkins stared at him, surprised. 'Excuse me?'

'Yeah, I know. It's fucking amazing. They all reckon it'd be a goer if the price was right.' He pulled his cigarettes from his jacket pocket and threw one to Hawkins before lighting his own.

'But don't they have something already? I mean, what do you have here?'

Billy shook his head and shrugged his shoulders. 'Lights and dummy cameras but nothing else. I've never really had a problem. Not with kids or vandals, which is what they're all moaning about.'

'What... no one's ever nicked anything?'

'Only once,' said Billy with a wry smile. 'Couple of years back some little fucker nicked a set of alloys off a BMW 3 series. Took me a week to track him down. It was one of the local boy racers. Silly bastard had only put the wheels on his own motor, hadn't he.'

Hawkins laughed. 'What d'you do?'

'Went round his house and took 'em back. Then I taught him the error of his ways.'

'Oh yeah?'

Billy nodded. 'Oh yeah. I slung 'im in the boot and then took a baseball bat to his windows. After I'd put every one through, I told him to spread the word that if anyone ever tried ripping me off again, I wouldn't be so nice about it. Funny, I ain't had a problem since.'

'What... did you leave him in there?'

'Too fucking right. I bet he shit himself.'

'Well,' said Hawkins with a grin, 'seeing as half the lads in Essex are on the nick, if your mates reckon this idea, it might not be such a bad thing. Maybe we should give it some thought.'

With a sigh, Billy got to his feet. 'I'm knackered. How you getting on with that? Will it be ready?'

'No problem,' replied Hawkins, grinning. 'It'll be at Upton Park by knocking-off time tomorrow night.'

'You're a good man, Hawk,' he said. 'When you fancy a break, come over and have a beer.' And with that, he headed back to his own office.

The figures on the monthly sales sheet made for good reading. March had been a better-than-average month for the garage, and Billy was more than happy. So much so that when he'd first seen the numbers he had immediately gone down to the garage, slipped all the lads fifty quid each and told them to have a few beers on him. It had cost a few bob, but he'd always been fair with the people who worked for him. And they'd certainly made him a lot more than he'd just handed out.

After a final look at the sheet, he slipped it back into the folder and flicked it into his 'out' tray before picking up his mug of coffee and walking over to the window. The early spring sunshine cast a soft, warm glow over the cars spread out below him and Billy was pleased to see a few people milling about in shirtsleeves.

The sight of the forecourt reminded him of his morning and the response to his security idea. He hadn't expected that, not at all. But the more he thought about it, the more he realised that it did make sense. He couldn't even begin to imagine how pissed off he'd be if someone ever ran a key down the side of one of his motors. And bitter experience had taught him that nothing put the shits up a thief quite like the sound of an approaching car engine and the flash of a car's headlights. Maybe Hawk was right and they should have a think about it. If there was a market there, why not? He sighed and returned to his desk. What with the pubs, Upton Park and now this, bloody security was taking over his life - and he'd only got into it to help Sal and Steve out.

Billy finished his coffee and lit up, leaning back in his seat to watch as the smoke drifted up and spread itself across the ceiling. He suddenly felt shattered.

A loud thump shocked him back to consciousness and he woke with a start to find Hawkins standing over him with a bottle in each hand.

'Wake up, you idle bastard! Anyone would think you work for a living.'

Billy leant forward and rubbed his eyes. 'Fuck me! I must have dozed off. What time is it?'

'About ten past five ... here.' He placed a beer down on the desk and settled into a chair. 'So, we all set for Saturday?'

'Yeah, I reckon,' said Billy after taking a mouthful of beer to wake himself up. 'The lads'll start ringing in tomorrow, so we'll have a better idea of the turnout. But it should be a good day out. You still up for driving?'

Hawk looked at him and smiled. He wasn't totally convinced that going to Manchester, and giving it the large one was a wise move. United were a major firm, and there was no love lost between the two sets of lads. More importantly, their bid had little enough chance as it was; this could kill it stone dead if either of them were seen and someone managed to put two and two together. But Billy had said that he thought it would be a good idea to give the club, and the plod, a wake-up call. And the bottom line was that he was top dog, so he called the shots. And he'd never been wrong before. 'No problem. It'll be nice to have a day without Al bloody Green. And you look like you could do with the kip.'

'I tell you, I'm shagged out, mate. Don't know why, must be all this excitement. You finished the bid yet?'

'No. I'll take it home and work on it there but there's not much to do. Just a case of copying out what the last company put forward and jigging it around a bit. You best have a look in the morning and I'll take it over. Oh, and I've put it down under St George Security Ltd, is that OK?'

Billy stuck out his bottom lip and nodded. 'What d'you reckon to the chances of us actually pulling this off, then? Seriously.'

'I've got no idea, mate. That's the truth. But let's face it, leaving aside our standing with the club and the Old Bill, we've got no track record and no employees, apart from that... Well, what've we got to lose? And you know what they say, you gotta be in it to win it.' He took a mouthful of beer and gulped it down, a loud belch signalling that it had hit the spot. 'So what's the story with this car thing then?' he continued after a pause. 'That could be interesting.'

'To be honest, I haven't given it much thought, mate. It kind of threw me a bit.' He stared at Hawkins for a while and smiled. 'I'll say one thing for you, Hawk, you're keen as fuck. You don't sell motors as well, do you?'

Billy was staring at the back of an old blue Ford Transit van and waiting for the lights to change, when his mobile rang and snapped him back from his daydream. He listened for a moment and then, as the traffic in front began to move away, thanked the caller and put the phone back into its holder.

A sly smile spread across his face as he pulled the gear lever back into drive and headed off after the Transit. For a second, he considered ringing Hawk and coming clean, but decided against it. Best keep his thoughts to himself, at least for now. Besides, he hadn't even decided what he was going to do yet. That's if he was going to do anything at all. There was a lot to think about first but, either way, he'd have to make a decision soon.

Reaching forward, he pushed the 'power' button on the stereo and, with the sweet sounds of Al Green pumping from the speakers, Billy headed for home.

'What you doin'?'

'Just checking the kids, that's all. Look at this little bleeder. He's all over the place.' He felt an arm slide around his waist and smiled to himself as Sam leant against him and shook her head.

'Don't leave him like that,' she whispered, before pulling away and moving into the bedroom. 'He'll wake up with a stiff neck. Is Alfie OK?'

Billy watched her as she tucked their youngest son back under his quilt and the smile spread even wider across his face. 'He's fine.'

'Good,' she said, walking out and kissing him on the cheek as she headed back down the stairs. 'Don't be long. Your programme's just about to start.'

Billy's eyes followed her and, when she had disappeared from view, he returned his gaze to the semi-darkness of the bedroom and the sight of his sleeping child. He often stood like that, staring at the kids or even at Sam when she was asleep. It helped him focus on what was really important. He was a lucky bastard, and he knew it.

But for the first time in a long time, he suddenly began to wonder if he was starting to push his luck a bit too far. Yet even before he could begin to think about that too deeply, the germ of an idea sprang into his mind. And with a wry smile, he pulled the bedroom door closed and headed for the sofa.

CHAPTER 10
Friday 31 March 2000
10.30

Hawkins placed his coffee down on the desk and stared across at Billy. To say he was shocked was an understatement. 'So let me get this straight. From Monday, you want me to concentrate on setting up a company to supply security cover for garage forecourts?'

Billy nodded but said nothing.

'And the thing with the pubs is dead in the water?'

Another nod.

'Well,' said Hawk, sitting back in his chair with a sigh, 'I've gotta say I'm relieved, mate. I wasn't happy about that. Not one fucking bit. But why the change of heart?'

'Like you say, getting The Squad involved in something like that... it's too bloody risky, what with the Euros coming up. I don't give a shit about the Old Bill; I just don't want to attract any grief from the local heavies. It ain't worth it.'

'That's the bloody truth,' replied Hawkins with a grunt. 'So what you gonna do about Mickey? And the lads, for that matter? They won't be best pleased.'

'Leave all that to me. I'll sort it. You just make sure that we get that bid finished and into the club today, that's all.'

Once Hawkins had left to return to his own office, Billy sat for a while and reflected on what he'd done. He actually felt a bit gutted. Running a scam to fund The Squad would have been a buzz. It would certainly have elevated him into the ranks of some of the more infamous hooligan leaders of days gone by.

But what he'd told Hawk had been the truth. Well, half-truth anyway. There was a big prize at stake. And last night he had realised just how much he wanted it. He'd also realised how easy it would be for him to get it, as long as he kept himself and Hawk focused. But this pub thing was causing his friend all kinds of problems and so it had to go. It just wasn't going as far as Hawk thought it was.

He lit a cigarette and picked up his mobile, selecting the number with one hand and inhaling as much nicotine as he could with one breath as he waited for an answer. When it came, it was abrupt, and familiar.

'Mickey, it's Billy. Listen, cheers for the information last night. Any chance we could meet up for a beer this afternoon? I have a proposition you might be interested in.'

Billy closed the folder and gave it a friendly pat. 'That, my man, is fucking sound.'

Hawkins grinned back across the desk. 'Cheers, chap, I appreciate it.' He paused for a second and placed the precious work into his briefcase. 'Well, I'm gonna get this biked over to the club straight away. Best not show my face if I don't need to. When I've done that, fancy shooting out for a celebratory beer or three?'

'No, mate,' said Billy with a gentle shake of his head. 'I'd best not. Besides, I've got somewhere to be later. Any news on the war front?'

'Looks like we'll have a tidy number up there,' said Hawkins. 'The lads have pulled a fair few old faces out of retirement as well, so Paul's had to get us some more tickets.' He stopped talking as Billy started to laugh. 'What the fuck's up with you?'

'You,' said Billy. 'Sitting there in your bloody suit with your briefcase and your Mercedes, talking about taking a mob to Manchester. Your mum would be so proud.'

Later that afternoon, Mickey James finished what was left of his scotch and stood up. He looked down at Billy for a second and then spat into his hand and held it out. Without even the slightest hint of hesitation, Billy got to his feet, looked him in the eye and took it.

Billy stepped calmly to one side as a single brown bottle came flying through the air and bounced off the pavement beside him. With a line of helmeted policemen separating them from the baying mob on the opposite side of the road, it was impossible to see who had thrown it, so he just shook his head and smiled to himself, revelling in the occasion and drinking in the atmosphere.

'Why the fuck do they do that?' said Hawk to no one in particular. 'Waste of good lager if you ask me.'

After a quick glance at him, Billy turned his gaze to the horizon, stepping forward as another bottle came sailing across in a steady arc before shattering against the wall behind him. Slinging missiles around might well be a cowardly way to conduct business, but they still hurt if they hit. Your pride if nothing else.

'This is bollocks,' muttered Darren, before walking out into no man's land and strutting around until he found one of the few policemen who had their rank and number uncovered. 'Here, Officer Dibble, you gonna do anything about these tossers lobbing stuff at us?'

Billy watched and smiled as the sergeant looked him up and down, barely attempting to hide his contempt for the man standing in front of him. 'Why don't you do yourself a favour and fuck off.'

'So that's a no then, is it?' responded Darren dryly.

'Get back in with the others, you smarmy little shit,' sneered the uniform. 'Or I'll nick you for resisting arrest. And you know what that'll mean, don't you?'

Darren looked at him and sighed. He did indeed know what that meant. It meant a revenge kicking. Time for the Old Bill to get their own back and settle a few scores. 'Resisting arrest' on the charge sheet simply explained away the wounds. 'Fair enough,' he replied before turning away and walking back over to the others. 'Bloody coppers up here. No respect for decent folk.'

Billy flicked his cigarette in the direction of the thick blue line and then burst out laughing as a chorus of 'Bubbles' broke out behind him. He knew what effect that was going to have on the lads opposite, especially after everything that had happened that morning. It would be like a red rag to a bull. One more stinging insult in what had been a humiliating day for the Manchester firm.

PJ had gleefully claimed the honour of the first result. In an effort to throw the police off the scent, he had hired two mini-buses and taken the Plaistow boys to Watford, jumping on the Manchester train with the Hornets lads heading north for their game with Everton. But within a quarter of an hour of the train pulling out, they had stumbled across a group of Cockney Reds drinking in the buffet car and it had all kicked off. Their fun stopped only when the British Transport Police took them off at Milton Keynes and escorted them back to Watford.

Yet even as they had jumped in the buses and begun the long drive northwards, others had begun to arrive in Manchester. The numbers were swelled by the presence of many old and experienced faces, together with a huge contingent of Under Fives and ticketless young wannabes, the majority of whom had made the journey simply to experience the thrill of being with the main firm when they went on the offensive - a thrill which, thanks to the attentions of the police, was becoming all too rare.

And as a result of their early start, most of them had made it into the city centre before the local plod had woken up to what was happening. So they drifted away from the station in small groups, only to mob up and invade the numerous cafés and fast-food restaurants, larging it up and letting everyone know they were there as they waited for the pubs to open. By the time United's lads had finally got their act together and turned up, it had been too late. They arrived to find a small army sitting on their doorstep and aside from the odd stand-off, there had been fuck-all they could do about it.

However, the influx into the city centre had only been a part of it. For the CSS hadn't just shown in the centre, they had turned up all over. Geoff had taken about thirty lads to Deansgate, while Stretch and some of the others were holed up in a Salford Quays pub. Aside from that, over the past two hours Billy had received a steady stream of calls bringing reports of trouble from as far afield as Stockport. And although a couple of groups had been turned over, most had given a good account of themselves before the Old Bill had arrived and stopped the fun.

But even as Billy was taking these calls, more lads had been turning up in the centre, until eventually Hawk had estimated that they had almost five hundred fighters in the city. And then, as Billy knew they would, the Old Bill had gone through and swept up, herding the West Ham lads together and moving them off until they were out of sight of the shoppers and could be held until kick-off time.

And then United had shown. In numbers. But it was too late. The CSS had come to make a point and it had already been made. They had walked into Manchester almost unopposed and taken liberties. Whatever happened now would be nothing more than a vain attempt to save face.

The shrill ringing of his mobile cut through the singing and Billy pulled it from his pocket and pressed it to his ear. Cupping his hand around it in an effort to drown out the noise, he listened intently for a moment before letting out a sarcastic laugh.

'You know the score, you mug. We come to your town, you find us ... Fuck me, we've been in the centre all day, how easy d'you want us to make it?' He listened for a second or so longer and laughed again. 'Yeah, right-oh. Dream on, son!'

'What's the story?' asked Hawk.

'Twat reckons they were expecting us in Cheadle or somewhere. How the fuck did they expect us to know that, then?'

'Telepathy, I guess,' laughed Hawk. 'Maybe we should bring Mystic Meg along next time.'

'Heads up!' someone shouted, the sharp cockney accent struggling to be heard over the sporadic shattering of glass and a hundred bellowing voices. 'Here we go!'

More missiles came flying over. This time not just bottles, but coins as well. Billy stole another glance at Hawk and they both grinned as they readied themselves for the inevitable attack. 'Football,' laughed Hawk. 'Don't ya just love it?'

The buzz intensified, almost crackling now. But it wasn't the buzz that knotted up your stomach when you were hunting, or even being hunted. This was a different one, the best one. It came when the enemy was right there in your face. Pissed off and hating but helpless. Reduced to throwing missiles and slapping scarfers rather than toe-to-toeing it. And you looked on and laughed at them as you wallowed in the buzz of victory. Fucking awesome.

And then, from the other side of the cordon, a roar went up. Bellowing across the road towards them like a solid, living thing, the Manchester lads poured forward in a desperate effort to get through the blue cordon and attack the blue and claret cancer that had invaded their city. But even as Billy and Hawk marshalled their troops, screaming at them to hold it together and stand firm rather than attack, the United lads were driven back by batons and gloved fists.

Within seconds, another salvo of glass and metal came flying across. This time it was not to wound, but it was a last-ditch effort to provoke a response and invite the West Ham mob to attack from their side. But as more police arrived and began driving Billy and his troops away in the direction of the ground, the only response from the CSS was jeering and yet more laughter. The greatest weapon of all in the propaganda of pain.

Billy was happy. Very happy.

The long column of lads headed towards Old Trafford shadowed by an equally long line of policemen, some on foot, others in vans and a few on horseback. At the front were the boys from Bermondsey. Nutters all of them, but game as fuck no matter what the odds. Just behind them walked the bulk of the Under Fives, each one looking to make the jump from periphery player to regular first teamer and well aware that the only way to do it was to prove you were solid and would stand. Show that you understood that it was better to take a kicking than to run. Run and you were out. Forever. As a result, a few already bore battle scars from earlier exertions, but despite their wounds and excited chatter, it was clear to all that if the chance for action presented itself again, it would be taken. Without a moment's hesitation. This was history in the making.

In the centre of the column, Darren, Stretch and Geoff marched along with all their lads, laughing about their morning and ignoring the presence of a few local youths giving it large from behind the safety of the boys in blue.

Billy and Hawk, meanwhile, were content to stroll along towards the rear, sure in the knowledge that with the quantity and quality of the lads in the column, anything else that went off now was going to be a bonus. There was only one firm that could live with West Ham on their day and they wore uniforms and had the law on their side. No one else came close.

But equally, both Billy and Hawk knew that if anything else *was* going to happen, it wouldn't be until they got nearer the ground. So this was the time to recharge the batteries and calm things down a bit. Everyone knew that and, as a result, the tension had eased considerably while the level of banter had increased. Even the mounted copper riding along beside them had relaxed and become involved. Laughing out loud at the stereotypical jokes about *Coronation Street* and flat caps, even though he'd probably heard them a million times before.

But even as he was responding to a stream of anti-Beckham jokes, a deep roar echoed back from the front of the column and he stopped talking. Standing up in his stirrups, he strained to see what was going on. Billy stared up at him and smiled as the electricity of anticipation began coursing through the air. Whatever was happening, his lofty perch was giving him a far better view than they had.

'Oi copper, what's occurring?' The policemen shot them a nervous look, but Billy could tell from the movement of the horse that whatever was going on was serious.

The roar came again, louder this time, and the column pulled away from them as people surged forward to get involved and play their part. Billy could see the cockney faces wearing angry smiles and gleaming eyes.

'It's the crossroads!' shouted someone. 'United are all over the fucker!'

By now the police horse was fidgeting like mad, its front legs rearing up and scattering what remained of the column as people tried desperately to avoid getting kicked or stamped on. The rider looked equally nervous but suddenly, he turned the huge beast around to regain control and then drove it forward towards the fighting. Its bulk cleared a path through the crowd, giving Billy and Hawkins a perfect view of what was going on ahead.

'Fuck me!' said Hawk excitedly, as a helicopter appeared overhead, the distinctive throbbing of rotor blades adding to the noise and the sense of occasion. 'That looks naughty.'

The pair watched as a swarm of people ran around about fifty metres in front of them. Backward and forward they went, the sun glinting off the flying glass and the polished black batons flashing above the heads. The noise level rose again and Billy had to hold himself in check and fight the desire to steam up the road and join in. It was the golden rule, never get involved in anything outside a stadium. Too many cameras equals too much risk.

By now, the column was no more. The regimented order had been replaced instead by numerous small cliques: groups of mates sticking together among the mêlée and watching out for each other. Some were heading towards the battle, others held back and jostled for a view as they waited patiently for their turn. One punch, that's all it took. One punch. Enough to prove to yourself that you were there and did your bit on the glorious day that West Ham went to Old Trafford and took the piss.

And there they were. Not up ahead, but right next to them. Mouthy Manc fuckers stripped of their blue protective shield and suddenly face-to-face with their worst nightmare. They might not be real lads, true enough, but if you're big enough to mouth off, you're big enough to take the consequences. Someone should have told them that. Maybe they had but they hadn't listened. Big mistake.

Billy watched the United mob with a wry smile on his face as a few tried to run for it while others tried to hide among the chaos, each one standing out a mile because of their pointed rat faces and shite clothes. They deserved a kicking for that alone. A shout went up behind him and he turned to stare at a few who had gathered together and were standing firm, bouncing around on their toes and screaming abuse to hide their fear and boost their nerve. They had bottle for sure, but didn't stand a chance.

The West Ham lads, their faces twisted with hatred and blood lust, gathered around them. The two groups jostled for position as each waited for the other to make the first move. To those involved, nothing else mattered now, just this single engagement. This was the moment.

An angry roar went up as a foot flew out across the narrow no man's land and caught one of the Manchester lads who had jumped out to try and land a punch. The force of the kick almost lifted him off the floor before he was dragged back towards safety. But before he was inside the protective enclave of his fellow fighters, a young lad, fifteen at most and wearing a cream Stone Island jumper he'd almost certainly bought in an effort to look the part and fit in, broke from the ranks of the West Ham and ran straight at him, seizing the chance to make a name for himself. Before he could land a blow, he took a vicious right-hander to the side of his head and staggered backwards, only to be swallowed up as other, slower lads poured forward and delivered the battering he had wanted to start. The rhythmic thudding of boot and fist provided a surreal drumbeat to the visual imagery of the beating.

Billy ignored that and kept his eye on his boy. One thing he had learnt over the years was that anyone could deliver a right-hander, but not everyone could take one. The key was how you reacted to the first. And from the look of him, this was the first. The kid was all over the place. But just as Billy was about to give up on him, he gathered himself together and ran back in, delivering a kick that, if nothing else, almost certainly made him feel better.

'Good lad,' Billy said out loud to himself as a group of policemen came steaming up from behind, shoving people to one side in a desperate effort to get through and get involved. Billy watched them break up the ruck and shook his head. The bastards loved it every bit as much as they did.

No sooner had they dealt with that and vanished into the mêlée at the crossroads than everything began to come back up the road towards where he and Hawkins were standing. The Old Bill were driving his lads back in an effort to create space between the two factions and give themselves some time to sort it out. But just as it seemed they were winning, thick cockney accents screamed out: 'Stand, you cunts!' and then 'Go again! Go again!' And the game lads at the front turned and ran back towards the crossroads and the enemy, leaving the wounded and the unwilling in their wake. Some of them were limping, others had eyes which reddened and closed even as Billy watched them.

And then, as quickly as it had started, it was over. The incessant barking of dogs signalled the end of that particular game. Everyone hated the dogs. Vicious little bastards.

Hawkins steered the Mercedes off the motorway and into the service station. He needed a slash and something to eat. But most importantly, he needed to wake himself up. He was shattered, and Billy crashing out and falling asleep as soon as they'd hit the M6 hadn't helped. With no one to talk to, Hawk had been forced to resort to the radio and the usual football phone-in mix of sad wankers moaning about referees and gloating Manchester United fans telling the world how great they were from the safety of their Kent front rooms. Then again, after giving The Hammers a 7-1 trouncing, they'd certainly had something to gloat about. On the pitch at least, it had not been good.

Off it, however, things had been entirely different. Billy had asked for a serious piss-take and he had got it. Some of those who had left early had even kicked it off with the police gathering on the Old Trafford forecourt, just to drive home the point. But apart from that, and a few exchanges of missiles on the way to Piccadilly Station, the Old Bill had held the upper hand in the post-match competition, meaning that their red opponents hadn't even had the chance to try and even the score. Shame. The CSS would have plenty to celebrate when they gathered again at the St George. That's when all the stories would come out.

Hawkins parked the Mercedes at the back of the car park and turned off the engine, rubbing his face as Billy finally returned to consciousness and stretched his arms above his head before asking where they were.

'Corley, just near the end of the M6. I'm totally fucked.'

Billy yawned. 'Me too, mate,' he murmured as he climbed out. 'I don't know what's up with me lately.'

They wandered over towards the restaurant, instinctively looking at the cars and coaches to check for evidence of club colours or possible trouble. But aside from the normal scarfers' cars, bearing allegiances ranging from West Ham to Dover Athletic, nothing seemed out of the ordinary; certainly nothing to worry them. Then, from behind a coach over to their left, a shout went up and they both turned to look; more shouts, then laughter. A ball appeared, closely followed by a young lad in a Watford shirt. They both breathed an inaudible sigh of relief. 'How'd they get on today?'

'Lost 4-2,' replied Hawkins. 'They're fucked now. Back to division one.'

With their hearts still racing slightly, they carried on and, as they walked, the apprehension began to rise; just as it always did when they approached such places without any serious back up. You never knew who, or what, was waiting inside. With the mirrored plate glass, they could have been clocked already and wouldn't know until they walked through the doors and it was too late.

Hawkins gave a loud cough as they passed between a couple of brand new Mondeos and Billy glanced inside to see the parcel shelves and back seats of both cars were strewn with screwed up copies of the *Sun* and empty food containers - a sure sign that they were hire cars. Lads' cars. He cursed to himself as he realised that they were facing forward, removing the opportunity to check the back windows or number plates for clues. He dare not walk back though. If they were being watched, it would give out the wrong signal. The apprehension rose another notch. 'The two of them on to how many?' he wondered. 'Four, six, maybe even eight or nine.' Not good odds. Not if they're game.

The two of them continued onward, their pace not varying at all and their eyes fixed firmly on the large electric doors at the end of the path in front of them. But when they opened, it was only to reveal a foyer full of people. Normal people. Some in replica shirts from a variety of clubs, others on their way to or from wherever. Who cared?

Both felt another blast of relief as they headed for the toilets and the obligatory first call, Billy hanging back a bit to make sure that if they were going to be jumped, at least they'd have a chance. It was like a routine, carefully developed over the years and practised without thinking. This time, as with most times, it proved to be a needless precaution.

But when they left the toilets and walked into the restaurant, their mood changed. Hawkins saw them first, Billy a split second later. Seven lads, staring across at them, their expensive clothing and arrogance marking them out as fully paid-up members of the Saturday scene, like secret signs to those in the know.

'Bollocks,' hissed Hawkins as they walked over to the counter. 'Any idea who they are?'

Billy raised his eyes as if studying the menu above their heads, the polished chrome providing a perfect mirror in which to view their potential foe. 'Fuck knows, they could be anyone. They're not ours, though, and that's what matters.'

Hawkins glanced up at the reflection. 'Well, judging by the looks on their faces, it looks like we're in the shit, mate. How d'you wanna play this?'

'Only one way really,' he replied after a second's thought. 'I'll get the drinks; you get the grub.'

'Quality call,' muttered Hawkins as he poured out two bowls of boiling hot tomato soup. He waited until Billy had returned with two chrome teapots and then the two of them walked directly over to the group of bemused young men, bypassing the tills and the baffled assistants.

'All right, lads?' said Billy almost merrily. 'How d'you get on?'

A chubby man aged about thirty in a blue Teddy Smith shirt looked them up and down and smiled nervously. He hadn't expected this at all. 'Lost 1-0 at Oldham,' he said. 'You?'

'Spanked, mate. Lost 7-1 at Old Trafford.'

Hawkins could see their facial expressions change even as Billy spoke. And in that instant, he knew that the danger had passed. A, at least for the two of them. He smiled to himself as he tried to imagine what was going through their heads. One minute, you're eyeing up two potential targets, the next they're standing over your table with boiling hot liquid in each hand. Then, just to add insult to injury, you find out that they're West Ham. Bloody psychos, the lot of them. 'Sorry, mate, you're ...?' Hawk left the question hanging, just to belittle them a bit more.

'Cambridge,' said chubby, almost too cheerfully.

'Oh right, tidy little club. Had a few tear-ups with your lads in my time,' said Billy, by now confident that the boiling water could remain in the pots and wouldn't have to become a weapon. 'Here, shift up. We're fucking starving.' He moved forward and put down his tea, easing the lads along the already cramped seats.

Hawkins almost burst out laughing as he wandered over to collect the cups, partly at Billy's cheek, but mostly with relief. And by the time he returned to the table, the group were exchanging cigarettes and telling war stories about various mobs they had run into at service stations on their travels. It was as if they were old mates.

Billy and Hawkins stood in the car park, shook hands with each of the Cambridge lads and wished them well. Their meeting had turned out to be quite a laugh, although neither of them was under any illusions that a great deal of that was because their companions had quickly realised who they had been sitting with. Billy, Hawk, the CSS; it didn't take a genius to work it out. And with the leaders of the major firms traditionally being regarded with a strange kind of reverence, both took a perverse pride in knowing that the Cambridge lads would dine off the story for months.

A short blast on a horn indicated that the first of the Mondeos was about to pull away, but, as soon as it began to move, Billy suddenly stepped forward and banged on its roof. The young driver stopped the car and nervously wound down the window as Hawkins and the passengers looked on, unsure of what was going to happen.

Billy crouched down and spoke, his face deadly serious. But, within a second the driver and his passengers were laughing. And then, with a final blast of the horn, they were gone. Billy watched them go and smiled. 'See them? They bloody shit themselves just then.' 'What did you say?' asked Hawkins. Billy pulled out a cigarette and lit up. 'I told them not to forget that tomorrow's Mother's Day.'

Part Two

CHAPTER 12
Thursday 13 April 2000
15.00

Billy stepped out into the warm spring sunshine and lit a cigarette. He hated hospitals, hated them. The stench of Domestos and death seemed to linger in his nostrils and on his clothes for weeks, as if to remind him of something bad. It was even rare to find a tasty nurse these days. Most of the ones he'd seen this afternoon had been as ugly as sin.

He turned and waited for Hawkins to catch him up; willing him to hurry so that he could get as far away from the place as possible and go for a pint - a much-needed pint.

Seeing PJ like that had been a shock - a big shock. He'd heard that he'd taken a kicking the other night, but he hadn't expected him to be in such a state. It would be a long, long time before he was back to his old self again.

Behind him, the electric doors hissed open and Hawkins came bursting out into the daylight, his face red with anger and his hands shaking. Billy looked at him for a second and then handed him his half-smoked cigarette. He watched as his friend took it without comment and drew heavily on it, desperately sucking in as much nicotine as possible in a futile attempt to calm himself down.

'Come on, son,' Billy muttered. 'Let's get the fuck out of here.'

Two hours later, Billy was back in his office. He'd told Hawk to go home and chill out for a bit but, unable to take his own advice, had returned to work rather than sit in his living room brooding and annoying Sam and the boys. He needed to think, and his office was the place to do it.

After the euphoria of Manchester, Tuesday night had not gone so well. Newcastle hadn't shown with any kind of mob and so, rather than kick things off with their scarfers, Billy had told The Squad to give the Old Bill as much hassle as possible, a task they undertook with not a little relish.

But with Chelsea also at home, and Sheffield Wednesday at Wimbledon, the police had been on a high state of alert and the longer the night went on, and the more grief they got, the worse their mood became. By 10.30, they were spitting bullets, and when word came through that Chelsea were all over King's Cross kicking things off with anything that moved, it got even worse.

A few of the lads had then come to Billy and suggested that they mob up and make their way to north London to join in the fun; build on the success against United. But he had held them back, preferring instead to continue his tactic of winding up the police. He had stuck to his guns, even when the calls had started to come through, taunting them for not showing. And then it had all gone wrong.

From what he had been told, PJ and a few of the others had begun to make their way towards Plaistow when the Old Bill had turned up in force and tried to stop them. When PJ had moved forward to tell them that they were simply going to Plaistow because that's where they all lived, a copper had grabbed him and tried to sling him in a van. At which point, it had all kicked off. Big time. Next thing they knew, PJ was in hospital having been badly beaten; according to the coppers, as he tried to resist arrest.

It was a joke. Everyone knew it. And Billy blamed himself. Not just because PJ had been one of those wanting to head to King's Cross and he had told him to stay put, but also because he had a sneaky feeling there was an element of revenge involved. Payback for him getting one over on the coppers after Italy. And what made it worse was that there was nothing they could do about it. For even if PJ made a complaint against the police, eventually it would come down to the word of a known football hooligan against that of a serving officer. There could, and would, only ever be one winner.

But what had really rankled Billy was the irony of his own situation. For although he was gutted that his friend had been put in hospital, there was no doubt that as a direct result, he had achieved exactly what he had set out to do: remind everyone who needed to know that as far as West Ham were concerned trouble was never more than a quiet word away. Even the *Evening Standard* had given the trouble in the East End some decent coverage, which was a massive result.

He sighed and took a beer from the fridge. Despite his guilt, he knew that if he was going to achieve what he had set out to do, he had to keep pushing, making sure that everyone was kept unsettled. But with tension rising among The Squad, he had to keep control of things. If he didn't, all kinds of shit could pour down on them, and him - especially with the press and politicians jumping on the Euro 2000 bandwagon. His next move, whatever it was going to be, would have to be carefully planned.

A knock on the door broke his concentration and he turned as Jill half-entered the room. 'There's someone here to see you.'

'If it's not my wife or my accountant, tell them to piss off,' he replied irritably.

She frowned at him and pushed the door open. 'No, you tell him.'

Billy was about to give her a mouthful when she stepped aside to allow the familiar face of a heavily built policeman to enter his office.

'Well, well, Sergeant Roberts. To what do I owe this unexpected pleasure?'

'I just brought you this, Billy.'

'Mr Evans, to you, Sergeant,' he interrupted. 'You are in my office; at least show me a bit of courtesy.'

Roberts smiled. He'd played this game a thousand times. Not just with Billy, but with countless others. 'I apologise ... sir,' he said sarcastically. 'But I thought I'd return this.' He dropped a large envelope on the desk. Billy immediately knew what it was and, despite the inevitability, his heart sank.

'What is it?' he asked, matter-of-factly.

'Your tender for the security contract at Upton Park. I have to say Bi—, I mean, Mr Evans, I do admire your cheek. But I don't think you'll be too surprised to hear that on this occasion, you weren't successful.'

'What's cheeky about submitting a legitimate tender for an available contract?' asked Billy after a pause. 'After all, I do run a security company you know.'

The policeman laughed. 'Oh yes, I'd forgotten. St George Security Limited. What is it you do now? Garages. That must be profitable.'

'Well,' replied Billy smugly, 'it's a living. And let's face it; someone has to keep an eye on things these days. We certainly can't rely on the Metropolitan Police. Only the other night, a good mate of mine ended up in hospital after getting the shit kicked out of him. By some of your colleagues apparently.'

Roberts smiled but said nothing for a moment. When he did speak, his tone was lower than before, almost friendly. 'Look, Billy, let's cut the bullshit, shall we? We're not stupid and we know exactly what's going on.' He moved forward and leant on the desk, as if to emphasise his words and give them more meaning. 'But, more importantly, we always win in the end. One way or another.'

Billy noticed the veiled threat but the half smile never left his face. 'Look, Sergeant, I don't know what you're getting at, but if you're suggesting that I'm involved with something I shouldn't be, well... haven't we been down this road once before? Last time, if I remember right, you and your mates from Scotland Yard followed me all the way to Italy because you had me down as a either a drug runner or a major league car thief. You didn't seem to know which,' he said with a wry smile. 'By the way, what did happen to those coppers? Is the one who murdered my mate still in prison?'

Roberts stared angrily at him across the desk. 'OK, Billy, off the record. Let's put our cards on the table, shall we?'

Billy shrugged his shoulders and sat down, lighting a cigarette and pushing the packet across the desk as he did so. 'I'm listening.'

'You know as well as I do,' began Roberts, 'that if anything kicks off in Belgium or Holland over the summer, the press and the politicians will be screaming blue murder and it'll be us who get all the flak. So to avoid that, whatever steps we need to take to keep trouble away from the tournament will be taken. If that means taking a hard line for the rest of the season or even making a few early morning wake-up calls, then so be it.'

'What is it they say?' cut in Billy as he blew out a lungful of smoke. 'If you can't take a joke, you shouldn't have joined.'

'Now,' continued Roberts, almost without taking a breath, 'I can understand why you would want to—'

'Hang on,' interrupted Billy. 'Not me, Sergeant. In case you'd forgotten, I haven't actually *done* anything.'

'OK then, I can understand why the CSS would want to have a dig at Manchester United, but the trouble the other night was different. That upset a lot of people and, if anything like it happens again, well, let's just say it'll bring down a lot of shit on a lot of people very quickly.'

'Is that a threat?' asked Billy with a faint glimmer of a smile.

'No, Billy. It's a friendly warning, that's all. And as I say, it's off the record.'

'Well then,' replied Billy. 'If we're talking off the record, I haven't got the faintest idea what you're talking about. The only thing I know for certain is that I bid for a contract and lost out.' He lifted his arms and shrugged his shoulders. 'That's business. Shit happens.'

Roberts stood up to leave. 'Like I say, Billy, we won't put up with any more grief like the other night. Some of your lads are in enough trouble already.'

Billy looked at him but let his remark pass. 'By the way, Sergeant, who did win? The contract I mean?'

'We did, Billy. Like I say, in the end we always do.'

Billy waited until Roberts had left before he allowed the smile to cross his face. 'Is that right, you cunt,' he muttered to himself as he picked up his mobile and dialled in a number. 'Well, we'll see about that shall we?'

'Mickey, it's Billy. Listen, what we spoke about the other night. It looks like we're on, mate. I'll be over to see you in the morning.'

Billy burst into the office and sat down with a grin on his face. 'How we doin' then?'

'OK,' said Hawkins, somewhat bemused at his friend's jovial mood, especially given the week they'd had. 'Where the fuck have you been all day?'

'Just doing the rounds. Meeting people, catching up. You know how it is,' said Billy cheerfully. 'But never mind that. How's things been going here?'

'Well, I signed up another three garages this morning; that's twenty-eight now. The two vans will be getting sign-written on Monday and the uniforms will be here Tuesday. So I guess, as from Tuesday night, we'll be in business.'

'Sound! And you're happy with the lads?'

'No problems at all,' said Hawkins, nodding. 'It's not as if we don't know them, is it? Christ, we've been seeing them most weekends for years.' He paused and frowned as he looked across the desk. 'What the fuck's up with you? You should be as pissed off as I am, what with Wednesday night and PJ. Not to mention losing that contract.'

'Oh, so you got my note then?'

'Yeah, pisser or what? I really thought we might pull it off you know.'

'Fuck off, Hawk!' replied Billy, with a laugh. 'You must have known that we never had a chance. Even if that bastard Roberts hadn't cottoned on to us, old man Mirren was always going to get it.'

'Yeah, I guess you're right,' replied Hawk quietly. 'But that still gets me. How can some old duffer who supplies supermarket guards and car park attendants end up running the security at West Ham? It's a fucking scandal.'

'Just got lucky I guess. Right place, right time. Anyway, it's done; forget it.'

'You must have lost a bloody fortune, though. What, with your erm ... activities.'

'Like I told you,' said Billy with a shake of his head, 'it was stuff I wanted rid of anyway. It's no loss - and besides, we're not finished yet.' He let out a silent curse even as he said it, hoping that Hawkins wouldn't catch the comment but knowing that he would.

'Pardon?'

'I mean we might have blown the Upton Park contract, but we've still come out of it all with a tidy little business. That's all I meant.'

Hawkins looked at him, his head tilted to one side, his expression deadpan. 'Bollocks. This is me you're talking to remember. I know when you're bullshitting. So, come on, what's going on?'

Billy took a deep breath and scratched the side of his head in a desperate attempt to avoid making eye contact with his friend. But in the end, he gave up and glanced across at him. 'OK, but if I tell you everything, promise me you're not gonna freak out again.'

Billy stared at Hawkins as he paced up and down the room; unable to work out if he was glad, relieved or furious. In the end, he guessed from the look on his face that it was a mixture of all three. 'Let me get this straight,' he ranted. 'You've gone into partnership with Mickey James?'

'Kind of,' said Billy quietly. 'He keeps my "connections" and we work together on the pubs and clubs. Plus he's doing this little job for me. So, what do you think then?'

Hawkins stopped pacing and sat down. 'I think you're a cunt, that's what. You should have told me all this before - if only to stop me wasting all that bloody time and effort.'

'Maybe I should've, I don't know. I just figured that the less you knew, the better. That way, if anything went wrong, nothing would come back on you.'

'Like fuck it wouldn't,' replied Hawkins angrily.

'Look, there's no way anyone can tie you in with this, so don't worry about that. But this really could work, mate,' he said excitedly. 'And if it does, we'll be fucking quids in.'

Hawkins thought for a moment and then leant forward in his chair, his elbows resting on the desk as he pulled a smoke from its packet, his calm, almost resigned voice totally at odds with the turmoil going on inside his head. 'D'you know what really worries me Billy? It's that despite everything I said to you about not wanting to cross the law, I actually think it could.'

Ian Mirren walked from the maternity ward and, arm in arm with his wife Kathryn, strode along the corridor towards the hospital exit. It had been a good week. No, it had been a great week.

Not only had Sarah, their one and only child, produced their first grandchild that very afternoon, but yesterday he had been officially told that his contract with Upton Park would be renewed for a further two years. Unofficially, of course, it had never been in any doubt. But it didn't do to take such things for granted, especially when it was probably the easiest money he had ever made. After all, it wasn't exactly difficult to manage. Most of the people he employed at the ground had worked there long before he had come on the scene and, as a result, he hardly ever even needed to go down there these days. He much preferred to watch his football at Highbury anyway. It was far more civilised.

The only downside to the past few days had been the trouble at the ground on Wednesday night. When his head of security had rung to tell him what had happened, he had begun to wonder if the club might get twitchy and start to consider the idea of someone new. It was unlikely, but a worry he could have done without, especially with the baby imminent.

Still, having signed the contract yesterday, that was no longer a concern and he could return his attentions to his golf and his new granddaughter. Other people could do the worrying; that's what he paid them for.

He led his wife through reception and out into the dusk. But, suddenly, he began to feel uneasy. And despite the happy chatter of his wife, the further across the half-lit car park they got, the more nervous he felt. And then he saw it, his month-old Jaguar. Every window put through and all four tyres slashed.

He looked at it for a second in absolute horror before grabbing his wife and comforting her as she burst into tears, her sobs covering the whisper of the black BMW's engine as it eased quietly from the car park behind them.

CHAPTER 14
Sunday 16 April 2000
10.15

The four men stood on the tee and stared down the fairway at the man standing in the semi-rough about a hundred metres away from them. 'What the bloody hell is that idiot doing?'

They began calling and gesturing at him to move but in the end gave up. 'Come on Ian, just play,' urged John Morris, a tall, distinguished but short-tempered man who had made his fortune from haulage and scrap metal. 'If the bloody idiot gets hit, it's his own fault. By the look of him, he shouldn't be here anyway.'

The others nodded in agreement and then glanced back up the fairway. John was right. This was an exclusive club, the membership fees alone saw to that. That's why the four of them came here and was why, even on this bright Sunday morning, the course was almost deserted. Besides, whoever, or whatever, this chap was, he was clearly no golfer. He had no clubs for a start.

Ian Mirren stepped forward, pushed his tee into the ground and stood upright. He took a few practice swings with his three wood and then, crack! The monogrammed ball took off into the distance like a small white missile; almost invisible to the eye, until it bounced on the lush green turf and rolled to a halt in a near-perfect position for the dogleg - a short iron to the green.

'Oh, good shot, Ian,' said the others in unison, as Mirren walked forward to collect his plastic tee. 'Let's see if I can ...' John Morris let his voice tail off and Mirren stared at him for a second before turning to follow his gaze up the fairway. 'What's he doing now?'

The four of them looked on in amazement as the man moved out of the semi-rough and walked up the fairway after the ball. When he got to it, he turned and looked back at them for a second before bending down, picking it up and walking off into the distance.

Ian Mirren watched him go in shocked silence, and began to wonder what the fuck was going on.

'Well, what did he say?' Kathryn Mirren's voice, normally so strong and confident, was anxious and unsteady. 'They must be able to do something.'

'All David said was that he'd ask the local police to keep an eye on the place,' replied her husband, struggling to keep the concern from his own voice. 'But really, there's nothing they can do. After all, aside from the car, nothing has actually been done. Man steals golf ball ... so what?'

'But what about the man I saw in the garden last night? He's a police inspector, surely there's ...'

He walked over and drew her to him as a tear ran down her cheek and dropped on to her cream blouse. 'Just because David's a policeman, Kathryn, doesn't make any difference. They can only do something if someone breaks the law.' He held her away from him and smiled as he stared into her damp eyes. 'Look, love, it's just like he said. We're probably worrying over nothing. You know what it's like for joyriders around here and, even if you did see someone in the garden last night, they were probably just looking for a dog or something.' He bent down and kissed her on the cheek. 'Come on, we've got to be strong for Sarah and little Becky. With any luck the infection will have cleared up and they'll be able to go home today.'

She smiled and pulled a tissue from her sleeve, wiping her eyes and blowing her nose before dropping it in the bin. 'You're right. Of course you're right. I'll go and get ready.'

Mirren watched her walk up the stairs and then made his way into the kitchen, his hand shaking slightly as he poured himself a glass of water. Was it fear or was it anger? He couldn't tell. But something was going on. And one way or another, he had to find out why. Then find some way of putting a stop to it.

He glanced at the ceiling as he heard his wife walk across the landing above him and wondered how she'd react if he told her that she wasn't the only one who'd seen someone in their garden last night. The difference was that in his case, there was no doubt, no doubt whatsoever. The half-covered face he'd seen had been staring through the kitchen window - directly at him.

By the time Kathryn Mirren had parked her tiny silver Nissan in the hospital car park, her eagerness to see the baby had blotted out every negative thought in her head and the smile was back on her face. Her husband, however, had not been so fortunate. If anything, his unease had deepened and he was surprised at the level of relief he felt when he saw his daughter sitting on the edge of her bed with the baby lying in the carrycot.

'How is she, love?' he said, embracing her and smiling down at the baby.

'She's fine, Dad. Kevin'll be here in an hour or so and we'll be taking her home.'

Kathryn beamed. 'That's wonderful, Sarah. Can I hold her? Oh look, Ian, she's so gorgeous.'

He smiled at his wife as she lifted the baby and began walking up the ward away from them, bouncing the small bundle up and down like the doting grandmother she was; proudly showing the baby to everyone who cared to look. 'You know that child is going to get spoilt rotten, don't you?'

'Oh yes, Father!' She pulled him down so that he was sitting on the bed next to her, a mock frown on her face and a disapproving tone in her voice. 'You need to speak to the florists tomorrow. The nurses were moaning about it all morning!'

'Why, what for?' he asked.

'The flowers you sent... the florists should have known better than to send red and white carnations to a hospital. Everyone knows it means bad luck. We had to mix them up with the ones Kevin's mum sent. And they forgot the card. We only found out they were from you because the man who made the delivery to reception told them.'

He stared at her open-mouthed. He hadn't sent any flowers to anybody, certainly not to his own daughter. And red and white carnations didn't just mean bad luck; they meant blood and bandages.

Billy Evans sat on his sofa and inwardly congratulated himself as he placed the phone back into its charger.

He'd never met Ian Mirren, never even seen him. But thanks to Mickey James, he now knew almost everything he needed to know about the man and his business. The most important detail was that he was old school, totally legit. The only connections he had were with a few old coppers who were mates. Nothing to worry about.

He looked up as his wife walked into the room and placed a steaming cup down beside him. 'I'm going up, love. You coming?'

'In a minute, gorgeous,' he said. 'I'll just drink my tea first.'

'Well don't fall asleep this time,' she scolded, 'or I'll leave you here.'

'You wouldn't do that to me. You love me too much.'

'Maybe I do, maybe I don't,' she said cheekily. 'And maybe if you come to bed, you'll find out.'

'Is that right?' he said, raising his eyebrows. 'I'll be two minutes then.' He watched her leave the room and leant back with his hands behind his head; staring at the television but not registering what was on the screen as he returned his thoughts to Ian Mirren and tried to imagine how he must be feeling at that very moment. He would be shitting it. Wondering what was going to happen next and, more importantly, when. When, that was the big thing. Would it be tonight, tomorrow, never? It was surely debilitating him, wearing him down and eating him up from the inside.

Billy smiled to himself as he downed his tea. What else could get under your skin like that? Fear, it was such a great weapon.

Ian Mirren lay in bed and stared at the ceiling as he tried desperately to make some sense of what was going on. But it was proving to be a futile exercise, because it didn't make sense; any of it. This was the kind of thing you saw on the television or read about in the *News Of The World*. It happened to celebrities or politicians, not to grandfathers from Essex.

Why? Why him? That's what he couldn't understand. What had he ever done to warrant such malice? He might have been in the security game for a good few years, but he had always stayed at the softer end of the business - shying away from supplying bouncers and bodyguards and sticking to what he knew best: supplying people to act as visible deterrents, not legalised thugs. By doing that, he'd been able to employ only older, stable men who used their heads rather than brute force. Surely none of them was behind this? A disgruntled ex-employee with a grudge? No, the very idea was laughable. He had always got on well with his employees. He was known for it. And besides, he couldn't even remember the last time he'd had to sack anyone. A few had left, sure, but mostly to retire or move to another company; and always with his blessing.

He let out a quiet sigh and gave up trying to work it out, consciously switching his thoughts to his new granddaughter in an effort to blank the nightmare from his memory. But thinking about the hospital only served to remind him of the episode with the flowers, and that had genuinely scared him - mostly because it proved just how vulnerable he and his family were. The one saving grace had been that he had managed to stop Sarah telling Kathryn. Goodness knows how she would have reacted to something like that. As it was, he had made her take a sleeping tablet to knock her out. She would never have slept otherwise.

He glanced across the bed at her and listened for a moment to the sounds of her shallow breathing before rolling over on to his side and staring into the darkness, hoping for sleep but knowing it would never come.

Ian Mirren opened his eyes and was surprised to find that he'd been asleep for almost four hours. Even more surprising was the fact that he actually felt quite refreshed. The worries and concerns of last night had been replaced by a sense of relief - maybe even hope.

A glance at his wife showed that she was still fast asleep so, rather than lay there and start worrying again, he climbed out of bed and made his way downstairs, almost reaching the bottom before it caught his eye: a small shape, barely visible through the frosted glass. He walked up and stared at the shadow for a moment before sliding off the chain and slowly pulling open the door, his throat tightening as he realised what it was.

He stared at the small plastic bag for a moment and then, without pulling it down, closed the door and walked into his front room to call the police.

The two young policewomen could not have been more apathetic if they had tried. Less than half an hour to go until the end of their shift and here they were, sitting with a man telling them that someone had stuck a golf ball to his front door.

Billy leant back in his chair and let out a roar of frustration as he rubbed his hands over his face. He had spent almost two hours wading through the pile of paperwork that had built up over the past week or so and had just about managed to get his nose in front.

After downing the remains of his coffee, he reached over and lifted the cover of the next file sitting in his in-tray. But after surveying its contents for a moment, he dropped it back down again. He'd had enough for a while and needed a break.

So he wandered over to the window and turned his thoughts to the far more interesting subject of Ian Mirren.

If what Mickey had told him last night was true, then he and his lads had been doing a bang-on job. There was more to do, for sure, but at least the process had begun. The most important thing now was to keep the pressure on and for Billy to work out when to make *his* move. If his plan was going to succeed, that had to be timed to perfection. But it had to be soon.

He was still pondering this when his thoughts were interrupted by the shrill clamour of his mobile. He answered it, only to find Mickey James on the other end.

After the inevitably brief small talk, Mickey paused for a second and then said, 'Listen. Seeing as we're partners, any chance I could borrow a few of your lads tonight? I've got a bit of a problem.'

Billy thought for a moment and smiled to himself. 'No problem.'

Ian Mirren had also spent the morning wading through files and paperwork. But, unlike Billy, he didn't resent it; he was glad of it. For, once the police had left his house, Kathryn had insisted on going to work to take her mind off things. And after dropping her off, he had continued on to his own office, rather than return home. The idea of going back to the house and being alone had not been an attractive one: far better to keep busy and avoid worrying.

But his unexpected appearance had shocked the five staff that worked for him. Not only was he unshaven, it was the first time any of them had seen him not wearing a suit. Tracey, his secretary, had even told him he looked tired. What she really meant was that he suddenly looked old.

Hawkins had just climbed into his Mercedes to head for home when Billy's Range Rover pulled in beside him. He climbed back out and was surprised to find that Billy wasn't alone, the remaining seats being occupied by four junior lads from The

Squad. He greeted them warmly as his business partner looked sheepishly on. 'Should I ask?'

Billy shook his head and smiled. 'Best not. I thought you'd have gone by now?'

'Just tidying up a few loose ends. We'll be up and running from tomorrow night.'

'That's great, mate, really. You've done a top job. If you weren't so fucking ugly, I'd give you a kiss.'

Hawkins laughed. 'If *you* weren't so fucking ugly, I'd let you.' He paused for a moment and then opened his car door again. 'Be careful.'

The dark wood and green glass exterior of The Porcupine epitomised everything Billy hated about the post-Canary Wharf East End. It was false and manufactured, existing for one purpose and one purpose only: to exploit.

The whole area was like that. Fuelled by corporate money and the Docklands Light Railway, it had become no more than a leisure park for the privileged few; packed to the rafters with wine bars and pretentious restaurants patronised by moneyed half-wits with no idea of the desperation being endured just streets away. If it hadn't been so tragic, it would have been funny.

Billy and Mickey had sat in the Range Rover for almost half an hour, watching the front of the pub as a succession of suited males and well-dressed women came and went - something which, if anything, had increased Billy's resentment. He'd enjoy watching his lads in action. It would be like his own little revolution.

The thought of his lads brought a smug smile to his face. Not one had baulked when he had rung and asked them to help. But then again, he'd known they wouldn't; that's why he had chosen them. They were lads on the way up, eager to gain acceptance. If the top man asked for a favour, he got it. Without question.

'What time is it?'

'Nearly nine,' replied Billy, without taking his eyes off the pub. 'Any minute now.'

Mickey smiled to himself, his confidence frighteningly obvious. 'You sure about your lads?'

Billy laughed and said, 'Don't worry about them. They know the score. Your man won't know what hit him.'

'Good. Serves the cunt right for stopping his payments,' Mickey said petulantly, before pausing for a second and pointing out through the windscreen. 'Here we go! It's show time by the look of it.'

The two of them watched as four men appeared among the pedestrians on the other side of the road. Each of them wore a baseball cap and sunglasses to avoid the prying eyes of the infrared CCTV cameras, which scanned every inch of every street.

With barely a break in their step, they strode out into the evening traffic and crossed the road, stopping on the pavement outside the pub and staring at it for a second or so before one of them stepped forward and pulled open the door, rolling something inside even as he did so. Immediately, a scream went up, piercing the clamour of the city and forcing pedestrians to stop and stare at what was happening. But before anyone could react, the four men stood back and unleashed a salvo of metal objects at the windows. The small canisters and their merciless contents shattered the glass, showering the people sitting inside with shrapnel.

And then they were off, running away in four different directions as the first of the drinkers poured out on to the pavement in an effort to escape the choking fumes and brightly coloured smoke. But it was too late, even for them. The stinging cruelty of the CS gas had invaded the eyes and lungs of everyone who had been inside, blinding and choking them, inflicting panic.

Billy and Mickey looked on from their air-conditioned comfort: Billy, with a kind of detached pride, Mickey almost in shock. 'Fuck me!' he gasped. 'I only wanted the frighteners put on.'

'We don't piss about,' replied Billy, as he started the engine and eased the car away from the pavement. 'You want a pub blitzed; we blitz a pub. What can I say? It's what we do best.'

Billy and Mickey stood on the roof of the multistorey car park, enjoying a quiet cigarette as they stared out over east London. The clear sky and orange glow of a million street lights gave it an odd kind of beauty, and both felt that unique feeling of satisfaction that can only come from being where you truly belong.

'D'you know,' began Mickey thoughtfully, 'we work well together, you and me. I reckon if we made our arrangement a bit more permanent, we could do big things.'

Without replying, Billy flicked his dog-end against the wall before walking round to the back of the car and taking a set of number plates and a screwdriver from under the carpet. He walked back round to the front and, noticing Mickey's puzzled expression, smiled. 'Fucking cameras everywhere down there. The filth would be at my garage before lunch tomorrow if I left the proper numbers on.' He crouched down and began the switch back to the originals. 'So, what did you have in mind?'

'I can always use muscle, Billy. Especially when it's as effective as your lads obviously are.'

'We don't do muscle,' answered Billy. 'We do numbers. It's safer that way, more anonymous.' He stood up and moved around to the back of the car to change the rear plate, Mickey following as he continued to speak. 'You want a place totalling or a rival mob driving out, we're your lads. But anything else... well, to be honest, I doubt many of them would be up for it. Not unless it was Squad business. It's just too dodgy.'

Mickey shook his head. He'd never understood this obsession with football. To him, it was a total and futile waste - both of time and of effort. Violence was a precious commodity: one to be used as a tool or traded as an asset. 'Well,' he sighed, 'that's a shame. But if anything else comes up, I'll give you a shout.'

Billy stood up as he finished changing the plates and smiled as he wiped his hands on a tissue. 'Any time, mate,' he said. 'But for now, you just keep on at old man Mirren for me.'

'No problem. My lads'll fuck with his head for as long as you want.' He pulled an envelope from his pocket and handed it over. 'Here, your half of the takings.'

'Cheers, partner,' Billy replied with a grin.

Mickey looked at him and paused for a second, unsure whether to ask the one question that had been buzzing around in his head since Billy had first contacted him about it. In the end, desperate to know, he went for it. 'So, you going to let me in on the reason?'

'It's personal. That's all. Just personal.'

CHAPTER 16
Tuesday 18 April 2000
08.15

Despite the amount of water that had been showered upon it, tiny wisps of smoke continued to drift up from among the remains of the small wooden building: evidence that somewhere under all that burnt wood, a few embers clung to life.

Martin Cooke stared at it with anger in his eyes. 'Fucking kids,' he said to one of the firemen who had begun to rake it over in a search for the stubborn spark. 'The little bastards need a good kicking.'

The fireman nodded his head in quiet agreement and studied the man standing next to him for a moment. He looked a decent enough bloke, late fifties, maybe older; possibly even ex-military, judging by his upright manner, and certainly not stupid. The copy of the *Telegraph* sticking out of his rucksack bore testimony to that. But whoever he was, and whatever he'd been, he'd somehow ended up working as a car park attendant. And now even that was gone; the poor bastard's job almost certainly ended by some little sod with nothing better to do, and no sense of right and wrong. After all, who else would waste their time doing something like this?

Graham Hawkins couldn't help but grin as he unpacked the new uniforms and hung them up in his office. He had done a lot in his life: some good, some bad. But he'd never been more proud of anything than he was of this. For despite the dubious origins, the fact was that from today, he was a partner in a brand-new, fully operational and totally legitimate business. More importantly, if the figures and projections were right, it was a business that was going to turn a tidy profit.

'So what d'you reckon then?' he beamed.

Billy sat on the edge of the desk and shrugged his shoulders disapprovingly. 'They're not exactly Paul Smith, are they?' He stared at Hawkins for a second and suddenly burst out laughing. 'Fuck me, you should see your face.'

'You twat!' Hawkins responded with a wry smile. 'You had me going for a minute.'

Billy pushed himself off the desk and examined the uniforms more closely. Not because he cared, but because he knew Hawk did. When he had finished, he punched his partner on the arm and said, 'Hang on. I'll be back in a second,' before walking out the door and instantly returning with the bottle of champagne and two glasses he'd left outside. 'Well done, my son,' he said, handing Hawkins a glass and bursting open the bottle. 'Here's to St George Security. God bless her, and all who sail in her!'

'Cheers!' replied Hawkins excitedly. 'And here's to the future!'

Billy nodded and downed his drink before refilling their glasses and looking sheepishly at his partner. 'Listen, how's about we all go out for an Indian tonight? To celebrate.'

'Well, I'd love to,' sighed Hawkins. 'But I'll have to call Jules and see what she says. Who knows?'

'She'll be OK,' responded Billy, more in hope than expectation. 'Tell her it'll be my treat. Now, what's the plan for this afternoon?'

Ignoring the double yellow lines, Mickey James pulled his car to the side of the road and walked into the newsagents to buy an early edition of the *Evening Standard*.

Scanning through it as he walked back, he was pleased to find a short story on the inside front page headed 'Police investigate gas attack on pub', and he stopped in the middle of the pavement to study the short paragraphs, ignoring all references to the number of injuries but noting with grim satisfaction that the police were appealing for witnesses. Media speak for they had nothing to go on.

Mickey finished reading and with a sly smile returned to his car, throwing the paper on to his passenger seat. 'Page two,' he thought to himself. 'Not bad. Not bad at all.'

Billy put down his mobile and allowed himself a brief smile of smug satisfaction. Everything was going well; the car lot, the new firm and even the thing with Mickey last night. He had quite enjoyed that. Not just seeing some of his lads in action, but watching Mickey's response. He had been seriously impressed, almost respectful. Never a bad thing when you skirt along on the edges of that particular world.

But uppermost in Billy's mind was the situation with Ian Mirren. Fair play, Mickey's lads were doing a good job there and he almost felt sorry for the poor bastard - especially since, according to the call he'd just had, things were about to get a whole lot worse for him.

But the truth was, Mirren had what *he* wanted. And his problems would only stop when Billy had taken it from him. The difficulty was deciding when, and how, to make the move.

He thought about that for a moment and then shrugged his shoulders and picked up the phone. 'Fuck it,' he said out loud. 'No time like the present.'

Tracey Smith had worked for Ian Mirren for more years than she cared to remember. But in all that time, she had never seen him as stressed as he had been these past few days. At first, she'd put it down to the impending birth of his first grandchild, but the baby had arrived safely and this morning, when she had told him about the fire at the Kings Street car park, he had gone as white as a sheet. That had thrown her a bit, and in her usual blunt manner, she had asked him what was going on; adding that whatever problem he had simply wasn't worth what it was doing to him. He was almost fifty-eight after all.

But he had dismissed her concerns, and a little too angrily for her liking. And now she was back at her desk, wondering what could possibly be having such an effect. The baby was fine, the business was doing OK and, unless something had happened to Kathryn since she'd spoken to her last week, it couldn't possibly be that. She'd been as right as rain; which left only unthinkable things. Was Ian ill? Was he having an affair? Or was it even worse than that? Could it be worse than that?

She sighed and shook her head. She was being stupid, letting her imagination run away with her. Maybe he was simply tired. He was due a holiday, after all.

The phone dragged her from her worries and, within seconds, she had the diary open and was scribbling an entry in for the following day. 'That's fine, Mr Evans. Mr Mirren will expect you at two o'clock.'

'Will you stop looking at your bloody watch?' hissed Julie Hawkins.

'I can't help it. I'm nervous.'

Billy laughed. 'Bless his heart. He's worried about his lads aren't you, Hawk?'

'Leave him alone,' said Samantha disapprovingly. 'I think it's fantastic what you've done Graham and you should be proud of yourself, not like this lazy git. I bet he did sod all.'

'He didn't,' replied Hawkins, loading as much self-pity into his voice as possible. 'I did everything.'

Billy smiled and bit his lip. Normally, he would have responded with an instant one-liner but, in this instance, he held back, wary of saying anything that Julie might possibly take the wrong way. After all, judging by the expression on her face when he and Sam had picked them up, it had almost certainly taken all his friend's powers of persuasion to get her to come out in the first place. And even though her mood had softened considerably, the last thing he wanted to do was spoil the evening. Besides, he needed to keep her on side - if only for Hawk and Sam's sake. 'He might joke about it,' he said thoughtfully, 'but Sam's right. Without him, this would never have happened.'

Julie glanced at her husband and smiled as she took hold of his hand. 'I suppose he's not a bad bloke really. It was a shame about the West Ham contract, though. You put a lot of work into that, didn't you, lover?'

Yeah. It would have been nice,' replied Hawk, his voice containing a slight hint of nerves. 'But never mind. You win some, you lose some.'

Billy looked at him and inwardly smiled to himself as he tried to catch his eye, but Hawk avoided making contact, his obvious embarrassment being saved by the sudden appearance of the waiters with their meal. Billy leant back in his chair as the food was spread out on the table in front of them and allowed the smile to spread across his face. They might not have won, but they certainly hadn't lost. Not yet. But, from the look on Hawkins' face, it was crystal clear that only one of them was ever going to be involved in the fight.

'How's your mum and dad, Julie? I haven't seen 'em for ages.'

CHAPTER 17
Wednesday 19 April 2000
09.15

Ian Mirren had barely walked through his office door when the call came through bringing him the latest instalment of bad news. He stood still for a moment as the full impact of it sunk in and then slumped into his chair with the handset still clasped firmly to his ear.

His life was turning into a living, breathing nightmare.

'So, how did it go then? Any panics?' Billy leant back in his chair and drew on his cigarette.

'No,' said Hawk happily. 'Nothing that I've heard about anyway. The lads would have rung by now if they'd have had anything to say.'

'See, I told you not to worry. It's sound, mate. Money for old rope.'

'I guess so. But I'll be making some calls today, getting some feedback. Oh, and thanks for last night, by the way. Sorry if Julie was a bit... well, you know.'

Billy raised his hand to stop him. 'Forget it, mate. Honestly. It's not a problem.'

The gates leading in to Upton Park were wide open, allowing Ian Mirren to steer the tiny Nissan straight in. He parked as near to the main entrance as he could and climbed out to see David Knight, head of security at the ground, strolling towards him, his face wearing an odd, almost bemused look. 'Where's the Jag?'

Mirren sniffed angrily. 'Don't ask. Just show me.'

The two of them strode from the car park and made their way out on to the pitch, where a line-marking machine sat right on the centre spot.

'Whoever broke in last night stole it from the garage under the stand. But that's the odd thing, there's no sign of a break-in or any other damage. Just this.'

'And have we any idea *how* they got in?' asked Mirren.

'None. There was a reserve game last night, so maybe they sneaked in and stayed behind. We're checking the security tapes though. Maybe they'll come up with something.'

'What about the police?'

'No, the club want them kept out of it. Bad publicity and all that.'

Mirren paused for a moment and then ran a hand through his thinning hair as he walked forward into the centre circle. 'So come on then, David. Why would anyone want to break into a football ground, steal a line marker and paint three Vs in the centre of the pitch?'

'Christ knows,' replied Knight, walking after him and bending down to study the markings. 'But I don't think they're Vs. I think they're ticks. Like the Nike ones.'

'Oh great,' said Mirren, throwing his arms up into the air. 'That'll be so much easier to explain to the bloody chairman.'

The offices of Mirren Events Ltd were nothing like Billy had expected. For some reason, he had imagined they would be a hive of open-plan activity but, instead, what he found was a large room containing three middle-aged women and décor which looked an odd combination of old-fashioned and homely. In a strange way, it reminded him of his mum's front room.

A fourth woman came over to greet him and, after introducing herself as Tracey, Mirren's secretary, she led Billy through to the far end of the room where a small area had been set aside as a reception. He accepted her offer of a drink and, after waving aside her apologies for Mirren's enforced absence, settled into the uncomfortable armchair and began his wait; noticing, as he sat there, that the pace of life wasn't exactly hectic. It was typical of a business that had settled into a comfortable routine and where expansion was a dirty word.

He finished his coffee and turned his attention to the woman sitting at the desk opposite him. She was slightly younger than the others, early forties at a guess, with an air of authority and confidence that went far beyond that of a humble secretary. Billy had met plenty of women like her over the years: protectors, he called them. And they were the real power behind a decent business, organising diaries and dealing with the day-to-day chores of office life while their bosses got on with more important things in a kind of remote bliss. It was exactly what Jill did for him, and was why she was so important.

'How long have you worked here, Tracey?' he asked cheerfully, adding, 'if it's not too rude of me to ask.'

She stopped what she was doing and smiled warmly. 'Not at all. I've worked for Mirren's since the company first started, in 1987.'

'Thirteen years! Blimey, that's a fair old time. You must like it here then?'

'Yes,' she giggled. 'I suppose I do.'

'And you've never fancied a change? There's a big demand for good personal assistants you know.'

She laughed out loud. 'Are you offering me a job?'

'No,' replied Billy with a sly grin. 'I couldn't afford you. Besides, my guess is that if you left, this company wouldn't be able to function properly. Am I right?'

Her cheeks flushed as she lowered her eyes and smiled, flattered that someone was paying her the kind of attention she rarely got anywhere else. 'I really should get on.'

Billy held up a hand to apologise and was about to ask if he could use the toilet when the door at the far end opened and a man strode in, his smart clothing totally at odds with the expression on his face. He looked like he hadn't slept for days.

'At last!' groaned Tracey. 'I'm so sorry you've had to wait.'

Billy looked Mirren up and down as he approached. Like the surroundings, he wasn't what he had been expecting at all. He looked older for a start, certainly more aged than the fifty-eight years Billy knew him to be. He stood up and held out his hand, Tracey appearing by his side as he did so.

'Ian, this is Mr Evans, your two o'clock appointment.'

Mirren smiled and, ignoring the reference to his poor timekeeping, shook Billy's hand with a weak, almost limp grip. 'Please, come through,' he said before leading Billy into a small office, which somehow managed to look even less dynamic than the outer one.

'So,' he began, gesturing at Billy to sit down as he took off his jacket. 'Tracey tells me you're interested in using our services.'

Billy looked him up and down for a second. 'No, that's not strictly true.'

'I'm sorry,' said Mirren, as he sat down, a puzzled frown on his face. 'But I was told that...'

'That *is* what I told your secretary, that's true. But it's not actually what I want.'

'Oh, I see.' Mirren leant forward and rested on his elbows. 'So what are you selling?'

'I'm not selling,' said Billy confidently. 'I'm buying. I want to buy your company.'

Mirren's jaw almost hit the floor. 'I beg your pardon?'

'I want to buy your company,' repeated Billy calmly.

With a slight shake of his head, Mirren took a second to gather himself together and then smiled, leaning back in his chair as he did so. 'And what on earth makes you think I'm looking to sell it?'

'You're not,' replied Billy. 'Or at least you weren't until about fifteen seconds ago.'

'OK, I'll rephrase the question. What makes you think I'd *want* to sell it?'

Billy rested back in his chair with his arms folded across his lap. 'Well, look at the facts, Ian. You're fifty-eight years old and the only child you've got is a daughter who's married to a building society branch manager. He's hardly likely to fancy a career change when you retire, is he? And your daughter can't run it, not with the new baby. So eventually, this business will *have* to be sold. All I'm offering is the chance for you to do it sooner rather than later. We'd pay a fair price. And even keep you on as a director if you'd like.'

'I think,' said Mirren, standing up and walking over towards the door, 'that you should leave.'

'I'm sorry you feel like that,' said Billy with a sigh, rising to his feet and reaching into his jacket pocket. 'But please take my card and think about it. I'm sure your wife would jump at the chance to have you at home more. And besides, do you really need all this stress?'

'What stress?'

Billy laughed. 'Come on, Ian, if it's not vandalism, it's shoplifting, break-ins or robberies ... well you know. And if no one gets caught, who does the customer blame? The security company. Why else do they pay us?'

For the first time, Mirren took a proper look at the man in front of him. He was vaguely familiar but he just couldn't put a finger on where from. The business card was certainly no help. 'St George Security Ltd. I've never heard of them.'

'We're fairly new,' said Billy proudly. 'But I'm looking to expand as quickly as possible. That's one of the reasons why your company is so attractive to us. It's small but well known. And you offer a range of different services. That's good.'

Mirren shrugged as he pulled open the door. 'I'm sorry you've wasted your time. But I've no intention of selling up, not for a few years yet.'

'Well, I wouldn't call it a waste,' said Billy warmly as he shook Mirren's hand and made to leave. 'And when you're ready to talk, give me a call. My mobile's on there as well if you need it.'

He gave him a final smile and turned away, but before he was fully out of the office, he paused for a second and then turned back, lowering his voice and his forehead as if in admonishment.

'Don't leave it too long though, will you? We can't hang about forever. After all, the clock's ticking.'

'Bollocks!' Billy climbed into his car and slammed the door. 'Bollocks, bollocks, bollocks!' He had fucked up and he knew it. Because although he had harboured a distant hope that Mirren would simply take the money and run, he'd known that it was far more likely that he would need a bit more persuading first. And with that in mind, Billy had planned to drop in a few well-chosen hints about some of the things that had been going on in the background; hopefully just enough to help him consider that there might possibly be a connection.

But instead, he'd been far too cool and had almost certainly achieved nothing except showing his hand and getting on Mirren's tits. Even the clock reference was obscure. For all Billy knew, he might never have even seen the bloody things.

He sat there for a moment and lit a cigarette, desperately searching for something positive he could take from the meeting. By the time he'd finished his smoke, he'd found it.

Ian Mirren sat at his desk and stared at Billy's business card, spinning it between his fingers as he ran the meeting over and over in his mind. Something was bothering him and he couldn't work out what. It wasn't the fact that someone wanted to buy him out - that was nothing new - he'd had plenty of offers in the past, most of them from people after the West Ham contract. And it wasn't even the fact that Evans had known so much about him and his family. That kind of information could easily be found if you knew where to look.

No, it was more to do with the man. He hadn't warmed to him at all. There was something about him, a strange kind of menace that made every word sound like a threat. And all that talk of stress, what was that all about? Christ, if Evans thought the security game was stressful, he should come round his house. Even the bollocking he'd had from the West Ham chairman that morning was preferable to the idea of another night lying in bed, listening to every sound and imagining the worst.

But he guessed that what was really irritating him about Evans was that although he was sure he knew him, he couldn't work out where from. And it wasn't just the face either; it was the name. He knew that name.

With a sigh, he reached forward and picked up the phone. 'Tracey, can you get hold of David Peterson for me please?

He's an inspector with the Met in Tottenham. His number's in the file.'

He sat back and waited as the call was connected, dropping the card on the desk in front of him but continuing to stare at it as he thought about his terrible morning, his terrible week. Sometimes the idea of selling up wasn't so bad after all.

A knock on the door interrupted him and he smiled as Tracey entered his office. 'Sorry, Ian, he's away until Friday afternoon. I've left a message, though, and they've promised he'll call.'

'What the fuck do I need a secretary for?' asked Hawkins. 'I've hardly got enough work for me as it is.'

'She's not just a secretary, Hawk, she got thirteen years' worth of contacts stored up here,' said Billy, tapping the side of his head as he spoke. 'D'you know what that's worth? Besides, if we can get her away from Mirren, he'll be fucked. That business would die on its arse within weeks and then the bastard will be gagging to sell.'

CHAPTER 18
Thursday 20 April 2000
13.15

After folding the letter and sliding it into the envelope, Billy sealed the flap down and threw it into his out-tray.

Despite Hawk's reluctance, he had decided to proceed with his plan to lure Tracey Smith away from Mirren's. Not, as Hawk had pointed out, because he necessarily needed her, but because it was simply another way to apply pressure on her employer. At the very least, the offer he'd just written out would unsettle her. At best, she would walk. And that would leave Ian Mirren in the shit and wide open for a take-over. His goal was getting closer. He could almost smell it.

Thinking about Mirren brought a wry smile to his face and so he dug around in his pocket for his mobile and rang Mickey, desperate to find out the latest.

'No, we didn't do nothin' to your man last night,' replied an almost cheerful voice when he posed the question. 'We couldn't. Wednesday and Thursday are collection days, mate. You should know that, you take half the bloody dosh. In fact, you should see what you're getting for your money. Why don't you go out with the lads tonight?'

'Fuck that!' replied Billy. 'What do I want to do that for?'

'I know it sounds daft, but it's a giggle. Honest.'

'How the fuck d'you make that out?'

Mickey laughed. 'Just watching the punters roll over. It's a power thing. Gives me a hard-on sometimes.'

Billy paused for a second. Up to a few weeks ago, the very idea of bullying would have left him cold. He'd been brought up to believe that it was cowardly and pathetic, and although people who knew no better believed that's what they did at football, they were wrong. For the most part, the Saturday scene only involved people who wanted to be involved. Sometimes you came out on top, sometimes you didn't. Everyone who played the game knew and accepted that.

Bullying was different, much different. Sure, as Mickey had said, it was about power - in that respect at least, it was no different to being in a firm. But in this instance it was about exerting that power over people who were weaker and scared, not equal. That was the big difference between what Mickey did and what he did at football.

But things had changed. The stuff with Mirren had shown him that no matter what his personal feelings, bullying was a useful weapon. One which worked. The money Mickey had handed him after they'd watched The Porcupine being totalled had proved that.

'Tell you what,' he said. 'I'll shadow them if you come along with me.'

There was a pause and then Mickey replied. His voice, if anything, sounding even more buoyant. 'All right then, where d'you wanna meet?'

Billy sat in the passenger seat of Mickey's BMW and stared out into the darkness. He was bored out of his mind.

The first few pubs he'd walked into had actually given him quite a buzz. Nervous energy had been hammering through him as he'd watched the landlords hand over their money. But, for him at least, the thrill had quickly diminished when it became clear that none of the publicans had given it a second thought. There'd been no moaning, no hesitation, not even any abuse. Two of them had even been quite chatty, handing over a free beer to all four of them and talking to Mickey like they were old mates. In the end, it had become so routine that Mickey had told the other two to carry on while he and Billy remained in the car.

'Not what you expected, is it?' asked Mickey, turning to face his passenger.

Billy shrugged. 'To be honest, mate, no it ain't. Then again, I didn't really know what to expect.'

Mickey smiled and lit a roll-up, the pungent smell filling the car and forcing Billy to open a window. 'Like I told you before, this game's a piece of piss. You just gotta be ready for anything. But, more importantly, the punters have got to know that you're ready. If they know, they'll pay up. It ain't worth their while not to.'

'So what's next, then?' asked Billy in an effort to make conversation. 'You gonna expand?'

'Sure am,' replied Mickey, starting the car as his two lads came wandering across the road towards them. 'That's why I wanted your lads on the firm. With clout like that, it'd be a stroll.'

'Not gonna happen though. Like I said, a few'd probably do it as a one-off. But regular? I don't know, mate. I'll have to think about that one. It ain't the kind of thing you just come out and ask people, is it?'

Mickey reached over and took an envelope from the two men who climbed in behind them and then, after dropping it on Billy's lap, grinned and pulled the car away from the kerb. Heading off in the direction of Stepney and their final call.

'What is that place?' asked Billy, staring across the deserted street at the dimly lit concrete façade of a seemingly derelict house.

'Illegal drinking den,' replied Mickey. 'Load of Bosnian refugees set it up in the cellar when the local pubs refused to serve 'em. Thieving fuckers the lot of them.'

Billy let out a sly sniff at the irony of Mickey's comment. 'Your lads've been a while, ain't they?'

Mickey glanced at his watch. 'Yeah, they have. Too fucking long. Come on, let's take a gander.'

He climbed out and wandered across the street, Billy following in his wake, scanning the area as he walked. He always felt uneasy around here, but had never been able to put his finger on why. There was just something about the place. If anything, it was just too rough. Even for him.

'What's that?' asked Mickey, stopping and leaning forward, straining to hear something.

Billy stood beside him and listened. A muffled noise was battling to be heard above the distant hum of the traffic. 'That's shouting mate. There's a row going on somewhere.'

'Bollocks!' barked Mickey angrily. He grabbed his phone and dialled a number. But when there was no answer, he thrust it back into his pocket and stared across at the building for a second. The noise was louder now, the shouting more obvious. 'Wait here a sec.' He ran back towards his car and opened the boot, returning within seconds, a glint in his eye and two baseball bats in his hands. He handed one to Billy and took a deep breath. 'Here, you might need this.'

Billy stared at him as his stomach jumped into his throat and pure adrenaline began pumping through his body. The speed with which Mickey had changed from a seemingly cocky chancer into an aggressive and obviously violent individual was astonishing. More so because for the first time since he'd ever been in his company, Billy actually felt like he was a subordinate, following for once rather than leading. It was a feeling he hadn't experienced for years, and it wasn't one he felt comfortable with.

'Come on!' Mickey snarled as he ran toward the cellar steps. 'Let's batter these fuckers!'

Billy trotted behind him, instinctively swinging the bat to loosen his joints, as well as to get a feeling for the weight. Finally, he broke into a sprint as, without hesitating, Mickey flew down the steps and burst through the doors, releasing the noise from inside and allowing it to explode out into the street. Ugly voices were shouting in a foreign language which shocked Billy with their sheer ferocity.

Then, even before he had made it through the doors into the brightly lit room, the voices were replaced by the high-pitched screaming of a single Anglo-Saxon tongue. The aggressive guttural language was punctuated by the sound of breaking glass and sickening thudding noises as the wooden club found its target.

Billy slowed as he walked in, his bat held firmly in both hands as he swivelled his head around and looked for an attack that was never going to come. For, despite their numerical superiority, the dark-haired eastern European men who minutes earlier had been battering the shit out of Mickey's two lads were now cowering against the walls as he stood in front of them, waving his bat around and lashing out indiscriminately with one hand as he pointed angrily at the man behind the bar with the other.

'Barry? Dave?' he called. 'Where the fuck are you?'

A noise from the other side of the room drew their attention and one of the two men stood up, helping the other to his feet as he did so. Billy smiled inwardly as he saw that they'd taken a major kicking. The dark-eyed character from the St George had come off particularly badly.

'Come on. Let's go,' scowled Mickey before turning back to the barman and shaking his head.

When the two men had made their way past him and out of the room, Mickey walked over to the bar and punched the barman full in the face. The blow shattered his nose and drove him backwards against the wall. But before he could fall to the ground, Mickey had jumped across the counter and grabbed him by the throat, only letting him fall when he was satisfied that a lesson had been dealt out. Billy glanced urgently around the room at the nervous customers as he hit him again. Mickey stared down at the prone body for a second and then, after emptying the till drawer, jumped back over the bar before walking past Billy and out into the fresh air without even glancing back. Billy followed in his wake like a nervous lap dog.

'What the fuck happened?' barked Mickey as he drove the BMW out of the street and away from the bar.

'Cunts jumped us as soon as we were in the door,' groaned Dave, the taller of the two men. 'We never stood a chance.'

'Shit! The bastards have stuck me!' gasped Barry. 'I'm bleedin' like a pig.'

'Watch the bloody upholstery, then!' growled Mickey. 'I don't wanna have to explain that away. How bad is it anyway? Take a look for us will ya, Billy?'

Billy turned and looked down. It was dark in the car but when Barry lifted his shirt, he could clearly see a stab wound. 'Not too bad. It'll need stitches though.'

Mickey nodded. 'Where's the nearest hospital?'

'The London in Whitechapel I reckon,' replied Billy. 'Don't know if there's a casualty department there though.'

'That'll do,' said Mickey. 'If there ain't one, they'll know where to go.'

He glanced in the mirror at the other man. 'What about you Dave?'

'I'll live. Just got a few bruises, but thank fuck I had a blade with me. At least I got a few of the bastards.'

Billy shook his head and turned to find Mickey looking at him with a broad smile on his face. 'See? I told you it gets exciting. All you gotta do is wait.'

After dropping his man at the hospital, Mickey took Dave to Bethnal Green, then he and Billy headed towards the St George for a much-needed pint and to recover the Range Rover.

'Tell you what, mate,' said Billy as he sank into a booth. 'I'm impressed. When we were younger, I always had you down as a bit of a mug - but fair play, you know the score all right. You certainly scared the shit out of me. Fuck knows what you did to them.'

Mickey swallowed a mouthful of lager and shrugged. 'Prison life, mate. Sharpens you up. You ever been inside?'

Billy shook his head. 'No fucking chance. And I ain't got no plans to go in, either.'

'Sound move,' replied Mickey without a trace of a smile. 'Forget what anyone else tells you, it's a fucking nightmare. Every day's a battle: against the screws, against time and against the other cons. I met some good blokes in the nick, fair enough, but I met some right evil bastards as well.'

'And I suppose you're some kind of angel!' laughed Billy.

'No mate. But the one thing I learnt inside is that you do what you have to do to get by. The key is always to think of the consequences first. Take tonight, I went in there with all guns blazing, but I knew that they'd back down and I knew that they wouldn't call the Old Bill.'

'How?' asked Billy.

Mickey laughed and lit another roll-up. 'Stands to reason. Most of the people who use that place are illegal immigrants, so the last people they wanna see is the law. But just as importantly, they got out of wherever it is they came from because someone else was treating them like shit. It's been like that for years out there. They're used to being oppressed so you stand up to 'em and give it large; they back down every time. They're fucking scum.'

Billy looked at him and shrugged his shoulders. He suddenly felt very uncomfortable in Mickey's presence. 'Listen mate,' he said with a glance at his watch. 'I gotta shoot. I'll give you a bell later in the week, OK? See what the score is.'

As ever, the front of his house was brightly lit but for once, as Billy sat in his car staring at it, he hadn't given it a thought. Instead, he was trying to clear his head of everything that had happened tonight. For the truth was that he hadn't enjoyed it, any of it. Playing second fiddle to someone had not been a pleasant experience, nor had being in a position where he'd felt out of control. But he'd also begun to feel uneasy about some of the things Mickey had said. Or to be more specific, the way that he'd said them. Referring to people as scum was one thing, but saying it with as much venom as he had was something else. He could have understood it if they'd have been at football, and the pub had been full of Chelsea, Millwall or even Old Bill. They really *were* scum, at least as far as Billy was concerned. But these had just been people trying to live their lives in a bit of peace and quiet and enjoy a quiet pint. OK, a few of them had decided to have a pop back, but did they deserve to get the shit kicked out of them for that? Especially for a poxy hundred and fifty quid.

With a sigh, he started the car and edged it along the road and into his drive. Maybe Hawk had been right about this after all. Taking Mickey's money was one thing, but actually being there when it was being earned was something else entirely.

All his life, Ian Mirren had played it straight. He could honestly say, with his hand on his heart, that aside from the odd traffic offence, he had never crossed the law in any way shape or form.

That said, there could be no denying that he'd made a good living from crime; as a business, trying to prevent it had served him well these past thirteen years. And for the most part, he'd enjoyed himself. Even though, deep down, he'd always been aware that in terms of actual crime fighting, what he was doing wasn't of any real value. He was just exploiting a bad situation and lining his own pockets at the expense of others. But because of that, he'd always had a suspicion that sooner or later, crime, as an entity, would turn round and bite him back in some way: extract its own revenge for his years of legalised pilfering. What he had never expected, however, was for it to be like this.

Speaking to his friend David, and hearing what he'd had to say about Evans, had shocked him. More than that, it had frightened him. And it wasn't just being reminded of who and what he was or suddenly understanding what it was he was after. It was other things, such as his absolute self-confidence, and the cryptic comments he had thrown into the conversation during their meeting. Each one had been carefully constructed to appear meaningless on its own, but when you added the one vital piece of information he had kept secret - his background - they suddenly assembled themselves like some mental jigsaw; screaming out that he was the man responsible for all the problems that had caused Kathryn and him so much distress in such a short space of time. And that had been another thing that had scared him: the fact that Evans had been able to exert such an influence on their lives so easily; terrifying her and making him feel more vulnerable and helpless than he had ever felt.

Realising all that had left him with a simple choice. He could go to the police and invite more trouble for himself and his family, or he could give Evans what he obviously wanted and get out, winning back his peace of mind at a stroke.

That had been the clincher. He was tired of being fearful and tired of seeing the look on his beloved Kathryn's face every time she turned off a light or opened a curtain.

And at least this way, if he played it right, Evans would give him a decent sum. Then he could retire, and play golf every day.

The mobile rang just as Billy was about to put his key in the front door and, after letting out yet another silent curse, he pulled it from his pocket and stuck it to his ear. To say he was astonished to hear Ian Mirren's voice was an understatement.

He listened in disbelief for a moment and then punched the air in silent celebration before calming himself down, desperately struggling to keep his voice composed.

'That's great news, Ian. It really is. Yes, I'm sure the accountants can sort it all out between them. I'll get mine to contact your office in the morning and we'll get this completed as quickly as possible.'

As the voice continued to speak, the smile faded from Billy's lips and he took a deep breath, releasing it slowly and silently to ensure his voice would appear as unruffled as possible.

'Well, I'm not too sure what this has to do with me, Ian, but, if I were in your shoes, I really wouldn't worry too much about it. In my experience, this type of thing has a habit of stopping as quickly as it begins.'

Part Three

In common with many of his colleagues, Sergeant Gary Roberts, West Ham's dedicated football liaison officer, had just returned from a hard-earned post-Euro 2000 holiday.

He had worked almost non-stop during the months leading up to the tournament. And with a further three weeks out in the Low Countries, acting as a spotter for the Belgian police, his fortnight's break in the Florida sunshine had been much needed and hugely enjoyable - if only because he had been able to reacquaint himself with his wife and two kids, and vice versa.

However, with the new season less than a month away, he was now back in harness. And although he could have done without having to spend the past two days with the lads from the National Criminal Intelligence Service, attending various post-Euro 2000 debriefs and hooligan related forums, today, at least, had not been too bad.

For, having endured the final debrief, the officers from NCIS had provided some much-needed relief by giving out some of the unofficial arrest figures for last season. And Gary had been singled out for particular praise as, according to their data, arrestable offences at the Boleyn ground had bucked the trend and actually fallen right across the board.

In fact, aside from the trouble on the night of the Newcastle match, things had improved so much at Upton Park that the last three home fixtures had seen barely any problems at all. Even the final game of the season, traditionally one of the year's most volatile, had passed by almost totally trouble-free, the only two arrests being for a touting offence and a drunk and disorderly. Considering that the visitors had been Leeds United, that was nothing less than incredible.

Gary, of course, had been happy to milk the praise that came his way from the other FLOs. He had even given a short impromptu talk about intelligence-gathering and community relations in the East End. However, the truth was he had been wondering what had been going on for some considerable time, and was at a total loss to understand why things had taken such a sudden and unexpected turn for the better.

For a while, he had put it down to Euro 2000 and a reluctance among members of the CSS to get involved in anything which might result in either a six o'clock knock or a banning order, both of which would have prevented them from travelling to the tournament. But then, just as the media were beginning their usual pre-tournament hooligan frenzy, they had surprised him by kicking it off at Old Trafford and, even more worryingly, at home on the night of the Newcastle game. The fact that both incidents had been so well organised and involved so many lads had shaken him a bit. And, when quiet had returned for the next few games, he had started to become seriously concerned that the two incidents had been nothing more than a sign of intent, designed to show the other English mobs that the CSS were going out to the Low Countries mobbed up, and would be in the thick of things.

However, he had been pleasantly surprised to discover that only about forty of West Ham's main lads had travelled to the tournament. And although a couple had been deported, for the most part, they had been well behaved. He wasn't even that convinced that the ones who'd been sent home had actually been doing anything. From what he'd heard, it seemed far more likely that they'd been victims of the Belgian police tactic of rounding people up en masse and sending them home. The trouble was the fact that the CSS hadn't shown had blown his already flimsy theory apart. And now he was as baffled as ever.

Still, at the end of the day, whatever was happening wasn't doing him any harm. And if, as was looking increasingly likely, trouble was genuinely on the decline at Upton Park, then who was he to worry about it? Maybe all his efforts were finally starting to pay off.

Tracey Smith placed a cup of coffee down on her desk and allowed herself a brief smile. After thirteen years working for Ian Mirren, she still found it difficult to believe how different everything felt now that the company had changed owners. And it wasn't just the new decoration or the fact that she had been given a promotion to company secretary either. There was a buzz about the place she had never known before.

It hadn't been all plain sailing though. For while Graham had quickly impressed her with the way he worked, it had taken a couple of weeks to get used to having someone else in the office behind her. And there had been all kinds of problems with the garage business he and Billy had brought in. That was until she had got sick and tired of dealing with complaints and spent a whole weekend re-writing all the patrol routes and working out a way of combining them to make things easier. It had been hard work, but she had done it. Now, each vehicle visited a variety of different locations using one of five patrol routes. More importantly, the way the routes criss-crossed meant that every location received frequent and random visits.

The customers certainly approved, and complaints had dropped right off. They had even begun to get recommended to other businesses and that hadn't happened for a few years.

Yet while she was certainly enjoying her work, and got on well with Graham, and Billy when he was there, there were still a few things she was puzzled about, one of which was why Ian had left so quickly. That had never really been explained at all. And, although he was still listed as a director, she hadn't seen or heard anything of him since the company had been sold and he didn't seem to be doing any work, so what was the point? He certainly wasn't getting paid.

Nor could she understand the decision to retain the name Mirren Events Ltd. Billy had said something about wanting to establish a personal relationship with existing customers before they even thought about a change, but that hadn't made sense at all. If anything, they were already giving a better service, so why not shout about it?

But the main thing that had been bothering her was that, for some reason she had not been able to work out, neither Graham nor Billy would have anything to do with the West Ham contract. They had looked at it, and had even had their lawyers go through it, but if there had been any communication with the club, they had insisted that she deal with it. Just as bizarre had been their request that she keep news of Ian's departure from them. Even David Knight, the head of security, had been included in that; although, what with the close season as well as the fact that he rarely came into the office anyway, it hadn't been that hard.

They had even turned down the standard invitations to the club's end-of-season function and, instead had asked her to attend on behalf of the company. Not that she'd complained, far from it. She'd had a fantastic time. But she had felt very uncomfortable whenever anyone had asked about Ian and had been forced to choose her words very carefully.

Still, it seemed as though that at least was finally going to change. That morning Graham had asked her to arrange a meeting with the club to discuss the security for next season, and both he and Billy were due to see the chairman at Upton Park tomorrow.

Maybe then all this cloak-and-dagger stuff would be over with. It had been fun for a while, but now it was starting to feel a bit childish.

The volume on the television had been turned down so low that Hawkins couldn't have made out what was being said, even if he'd been interested in listening.

Instead, with Julie on a night shift, he had spent much of the evening sitting alone on his sofa, thinking about the appointment at Upton Park in the morning. For despite all the work he and Billy had put in that afternoon, working out responses to the inevitable questions, he was starting to feel increasingly nervous. Not about failure - the pessimist in him only really rated their chances of pulling it off at fifty-fifty anyway - but at the sudden awareness of the possible consequences were the contract actually to be taken off them.

His biggest fear was that, despite the increasing success of the rest of the security business, if Billy lost out on the one thing that had been all but consuming him these last few months, he might lose interest in the whole thing and sell out. And if he did, where would that leave him? Almost certainly back on the dole and that would be a nightmare. He had enjoyed having money in his pocket again and, despite no longer being a full partner, having been unable to put any money in, Billy had insisted that he become managing director of Mirren's and had even given him a stake in the projected profits. So he stood to miss out on a tidy sum if it didn't work out.

But equally, for the first time he had begun to consider the financial loss Billy might have to take. For, when the worth of the company had been established, it had included the very lucrative contract at West Ham, a contract which had already been signed by Ian Mirren and which was due to run for another two years. It didn't take a genius to work out that without it, that value, even with the garage business added, would be much, much lower. And as far as he knew, Billy had bought the company at the initial price, almost certainly having to borrow to do it. Could he carry that burden and live with the reduced profits? Or would he be forced to cut his losses and salvage what he could, again with the obvious consequences for him?

Of course, there was always the possibility that they would pull it off and that he was worrying for nothing. He actually felt better prepared for a meeting than he had ever done before - which was something. And with so much at stake, they had to give it their best shot. After all, they had come so far and were so close. What did they have to lose?

Billy Evans was also alone, and also wide-awake. With Samantha out for the evening and the kids in bed, he had spent his time soaking in the bath and then playing *FIFA 2000* on his PlayStation. But unlike his friend, he had no fears or concerns about their meeting. Instead, he was buzzing.

For him, the past few months had been nothing less than one long plot-up. Admittedly, the stakes were higher, and the objectives different, but the basics had been the same as they were for any tear-up: know what you've got, know what they've got and then do whatever it takes to get a result. And although it had taken some time to pull it all together, he finally had everything he needed. He was ready.

But it hadn't been easy - far from it. After the battering PJ had been given on the night of the Newcastle game, the lads had wanted to spend what was left of the season taking it to the Old Bill. Thankfully, albeit after a struggle, he had persuaded them to hold back, convincing them that with Euro 2000 on the horizon, the filth would have free rein over the Saturday scene and would have no problem using that to settle a few old scores. Far better to bide their time and do things properly later on, than get banged away now, for nothing.

And then the situation with Mirren had come to a head; much earlier, and far easier, than he had expected it would. The problem had been raising the money to buy him out. But in the end, rather than go down the more traditional route, he had gone to see Mickey James and the two of them had come to an arrangement. One that meant that he got some interest-free finance and Mickey had access to the CSS until the loan was repaid. It was a facility he had wasted no time in employing - and with devastating effect. On at least eight separate occasions he had taken some of the less law-abiding and more substance-fuelled lads, and used them to exert influence over pubs and clubs who hadn't been willing to take part in his expansion programme. It had worked every time, and everyone was happy. Mickey's business was expanding, Billy was using his increased earnings to pay back his loan and the lads were getting their regular fix of fun as well as a few quid in their pockets.

However, the serious work had started once he had signed the contract to take over Mirren's. And that's when Hawk had really come into his own. Not only had he done a bang-on job running the company, but between the two of them, they had spent hours making sure that every single detail was straight, so that when they were ready to show their hand, there would be nothing which could trip them up.

And now, after weeks of work, the time *was* right. Everything they could possibly need was in place and tomorrow they would stage the hit that would elevate the CSS to a whole new level. And he couldn't wait.

Billy and Hawkins sat quietly in the black Range Rover.

Each wrapped up in their own thoughts, they stared at the front of Upton Park and indulged in a much-needed cigarette.

'It's ten to,' said Hawkins nervously. 'You ready?'

'Ready as I'll ever be,' replied Billy, pushing open the door and flicking out what remained of his Benson & Hedges. He reached across the car and held out his hand; for once, the smile absent from his face. 'Good luck, my son.'

Hawkins smiled at him. 'And you, boy. Come on, let's go and make some history.'

The legs of the young blonde secretary walking along in front of him were doing an excellent job of settling Graham Hawkins' nerves. Long and slim, they were as tidy a pair as he had seen in a long time. And along with the faint smell of perfume trailing along behind her, they had begun to invite the inevitable lurid fantasies.

Beside her, briefcase in hand and wearing his favourite Armani suit, Billy strode along making small talk and oozing confidence, seemingly without a care in the world.

She suddenly darted ahead of him and held open a door, gesturing the two of them through and providing Hawk with a tantalising glimpse of cleavage and another blast of perfume as he brushed past her. 'It's a shame Mr Mirren wasn't able to make it,' she said, 'but Mr Baines is expecting you both. Oh, and he's invited David Knight to join you if that's OK? He'll be along in a minute. Please come through.'

She rushed past them again and pushed open one of a pair of double doors on the far wall, walking through and proclaiming, 'The gentlemen from Mirren Events, sir. Would you like coffee?'

Behind her, Billy and Hawkins glanced at each other. They hadn't considered the possibility that Knight might be there. He could blow everything unless they acted quickly.

Hawkins shrugged and followed her into the chairman's office. 'Yes please, that would be wonderful.'

A tall, distinguished-looking man stood up and walked out from behind a large wooden desk, his silvery hair styled perfectly and his clothes immaculate. Money and power were written all over him, something echoed by the fact that he projected an impression of being completely at ease and totally unflappable.

'Gentlemen, Keith Baines,' he gushed, as he came towards them, hand outstretched. 'Thanks for coming. How's Ian? We haven't seen him for a while.'

Hawkins shook his hand first, introducing himself and then Billy, who studied the chairman's eyes for even the slightest flicker of recognition. If there was one, he never saw it.

'That's one of the reasons we're here ...' he began, only to be interrupted by the sound of the door opening behind him. He looked around as the blonde bombshell walked in and introduced David Knight. His reaction was almost instantaneous. 'What the fuck ...!'

'Thank you, Karen,' said Baines gently. 'That will be all.' Knight spun around, his face crimson as he blurted out an apology. But the second the door closed behind her, he turned back, staring at Billy in shocked bewilderment. 'Would someone mind telling me what's going on?'

'I believe that Mr Evans was about to do just that. So I suggest we all sit down, calm down, and hear what he has to say. I for one can't wait.' Baines gestured across the large office and led them to a leather suite. He sat down in an armchair, smiling confidently.

Hawkins and Knight followed, but Billy remained standing. He worked better that way.

'So, Mr Baines ...'

'Keith, please,' he said, holding up his hand and smiling warmly. Three tiny gestures, each one designed to disarm his opponent and throw him off his carefully prepared stride.

162

Hawkins settled back in his chair and watched as the two heavyweights manoeuvred themselves into position, immediately consigning both himself and Knight to the role of spectator.

'Sorry, Keith ... and David,' apologised Billy, smiling confidently as he began again. 'I think the best thing I can do is outline what's been going on behind the scenes, so that there can be no misunderstanding about the current situation.'

Baines nodded in agreement, his smile unwavering, while Knight simply sat and stared, unable to comprehend what on earth was going on.

Billy was about to start speaking when the door opened again and the bombshell walked in with a tray of coffee. Before she could put it down, Baines stood up and took it from her. 'Thank you, Karen. I'll take care of that. And could you get hold of Sergeant Roberts, the police liaison officer, for me? If at all possible, I would like him to join us.'

She smiled and left as he began to pour out the drinks, handing them around as if he had the vicar and his wife sitting in his office rather than two men he obviously knew to be among the biggest thorns in the side of his beloved club. Hawkins watched him and smiled as he took his cup. He was impressed that anyone could act so cool in what must have been an almost surreal situation. But he had noticed that the reference to Roberts had been made in a slightly different tone: one that suggested it was in young Karen's interests to make sure that she got hold of him and that, no matter what, he got here, or she'd be in the shit.

'As you know,' began Billy, once Baines had taken his seat again, 'the contract to provide both match-day and general security for West Ham United is held by Mirren Events Ltd. And you will obviously be aware that the contract was renewed at the end of last season for a further two years. However, there have recently been some changes at the company and the reason we are here today is to outline those changes and to discuss how they will affect the security arrangements here at the club.'

'What kind of changes?' asked Knight, growing uneasier by the second.

'On 29 April, Ian Mirren and I began negotiations for the sale of the company. That deal was completed on 29 May when I became the sole owner, and installed Graham here as managing director. Ian Mirren has been retained by the company as a director, although his position will be in more of a consultancy role.' He took a deep breath and took the briefest of glances around the room. Hawk had the slightest trace of a grin on his face, Baines still wore his smile and Knight had turned white as a sheet. 'As regards the situation at the club, nothing will change.'

'Like hell it won't,' said Knight.

'I think what David is trying to say,' interrupted Baines, 'is that you of all people must be aware of the sensitivity of the situation you are suggesting. You are, not to put too fine a point on it, one of the reasons why security has been and remains such a major concern, not just at this club but at others. Wouldn't putting you in charge of it be like putting a fox in charge of a chicken coop?'

'I'll answer that if I may,' said Hawkins, standing up as Billy took a mouthful of coffee. 'I think we can understand your obvious concerns, and they are legitimate ones. As supporters ourselves, we have thought seriously about the potential impact this could have on the image of the club. However, there is one thing you will not know which will hopefully allay some of your fears.'

He paused for a second and took a sip from his coffee, more for effect than anything. 'As soon as negotiations began, back in April, we effectively took control of the company and began working with the supporters to ensure that trouble at Upton Park would become a thing of the past. Indeed, I believe, as David will hopefully confirm, that there were almost no incidents in and around the ground towards the end of the season. Is that correct?'

He glanced down at Knight, who shrugged his shoulders. 'Well, yes that is true.'

'We are confident,' continued Hawkins with a smile, 'that we can build on that, using our connections with the various supporters' groups.'

'Can I ask one question?' asked Knight, his voice almost apologetic.

'Please, ask away.'

'Does this mean that you two are my bosses?'

'I guess it does,' replied Billy. 'Ironic, don't you think?'

Knight sat back in his chair and shook his head. The world had gone mad.

'But that is a good point,' Billy continued. 'I need to stress that as far as existing employees are concerned, apart from Graham here replacing Ian Mirren, nothing else has or will change. There will be some changes on match days though, but those will be for the benefit of the club. After all, we do have a certain erm ... expertise in this field.'

'Yeah, I know,' barked Knight. 'You two are convicted hooligans.'

'Actually, that's not strictly true,' said Hawk quietly. 'I was once deported from Italy after unwittingly becoming caught up in an incident but, aside from that, there is nothing on my record. My colleague here has never been convicted of any football-related offence.'

Baines leant forward to speak. For the first time, his smile had slipped a little. 'David, could you give us a minute, please.'

He waited until Knight had left the room and stood up. 'OK, enough of the small talk. Let's put our cards on the table, shall we? What's to stop me cancelling this contract and having you two ejected right now?'

Billy smiled to himself. He had hoped Baines would ask him this question. He had gone over and over it in his head a hundred times to make sure that both his answers, and his timing, were perfect. 'A number of things actually,' he said. 'Firstly, considering that all the security staff here are on my payroll, I can't see many of them being that keen on the idea of throwing me out, can you? Not unless they like being unemployed. And secondly, you're not stupid, Keith. You know that as far as the law stands, you have no grounds for cancelling this contract. After all, it's with Mirren Events Ltd, not with me. And Mirren Events as a limited company still exists. It has the same offices, the same staff and even has the person who signed the contract with you still listed as a director. What's more, not one of the clauses in that contract refers to a change of ownership or, for that matter, anything else that would stand up in court. And make no mistake, that's exactly where I'd take you. And I'd win, you know it. And it'd cost you a fortune. The final problem you'd have is that even *if* we decided to walk away right now, you'd never get anyone in to replace us in time for the start of the season - and that would mean no home games until it was sorted. I can't see the Premier League being exactly thrilled about that, can you?'

Baines straightened his back, making him appear even more imposing than before. 'And I dare say that over the coming months whoever took over would have a less than cooperative support.'

'I couldn't comment on that,' said Billy.

Baines raised an eyebrow in mock surprise. 'That has the sound of a threat to me.'

'I don't make threats, Keith. I'm simply saying that I couldn't comment because I don't know.' He held out his arms and added, 'Who does?'

'So if, and it's very much an if at the moment, but *if* I accept this, what assurances have I that you will not simply use it as a way of promoting your own interests or, more specifically, those of the CSS? And yes, before you ask, I know all about them. I might be the chairman now, but I have been coming here a long time, you know.'

Billy smiled. 'There are a lot of myths about the so-called CSS, Keith' he said. 'But the truth is that these days it's no more than a lads' supporters club. The eighties were two decades ago. It was a different time.'

'That doesn't answer my question.'

'Well, you tell me what interests we could possibly have other than simple business ones?'

'There's my problem, I can't possibly imagine,' said Baines irritably.

Hawkins suddenly realised what he was hinting at and butted in. 'If you're thinking along political lines, then please don't. My father was a printer at Wapping. I was brought up the son of a card-carrying Labour party member. Billy here, is a slightly different matter. He's one of Thatcher's children, self-made and very greedy. But that's as far right wing as either of us goes. No, Keith, sorry to disappoint you, but we're not the BNP, or members of Combat 18. We're just two lads who work hard and love West Ham.'

'So why then?'

'It's easy,' said Billy. 'We travel the country week in and week out watching the Hammers, and over the years we got sick and tired of watching other people get rich by supposedly making sure we were behaving ourselves. In the end, we thought: sod it. We can do that ourselves. It was a simple business decision.'

'But I take it you'll be exploiting the publicity to the full. Potentially, this is a big story. Talk about lunatics running the asylum.'

Billy furrowed his brow. 'You're looking for things that aren't there, Keith. Why would we want publicity? In the old days sure, but not now. It wouldn't do the club any good, or my other business interests for that matter.'

The phone interrupted them and Baines picked it up, listened for a minute and then asked if David Knight could be sent back in. 'Gary Roberts is on the way,' he said as Knight walked back into the room. 'So I suggest we wait and continue the discussion then.' He looked around and gestured to everyone to sit down before the smile returned to his face. 'Would anyone like more coffee?'

To everyone else in the room, Billy appeared almost indifferent to what was going on. Yet inside, he was roaring with laughter. Watching Roberts squirm in front of him was something he had been looking forward to since he had first decided to go after Mirren and, so far, it had not been disappointing. The look on the bastard's face as he raged at Keith Baines was almost worth the money he had paid out all on its own.

'You can't seriously tell me that you're even considering going along with this? You do *know* who these two are and what they're involved with?'

'I would appreciate it,' said Baines, glowering angrily at him, 'if you would moderate your tone in my office.'

'You don't get it at all, do you, Sergeant?' said Billy, from the comfort of his armchair, seizing the opportunity to score another point.

'Get what?'

'That you've already won. The CSS as you know it doesn't exist any more; it hasn't for ages.'

'Don't give me that bollocks,' barked Roberts. 'What about Manchester, and Newcastle? They were hardly peaceful affairs, were they? And don't tell me they weren't organised in advance or that you had nothing to do with them.'

'D'you know what your problem is, Sergeant?' smarmed Billy. 'You *want* to believe that someone controls everything because that would make *your* life easier to justify. But the truth is ...'

'To return to the point,' interrupted Hawkins, desperate to avoid any chance of Billy falling into a slanging match and making them look like idiots. 'I think you're missing something here, Mr Roberts. The fact is that since we took over Mirren's, trouble in and around the ground has all but stopped. There's no reason why that trend shouldn't continue right through this coming season. After all, as I'm sure everyone in this room will agree, that's what we all want. Isn't it?'

An hour later, with Billy and Hawk having left, the three men sat in Baines' office and reflected on what had gone on earlier. Each had very different feelings and for very different reasons.

'We will be registering the strongest possible objections to the licensing authority,' said Roberts. 'You do know that, don't you.'

'On what grounds?' replied Baines with a shrug. 'Safety has actually improved since they took over, which does kind of render your case invalid.'

'On the grounds that these are two of the kingpins of one of the most violent groups of hooligans in the country.'

'So why haven't you proved it?' asked Knight ruefully. 'If you're so bloody sure, why are they still walking around?'

'Well, whatever they are,' said Baines before Roberts could even attempt an answer, 'they're hardly stereotypical thugs, are they? They've got me by the balls here and no mistake.'

'Couldn't you just buy them out?'

Baines shook his head. 'They wouldn't sell. If that was what they were after, they would have dropped a hint and I'd have gone for it. I doubt they would even settle if we ended up going to court. They'd take it all the way just for the publicity and in the end, it would still end up costing this club millions. That's without the lost revenue. You forget, I was the one who gave that contract the OK. Believe me, there's no way we could get out of it.'

'But there must be something relating to performance,' said Roberts, almost pleading.

Baines laughed out loud. 'That's another irony. The only way we can get out of it is if the security is ineffective. That's hardly going to be a problem here, is it?'

'So what are you saying then? That we have to accept it? And work with them?'

'That's exactly what I'm saying, Gary,' sighed Baines. 'Because as it stands, I don't think we have any choice.' He paused for a moment and leant forward on his elbows. 'But ultimately, my job is to do what's best for West Ham United. And the plain truth is that while I'm not exactly thrilled, if you look at it objectively, this might well turn out to be the best anti-hooligan measure this club ever took. After all, as a wise man once said, keep your friends close and your enemies closer.'

Gary Roberts shook his head and stood up. He pulled open the door angrily and snapped: 'Let's just hope you're right, Keith. For all our sakes.'

CHAPTER 21
Wednesday 26 July 2000
15.00

'I'd like to be a fly on the wall when that twat gets on the blower to NCIS,' said Billy with a laugh, as he watched Roberts climb into his unmarked Vauxhall Vectra and drive out of the car park. 'They'll go bloody apeshit. Did you see his face when he walked into Baines' office?'

Hawk let out a low grunt and watched the car vanish from view as Billy continued his tirade. 'I tell you, that was the biggest buzz I've had in years. He must hate you and me with a passion.'

'Come on,' said Hawk abruptly as he opened the car door. 'He's fucked off. I want to have a word with that little shit, Knight. Remind him who butters his bread for him these days.'

Billy suddenly reached out and grabbed his arm. 'Listen, mate,' he said. 'This is your gig. You call the shots. That's what you're paid for.'

Hawkins looked at him, surprised at the tone of his voice. He sounded almost pleading. 'But...?'

'I know what you think about playing all this dead straight,' said Billy nervously, 'and you're right. But chances are his office is full of stuff about the lads and us. We should try and get a look at it.'

'Don't worry, mate,' said Hawkins with a sly grin. 'That very idea had already occurred to me.'

Ten minutes later, they were sitting in Knight's office, a pokey little room cluttered with filing cabinets and walls barely visible behind a collection of cork noticeboards and club memos stuck up with Sellotape. From the mound of paperwork covering both the desk and the top of a large photocopier, it looked as if the place hadn't been tidied for weeks.

Billy looked on silently as Hawkins began talking to Knight; laying out their position and making it clear that, unless he had a problem with the change of ownership, his job was safe. But he then went on to remind him that at the end of the day, it was Mirren Events who paid his wages, not Roberts or even Keith Baines, and his loyalty had to be to them. If it wasn't, then he had no future. Pure and simple.

Knight's face had been a picture. As the conversation went on, Billy had looked on in amusement as he had clearly struggled with the rights and wrongs of consorting with what he obviously believed to be the enemy, as opposed to the desire to continue paying his mortgage. But, inevitably, it hadn't taken long for the financial implications to win out — so much so that, by the time Hawk had finished reassuring him that they didn't intend to turn back the clock to the mid-eighties and cause mayhem at every match, he had visibly relaxed. He even offered to show the two of them around the ground, an offer Hawkins readily accepted, adding, 'I've never really looked around this place when it's been empty.'

They both stood up and looked at Billy. But he held up his hand and said, 'Not me, I've got calls to make. You go ahead.'

Knight hesitated for a second and then led Hawkins out into the corridor, leaving the door slightly ajar behind him.

Billy smiled to himself as he listened to their small talk receding into the distance and then, once he was sure they had left, pushed the door shut and began riffling through the filing cabinets.

The two of them were heading back to the Range Rover when a familiar vehicle turned into the car park and stopped a short way from them. Billy immediately made to turn towards it but Hawkins touched his arm as if to signify that it wasn't a good idea.

'You know why that cunt's come back, don't you?' he muttered as Billy hissed an expletive before changing direction and heading back towards his own car. 'Someone's reminded him about all the stuff in Knight's office and he's come to clean it out.'

'Yeah, well he's too fucking late,' said Billy. 'I tell you, some of the gear he's got in there is incredible. You wait till you see it.'

'How much did you get copied?'

'A fair bit, but there was loads I couldn't do. The poxy copier was crap. But I saw plenty. Enough to wonder how the fuck half of us are still wandering around.'

'What, photos as well?' asked Hawk as Billy clicked the remote locking and they climbed in.

'Believe it, mate. Come on, let's get the fuck out of here and then you can have a decent shufti.' He started the car and gunned it out of the car park, glaring at Roberts as he drove past him. 'Your time'll come you bastard,' he muttered. 'We owe you big time for PJ.'

Once they were out on to the Barking Road, Hawkins, unable to contain his curiosity any longer, reached over and took the bundle of papers from Billy's briefcase. It took only a few seconds before he was shaking his head, more in disbelief than anything. 'Holy shite!' he exclaimed. 'I see what you mean. No wonder Knight freaked out when he saw us. He must think we're all raving mental.'

'There's more than that in there,' said Billy, struggling to keep his eyes on the road. 'Look at the stuff at the bottom. Copies of the actual police reports on all the visiting clubs. Names, addresses, pictures, everything. He even had some copies of the reports they make after games. Fucking amazing!'

'Jesus,' gasped Hawk. 'Look at this!' He held up a photo of a group of lads obviously fronting someone up outside a pub. 'That's Darren, Geoff, a few of the Brentwood lads. You can see their faces clear as day.'

'I know, like I say, it makes you wonder why half of us haven't been nicked.'

Hawkins dropped the picture down on his lap and lit a cigarette, passing it over to Billy before lighting another for himself. 'So what's the plan, then?' he asked as the car filled with smoke.

'We best get the lads together at the St George next week. Fill them in on what's been going on and then show them this lot, see what they say. It's about time we had a pre-season plot-up anyway.'

Gary Roberts leant against his car and stared into space, trying to work out how his life had been turned upside down in the space of a few short hours.

This morning, thanks to the figures NCIS had given him only yesterday, he'd been full of pride and pre-season optimism. Now, he was shafted. Well and truly. Quite how he was going to explain all this to his guv'nor was beyond him. Not just the fact that he was somehow going to have to work alongside the very people he was supposed to be trying to bang up, but also the fact that they had almost certainly seen confidential police reports concerning both them and their activities; reports that David Knight wasn't even supposed to have seen, never mind copied and held on to. If only he'd remembered about that before he'd headed back to the nick, he could have taken everything away with him and no one would have been any the wiser.

David Knight, what a prick. Fancy leaving Evans alone in his office with all that stuff not even locked up. He must have realised what he was up to. Then again, what choice did he have? The poor bastard's on their payroll now. He could hardly tell them to piss off.

Roberts pushed himself away from the car and climbed in with a sigh. There was no doubt about it, he was in the shit. Big time.

The noise coming from the bar downstairs was in stark contrast to the almost eerie silence in the upstairs room of the St George.

Billy left them contemplating everything that had been said for a few minutes and then, with a shrug of his shoulders and a glance at Hawk, simply asked, 'Well?'

Geoff looked up from the sheets of A4 paper he'd been studying and shook his head as he passed them along the line.

'Holy shit!' he muttered. 'So I guess it's fair to assume that you two wankers have been busy during the off-season then.'

'You could say that,' said Billy with a grin. 'I haven't had me holiday yet if that's what you mean.'

'But the point is,' jumped in Hawk 'we need to sort out what we do now. The coppers will have guessed that we've got this stuff and, on top of us taking over the security contract, they must be freaking out. But, as far as we can see, they've only got two options. They can either pull back and wait to see what happens when the season starts or steam in now and come after us big time.'

'Well, come on then,' barked Stretch angrily. 'You two've got all the answers. You fucking tell us.'

Billy looked at him and frowned. 'What's your problem?'

'My problem? It's not my bastard problem. It's *our* problem. Have you *seen* this lot?' He grabbed a sheet of paper and began reading through it. His voice seemed to rise a pitch with every word. 'Look: dates, names, addresses, places ... the fucking works!'

'Stretch, mate,' said Geoff quietly. 'Calm down for Christ's sake.'

'Calm down! That's fucking easy for you to say. In case you'd forgotten, I'm already on a suspended. This fucking lot could get me sent down.'

Billy stood up and called for quiet as everyone began talking at once. Panic was spreading through them like it was going out of fashion.

'For fuck's sake, what is it with you lot? Look at the dates. They've had this stuff for ages. Some of it's a year old. No one's gonna get tugged because of this. If they were, it would have happened before Euro 2000. Am I right or what? And besides, if they're going to come after anyone, it'll be me and Hawk. So we've got more to lose than anyone.'

He waited until everyone had settled and then went on, speaking more deliberately this time, almost businesslike. 'So what we have to decide is how we go on from here. Because I think everyone realises that nothing's gonna be the same any more. Mostly because if any of you cunts step out of line in *our* ground, I'll nick you myself!'

The room burst into laughter and Billy stood and smiled as the one-liners came flying at him. Panic over. He glanced at Hawk and winked, a signal for him to carry on, and then sat down. Job done.

'Right, this is how we see it,' Hawk began. 'But before I go on, I think that it's only fair to say that if anyone wants to walk away from all this at any time, then we've got no problem with that and there'll be no hard feelings.' He paused for a second and when no one spoke, went on. 'OK, now as I reckon you've guessed by now, we're pretty sure that the filth won't come after us. Not yet anyway. Chances are they'll wait until the start of the season and see what happens. But, the fact that we're in charge of match-day security does change things slightly! For a start, it means that we have to be crystal clean. And that means that no one involved with The Squad, and I mean no one, is to step out of line in or around the ground again.'

The room burst into noise but Hawkins shouted them down. 'Will you shut the fuck up and listen! Jesus bloody wept!' Again, he waited for calm to descend. 'Now, we can't expect the other mobs to play the game so, whenever anyone's coming to us, we'll be doing things slightly differently. First off, as far as The Squad is concerned we'll be calling it well away from here. Stations mainly. For the London clubs, we'll be taking it to their backyards, rather than kick things off around here. We can't afford to shit on our own doorstep. Anything within a couple of miles of the Boleyn, and I mean anything, will be left to the Under-Fives.'

'So what you're saying,' said Geoff, 'is that we're becoming an awayday firm.'

'Absolutely,' replied Hawk.

'This is bollocks!' Everyone turned in surprise as a normally quiet voice spoke out.

'What is, Chris?' asked Billy. A tall, powerfully built man stood up and walked into the middle of the room. With his close-cropped greying hair and round face, he looked like a typical cockney hard man - which is exactly what he was. But although he'd been a member of the Cabinet since Billy had taken over as top dog, Hawkins could never remember him speaking out of turn at a plot-up before. Whatever he was about to say, had to be worth hearing.

'All of it. D'you really expect us to roll over and do fuck-all when the Yids or the Rent Boys walk in and start taking liberties? And what happens if we draw Millwall in one of the cups? Are we just gonna invite them to nip round here for a swift half and a chat?'

'You're bang out of order, Chris,' barked Geoff.

'Am I fuck!' he countered angrily. 'All I can see is these two selling us out and making a fucking bomb into the bargain.' He turned towards Billy, his eyes blazing. 'Come on then, Billy. You want all this from us. What do we get out of it?'

'If you sit down and listen, we'll tell you,' replied Billy calmly. Chris glared at him for a second and then sat down in his chair, kicking his legs out and folding his arms across his chest like a spoilt schoolboy. Billy waited a second and then spoke again. 'Listen, let's get one thing straight. There are two reasons why we've done this. The first, as Chris rightly says, is to make a few bob. Though I'll only do that when I've clawed back the small fucking fortune I've had to shell out. But, as Hawk was about to explain, the entire Squad will benefit in the end. You lot, and some of the lads downstairs, right from day one.' He paused for a second and took a smoke from a packet in his pocket, speaking again as he lit it and making the white tube bounce around in his mouth in time with his words. 'The other reason is because of this ...' He reached down and lifted up some of the papers they had been studying earlier. 'This just proves what we've all known for fucking ages. That there's only one decent firm these days and that's the Old Bill. There's more of 'em, they're full time and, no matter what happens, they can't lose. When was the last time a lad took a copper to court and won?' He looked around for a second, waiting for a response which never came. 'Exactly! So if we're ever going to get ahead of the game again, we have to play it a different way. Their way. Because if we don't, sooner or later they're gonna have us all inside. And I don't know about you, but a spell in the nick doesn't appeal to me.'

Hawk stood up and butted in. 'To answer Chris's question and explain what you lot will get out of it, the answer is simple. For away games, nothing much will change, but at home, to avoid problems with the Old Bill, if you lot are up for it, what we want to do is put together a small group of about twenty lads that'll work at the club during games and deal with any incidents that take place. A kind of rapid response unit. In return, that group will receive a few quid, plus free tickets to home and away games. The other bonus, of course, is that if you get involved in an off during the game, you're less likely to get nicked because you'll be on the club staff. And who's ever heard of a steward getting nicked for rucking?' He glanced at Chris, who shrugged his shoulders in unhappy acceptance.

'So what you're saying,' said Stretch 'is that we'll be working alongside the Old Bill.'

'Yep. But I reckon that, for most of the serious mobs, that'll be a bonus. You'll only need to be there from about half-hour before and after kick-off and you'll have the whole game to wind them up. After, of course, it'll be game on.'

'Any questions?' asked Billy 'Or objections?'

'What do the club and the Old Bill say?' asked Geoff. 'That twat Roberts must have gone up the fucking wall.'

'He was slightly upset, that's true,' laughed Billy. 'But the club seem sweet. We've met with Bainsey a couple of times this last week and he's cool. Besides, he's no mug. He knows we ain't gonna shit on our own doorstep. There's too much money involved. My fucking money as it happens.'

'And don't forget,' butted in Hawk, 'as far as the normal stewarding goes, nothing will change. It'll be the same people run by the same bloke. The only difference is that now, they work for us.'

Geoff sat up straight in his chair and sniffed loudly. 'Is the stuff with Mickey James involved with this?'

Hawk stole a puzzled glance at Billy who blanked him completely. 'No.'

'But is it still gonna go on? It's a fucking good earner for some of us.'

'Who the fuck's Mickey James?' asked Chris.

'Mickey James is someone I've been doing some business with that's all,' said Billy tersely. 'And a few of the lads have been working for him. Doorman stuff, nothing serious.'

'Yeah, fucking right-oh!' said Stretch. 'I tell you, we blitzed this fucking club in Grays last week—'

'OK, Stretch, we get the picture,' said Billy angrily cutting him short. 'The point is that's nothing to do with The Squad, so let's leave it out shall we? Now, is there anything else? 'Cause I'm gagging for a pint.'

'One thing, though,' interrupted Hawkins again. 'For obvious reasons, we want this kept as quiet as possible. So until we can tie everything together, just spread the word among the lads that things are going to be a bit different this season, OK? You know what some of the young 'uns are like. One sniff and it'll be all over the fucking Internet by the morning.'

Hawkins waited until the others had left the room before he grabbed Billy and asked him what was going on with Mickey James.

'It's nothing, mate, honest. Like I said, we're just doing some business together, that's all. Nothing to do with what's going on at the club, so don't worry about that.'

'Yeah, but the lads ...'

'Are helping him out with a few things once in a while, that's all. Like I said, forget it. Besides, I'll be putting the block on it soon. Now come on, I'm gagging.'

CHAPTER 23
Wednesday 2 August 2000
10.15

Billy slammed the phone down angrily and shouted out a curse to all things electronic before grabbing his laptop computer and logging on to the web.

Within seconds, he was staring at his favourite hooligan message board and the posting that was inevitably going to cause him serious problems. He studied it slowly and then followed the thread, reading all of the eighteen messages expanding on the rumour that the CSS were now running the security at Upton Park. Even as he was reading them, another was added.

'Shit! I fucking knew it!' he yelled out loud, grabbing the phone and dialling Hawkins' number as he did so. 'Have you seen the noticeboard this morning? Well do it, and then call me straight back!'

He put his finger on the receiver and quickly dialled another number. 'Craig, it's Billy. Yeah, cool. Listen, I need a big favour. There's a load of messages on your site about The Squad. Wipe 'em. Now. Any others that turn up, do the same. And is there any way you can trace who posted the first one? Well do your best, mate. Quick as you can. And one last thing, can you mail all the lads who were there last night, at least the ones who are e-mailed up, and remind them that this isn't for public consumption. Cheers, mate. Laters.'

He had just put the phone back on the receiver when it rang again. He lifted it to find Hawk on the other end. 'Yeah, I know... what a bastard. I've spoken to Craig already, and they'll be gone any second. He's also gonna try and track who posted it but it ain't easy apparently. I hope he can though, 'cause whoever did it had to have been there last night and if I get hold of him, I'll break his fuckin' legs. Let's just hope no one saw 'em ... that cunt Roberts for one. If he did, we're screwed. Sure as shit smells, he'll use that against us.'

Gary Roberts stared at his computer and smiled to himself. He'd known all along that sooner or later, someone would slip up - and now they had. More importantly, they'd given him an idea.

He downloaded all the messages on to his hard disc, printed them out and, after putting his mobile phone in his pocket, headed out into the car park.

'It's Craig. I've got your man.'

'Who?' asked Billy, his voice bristling with anger.

'One of the Under-Fives. Name of Steve Parry. I think he lives out in Grays.'

'You sure it's him?'

'Pretty sure. You know about IP codes and all that shite?'

'Not a fucking clue, mate.'

'Well I won't go into the details but, basically, every computer has its own code that gets logged on to every message. I just compared the one on this morning's post against some old ones. It's fairly close.'

'How close?'

'About ninety per cent.'

'That's good enough for me. Cheers, Craig. I owe you one.'

Billy clicked the receiver down and then dialled again. 'Hawk, who we got out in Grays? I want to know where a guy called Steve Parry lives. Yeah. He's our man.'

The silver Escort pulled into Palmers Avenue and for once, nineteen-year-old Steve Parry was relieved to find a space outside his own house. After a hard day's work, the last thing he'd fancied was the usual early evening parking scramble with the neighbours - or his mum and dad, come to that. Three cars in one house equals pain in the arse for everyone living nearby. Not that he gave a shit about anyone else.

He brought his car to a halt and reversed in, his relative inexperience causing him to shuffle it around until it was parked neatly between a blue Toyota and a white Transit van.

But by the time he'd turned the engine off, the Transit had pulled out of its slot and, before he could finish the expletive he'd begun to utter, it had pulled alongside him and stopped; so close that he was unable to open his own door.

Shocked, he reached for the window winder to give the driver a mouthful but, before he could put a hand on it, the Escort's passenger door was pulled open and a man dived in beside him, his face instantly recognisable, and decidedly unhappy.

'What!' exclaimed Parry, his face draining of colour even as he uttered the one and only word that, up to that point in time, he had ever spoken to a man he regarded with not a little reverence and an awful lot of fear.

'Shut the fuck up!' barked Billy. He waited until Parry had settled a bit and then allowed a smile to spread across his face as he reached into his pocket for his cigarettes. 'D'you know, Steve, I had high hopes for you. I did, really,' he said, ignoring the no-smoking sign on the dashboard as he lit up. 'And that makes the fact that you've let me down even worse. I actually feel betrayed.'

'Look, Billy,' he said, his voice shaking with fear. 'I don't know what you're talking about, but I ain't let no one down. Honest.'

'Don't insult my intelligence, Steve,' replied Billy calmly. He leant across and motioned to the driver of the Transit, who reversed back far enough to allow the door to open. 'Come on.'

'Where we going?'

'Just get in the van. There's a good lad.'

Parry leant back against the door like a frightened rabbit, reaching for the handle behind him as he continued to stare at Billy. 'No fucking chance!'

The punch, when it came, was immense, catching the side of Parry's head and bouncing it off the glass behind him before he could turn his head or pull it away. 'Get in that fucking van!'

'But I ain't done nuffin,' pleaded Parry, almost begging now and doing his best to shrink into the corner, as he fought to stop himself from crying - the ultimate humiliation.

'You lying little fucker!' screamed Billy, leaning across and punching him again as the anger and frustration welled up inside him. 'Get in that fucking van!'

'No, I ain't goin' anywhere. I ain't done nuffin!' shouted Parry, holding his hands over his head as the blows rained down on him, each one punctuated by more abuse.

'You lying little cunt!'

The blows were still coming when the door behind him was pulled open and Parry felt himself being dragged out and thrown through the side loading access into the back of the Transit. Next thing he knew, it was slammed shut behind him. And then they were moving.

Tracey Smith leant back in her chair and feigned surprise.

'Well, well. Hello stranger. We don't often see you here these days.'

Billy smiled cheekily at her and doffed an imaginary cap. 'It's a bit too posh for me out this way, ma'am. I know my place.'

'Have you come for me this time? Or is it him again?'

He held out his arms and laughed. 'I'm spoken for, Trace, what can I say?'

'My loss,' she replied sadly. 'He's in if you want him. Coffee?'

He winked and grinned at her. 'Two sugars. And don't try and smuggle any of them bloody sweeteners in this time. I don't want to have to sack you.'

Hawkins looked up in surprise as he walked in. 'Oi, Oi. What you doing over here?'

'I just fancied a trip out, that's all. Nothing important. How's it all going?'

'Don't give me that old bollocks,' said Hawk, dropping his pen down on the paper in front of him and leaning back in his chair. 'What's up?'

Billy walked over and sat down. 'I don't know, mate. Honest I don't. I just feel...'

'What?'

'Like something's wrong, you know? Call it a gut instinct.'

Hawkins looked at him and frowned. If Billy's sixth sense was talking to him, it was usually worth listening to. 'You sorted this Parry geezer yet?'

'Last night,' said Billy. 'That's one little bastard who won't be playing the keyboard warrior for a while.'

'Why? What happened?'

'Me and Geoff took him for a little drive. Just to help him see the error of his ways. D'you know how hot a Transit's exhaust manifold gets after a drive from Grays to Lakeside? It's fucking hot, let me tell ya.'

Tracey knocked on the door and walked in with two steaming cups of coffee. Once she had left, Hawk looked across the desk and shook his head. Billy had always had a thing about making the punishment fit the crime. If you ran, it was the knees; bottle it, and it was the hands. They all knew it and accepted it. It was why The Squad had so little dissent. 'So come on then, what d'you do this time?'

'You don't wanna know. You're too squeamish.'

'Just fucking tell me.'

'Let's just say that there's a van in my yard that's got a perfect set of young Steven's fingerprints imprinted on the exhaust. You get the idea.'

Hawkins winced and moved to pick up his coffee. But the heat made him pull his hand away and he decided to let it cool down a bit first. 'Fuck me, Billy. That's a bit extreme.'

'Is it bollocks! I told 'em. I told 'em all. Nothing was to be said outside the St George. So what does he do? He goes home to his bedroom and tells the fucking world!'

'You're the boss,' sighed Hawk. 'But it's no wonder you're twitchy this morning. I bet he screamed like a pig.'

Billy took a mouthful of coffee and shook his head. 'Nah, it's not that. I don't know what it is. Anyway, fuck it. What's been going on here?'

'Busy,' said Hawkins with a nod. 'Everything's sound, though. No problems at all. Had a break-in at an office in Hackney last night but looks like it was just druggies.'

'Fucking scum,' cursed Billy. 'What about the club?'

'Funny you should say that. The first of the incremented payments went into the bank this morning. Tidy wedge as well. Apart from that, not a lot going on really. At least not here. Knight is busy gearing up for the start of the season. He's got the stewards coming in on Saturday for a training day. He's turned out to be a good bloke. I just let him get on with most of it.'

'Have you told him about the erm ... enforcers yet?'

'Yeah, yesterday. He's not pleased. But he'll live.'

A knock on the door interrupted them and they both turned as Tracey entered the room carrying a pile of post. 'I thought you two might like these,' she said, holding out a large white envelope as she dropped the others into a tray on the desk.

Hawk took it off her and drew out the contents, a huge grin spreading across his face as he examined them. 'Well fu—, I mean goodness me. Looks like we've been and finally cracked it, boy. We've been invited to an official West Ham function!'

Billy was almost at his car when a shout made him turn back to see Hawkins running after him. It was obvious from the look on his face that something was wrong and within a couple of minutes, the two of them were back inside his office.

'This is down to that cunt with the Internet!' growled Billy. 'It has to be. Fuck me, he might as well have grassed us to the law and have done with it. I knew I should have let Geoff slice the bastard.' He took a cigarette and lit up, sucking heavily on it before throwing the packet at Hawkins. 'OK, let's calm down and get our heads around this. What did she say?'

Hawk lit his smoke and exhaled quickly. 'Just that she was from the *Evening Standard* and would we like to comment on the rumour that blah, blah, blah. You know the rest.'

'And what did you say?'

'Er ... some bollocks about this being an old-established firm and that, as the managing director, I would not take kindly to such a slur appearing in their paper.'

'Nice one. All those episodes of *Ally McBeal* you watch are obviously paying off. At least we've got some time now. Not long, though, so I reckon we need to go on the offensive. I'll get on to my brief and see what he says.' He grabbed his phone but before he could dial he looked up and frowned. 'We got anyone who works in PR or anything like that?'

'Fuck knows,' replied Hawk nervously. 'Call Craig, he knows everything about everybody.'

'Good idea,' said Billy as he began searching through the numbers on his phone. 'Craig, mate. It's Billy. Listen, have we got anyone who works in the PR game or anything like that? No fucking way! Well sod me, I never knew that. You got a ...? Cheers, my son. You're a diamond.'

He clicked the phone shut and dialled in the number he'd just scribbled down. 'Hello, could I speak to Mr Parish please. Yes, could you tell him it's urgent. My name's Evans. He *will* want to speak to me.' He held the phone away from his ear and looked at Hawkins. 'You ain't gonna believe this one. Darren, it's Billy.'

Hawk looked on in total shock as Billy explained what had happened. Darren was one of the biggest psychos in The Squad: one of those lads who were always first in, no matter what the numbers. The very idea of him even being employed was surprising; the thought that he was actually a professional was incredible.

'Yeah, sound. I'll get Hawk to mail you what we've got right now. And next time we get together, you've got some explaining to do! I always had you down as a daft fucker!' He put the phone down and shook his head. 'Well, you think you know someone ...'

'Shit,' said Hawk. 'I can't get my head around that at all.'

Billy laughed and shrugged his shoulders. The truth was that they knew very little about anyone in The Squad outside their immediate circle and even that was sketchy. More often than not, as long as a lad turned out, stood his round and wasn't a runner, that was all they really needed and wanted to know about him.

'Right,' he said 'mail him over everything that happened and he'll give it some thought. I'm gonna pop in and see my brief on the way back to my place. We gotta try and stop this before anything gets into print. You got Darren's mail address?'

'Yeah, it's on the message board.' He paused for a second and shuffled uneasily on his feet. 'Listen, if this comes out in the papers, we could be in the shit - you know that? And I'm not thinking about here or at the club, that won't be a problem. I'm thinking about at home. Julie would throw a fit if—'

'Well,' said Billy interrupting him. 'We best do what we can to make sure it don't. But it might be a good idea to give Keith Baines a ring. Just to warn him. That's if he doesn't already know.'

In the offices of the *Evening Standard,* Jenny Randall was reading through her notes and writing up her piece. This was going to be a great story. 'Football hooligan takes over club security' - it was perfect. And with the whole issue of football violence still in the news after Euro 2000, it was going to go down a storm with her editor; something that wouldn't do her any harm at all. If it went really well, the nationals might even pick it up. That would be awesome.

She owed her policeman friend a serious drink next time she saw him.

'Look, you must have realised that it was going to come out sooner or later.' Billy and Hawkins glanced at each other and shrugged their shoulders as Keith Baines stared across his desk at them in surprise.

'Of course we did,' said Billy, sighing. 'We just didn't expect it to be so soon, that's all.'

'Well, like I say, I wouldn't worry about it. We've already issued a press release saying how delighted we are both with the new contract and the fall in the arrest figures at the end of last season. And at the end of the day, that's what counts.'

'And ours has done much the same, with the addition of some information about the new management structure,' replied Billy. 'Let's just hope they do the trick.'

'Have they said when it's going to be in?' asked Hawk.

'Could be anytime,' replied Baines. 'Papers are funny like that. Now, if you don't mind, thanks for coming over, but I do have a pile of work to do.'

The two of them strode out across the car park in silence. It was only once the car was actually moving that either of them spoke. 'What d'you reckon then?' asked Billy pensively.

'I don't know, mate. Until we see what they print, what can we do?'

'According to my brief, fuck all,' said Billy. 'Let's just hope Darren's press release does the trick. Mind you, as long as Baines is cool, I can't see what harm it's going to do anyway.'

Hawk looked at him and raised an eyebrow. 'I've just got Julie onside after the last stunt. Having it splashed around the paper ain't exactly gonna do me any favours on the domestic front.'

Billy looked at him and winked, before powering the car away from the ground and headed in the direction of the St George. 'Come on, I reckon we could both do with a drink.'

CHAPTER 25
Friday 4 August 2000
11.30

Hawkins put the phone down and put his head in his hands as he tried to come to terms with the full impact of what Keith Baines had just told him.

While he had spent a restless evening hoping that the story wouldn't even appear in print, he had known, deep down, that it would. But he had naturally assumed that when it did make the papers, the article would focus on Billy. After all, he was the one who had the most colourful history. But to suddenly find out that his was the name in the frame and that his friend had been relegated to the role of a bit-part player was, to say the least, a shock.

He was about to go out and get a copy to read for himself when the phone rang again. This time it was Billy. He sounded as amazed as Hawk felt. 'Have you seen it yet? Jesus, mate, what can I say?'

'No I haven't. I was just on my way out to buy one,' replied Hawk irritably. 'Baines has just called and given me the basics, though. He ain't pleased, but he reckons that the quotes they've lifted from the press releases did the trick and they'll be able to ride it out.'

'Oh well, that's something I guess. But I'm er... sorry to have to break this to you, it's on their website as well.'

'You're fucking kidding me!' gasped Hawk. 'I'll call you back.' He grabbed his computer, logged on and flicked through until he'd found it.

"The *Evening Standard* can exclusively reveal that the general manager of the company responsible for match-day security at West Ham United has a history of involvement in football hooliganism.

Graham Hawkins (33) of Chadwell Heath, Essex, who took over the post with Mirren Events Limited in June, was one of a number of fans held and subsequently deported from Italy last year following the fatal stabbing of an England football fan in Rome.

Hawkins, who was not charged with any offence relating to that incident, is also believed to be a member of the notorious hooligan group the Cockney Suicide Squad, a group who, ironically, affiliate themselves to West Ham United.

After initially refusing to comment when the *Evening Standard* contacted them yesterday, the club later issued a press release announcing that figures just published by the National Criminal Intelligence Service showed that arrests in and around Upton Park fell to among the lowest in the country towards the end of last season. This confirmed their long-held belief that Mirren Events Limited was among the best in Britain when it came to match-day security.

However, it is believed that since those figures were compiled, the company has merged with St George Security Limited, which is owned by Essex entrepreneur William Evans. Unfortunately, we were unable to contact anyone at the company yesterday to confirm this.

A spokesman for NCIS said that they had been made aware of the sensitive situation at West Ham and would be monitoring it over the coming months."

Hawk read it through two or three times to make sure he'd taken it all in. Although it didn't make comfortable reading, even he realised that Baines had been right and it could have been a lot worse. At least there weren't any pictures. Christ, that would have been a nightmare.

He lifted his mobile to call Billy but suddenly realised that there was someone else he had to speak to first. He dialled the number but, even before it had begun to ring, cancelled the call and, with a sigh, printed off the article and headed for his car.

'You gotta be kiddin' me?' gasped Billy.

'No, mate,' said Hawk quietly. 'She's just given me shit for a solid hour and told me straight, the next time I pull anything like this, she's off. So that's it as far as I'm concerned, game over. It just isn't worth it any more. Not for me anyway.'

Billy looked at his friend and shook his head. Although he'd guessed that seeing his name in the papers would freak him a bit, this was a real bolt from the blue. 'So what happens now then?'

'That's up to you, son,' said Hawk. 'If you want me out of Mirren's, I'll understand.'

'You daft twat,' replied Billy, laughing. 'Just 'cause you want out of The Squad, don't mean I'm gonna give you the bloody heave-ho from work. Besides, who else would I get to run it?'

Hawkins looked up and smiled nervously at Billy's attempt to inject some humour into the situation. But the relief in his voice when he spoke was almost tangible. 'Cheers, mate, I appreciate it. You know—'

'Listen,' said Billy, holding up his hand to stop him speaking. 'We've been through a lot together, you and me. I owe you, big time. I always will. But even if I didn't, business is business, and you're the best man I could have or want in there. This ain't gonna have no effect on that side of things at all.'

'So what happens with The Squad then? I mean, you'll have to find a new deputy. Any ideas?'

'Fuck knows. I'll have to try and get my head around it before the next meet. But I gotta say, you've shaken me, mate, and that's a fact. I reckon the others might feel the same. For all I know, with you gone, they might even drop me.'

Billy stood and watched as Hawk's Mercedes drove slowly out of the car park and headed off towards Walthamstow for an afternoon of explaining himself to Tracey and the other women at Mirren's. The fact that he'd been prepared to put his wife above both his job and The Squad had quite impressed Billy. He didn't think much of Julie, but he'd always known that Hawk loved her. Now he knew how much.

Once he had vanished from view, Billy walked back to his desk and lit up. He suddenly felt deflated. It was like an era had just come to an end. But as he sat and thought about it, the more he began to realise that the newspaper article had simply been the final straw for Hawk and that his leaving The Squad had probably been on the cards for months. It certainly explained why he'd been so twitchy when they'd first thought about getting involved with the pubs *and* why he'd been less aggressive on the footballing front. A year ago, Hawk would have been the one who'd gone after that little runt Parry and would have done him without a second thought. Now Billy was doing his own dirty work. That was almost unheard of for someone in his position.

But as he reflected on this, Billy also began to consider the possibility that maybe, deep down, he'd known it all along. And as a result, be it through guilt or genuine concern, had subconsciously been shielding his friend from other stuff that might spook him. The things with Mirren, the business with Mickey James; he'd even kept the two of them in the background at Old Trafford. Because there was no doubt about it, over the past few months, Hawk had changed. It wasn't simply that he was more confident; it was something else. There was a drive and determination about him that Billy hadn't really seen before, most of which, he guessed, stemmed from his time out of work. Considering the way it came about, as well as the fact he'd struggled to get even job interviews, he must have begun to think he was unemployable. So getting back into it must have been a massive boost, both financially and in terms of his self-esteem. Having seen at first hand the positive difference it had made, Billy could well understand why he wouldn't want to risk losing it all and sliding backwards into what must have been a shit time.

And there was no denying that those risks were real ones. Billy might not give a shit about the Old Bill, but it was a fact that if you were involved with a firm these days, the stakes were increasing week by week. And the more he thought about that, the more Billy began to wonder if maybe Hawk had the right idea. After all, he had a lot of money wrapped up in a business that sat him firmly on the other side of the hooligan fence. One wrong move might open him up to big problems with the club and that could really cost him. Was it worth the risk? Ten years ago, when you could still have a decent toe-to-

toe without any interference, definitely. But today? With the Old Bill doing their level best to spoil everyone's fun, no chance. So, maybe with Hawk going the time had finally come for him to call it a day as well. Hand over the reins and move on.

He would miss the buzz though, that was undeniable. The thrill of plotting-up and watching the lads in action was a major blast. But the idea of heading up The Squad without Hawk by his side was strange. Unthinkable even. They had been through too much together. Yeah, it would definitely be a wrench, but Hawk was right. The time had come.

Graham Hawkins was just about back at the office when his phone rang and he took Billy's call. Hearing that his oldest friend had decided to follow him into the ranks of the West Ham old boys came as a total shock and it was only after he'd put the phone back in its holder that it began to really sink in. But as it did, he was suddenly overcome by an almost unbearable sense of emotion: a jumbled mixture of sadness mixed with elation that stuffed a lump into his throat and filled his eyes with water.

He pulled the car on to a garage forecourt and sat still for a moment before letting his head fall forward until it was resting on the steering wheel, sitting there in silence as he tried to work out if he was devastated or simply relieved. After all, it might be an old cliché, but The Squad really were like a second family to him. They were lads he had grown up with and who, through shared experience and time, had become like brothers. Yet, once he and Billy had announced their retirement to a hastily convened meeting of The Cabinet tonight, it would all be over. Despite his fears, he would miss it. Badly. A part of him already did.

Yet, equally, he felt as if a huge weight had suddenly been lifted from his shoulders. For the past year, ever since he'd been deported from Rome, he'd been increasingly paranoid about how much further he'd be able to push his luck until it ran out and he ended up inside. And although working for Billy had allayed a lot of those fears in recent months, seeing his name in the papers this morning, and having to explain himself to Julie, had brought home just how close he was getting to losing everything. He wouldn't have that worry any more. He'd got away with it. And that was the most important thing of all.

Billy put the phone down on Hawkins and stubbed his cigarette in his ashtray. That was that then.

He picked up the paper and started to read through the article that had caused him so much grief in such a little time. The fact that so few words could have such a major impact on people was something he had never considered before and he actually found it quite staggering.

But as he got to the end, he began to wonder how this woman had picked up on the story in the first place. And when he re-read the quote from NCIS, it suddenly fell into place. 'Fucking Roberts,' he thought as he sat back in his chair and smiled to himself. 'It has to be. Well my old piggy mate, I think the time has come for me to fuck you over one last time.'

Sergeant Gary Roberts was wading through a pile of expenses when the call came. He listened intently and then, after telling his guv'nor where he was off to, headed quickly out into the August warmth.

Billy drove into the supermarket car park and slowly cruised around until he spotted the car he was looking for. He pulled up alongside before lowering the window and motioning at the driver to join him in the Range Rover. It was always safer to be on home territory. Meetings like this one were no exception.

'Mr Roberts,' began Billy as the policeman climbed in beside him. 'Don't get too comfortable, will you? You're not stopping.'

'What do you want, Billy?' asked Roberts smugly. 'More of your schemes?'

'No,' he replied coolly. 'Not this time. I have news that might interest you. That's all. And I wanted you to be the first to know; for old time's sake.'

Roberts looked at him in surprise. 'Don't tell me you're turning into a grass, Billy?'

'Me ... grass?' he said, with a laugh. 'You bloody wish.'

'So what is it then?'

Billy turned to him and smiled. 'It's over, Gary. And you lost.'

'What is?' asked Roberts slowly, frowning as he did so, unsure of where this was going.

'The Squad. It's finished. Well, as far as I'm concerned anyway.'

'Bullshit!'

'No, straight up,' replied Billy with a slight shake of his head. 'As of today, I'm officially retired.'

'So what's brought this on then?' asked Roberts quietly after a pause.

Billy sniffed and lit a cigarette. 'It's time, that's all. I've had my fun, now it's over. I've got other things to keep me occupied. Well, you know all about them, don't you?' he added with a smirk.

Roberts turned away and stared out through the window at the late afternoon shoppers, his mind racing as he tried to take in the full implications of what had just been said. All that work, the background information and intelligence he'd spent months putting together and writing up, it was all wasted. Now he'd have to start again from scratch.

But, more importantly, he'd been involved with hooliganism long enough to know that for the most part it was a victimless crime: a game played out to a set of rules built around the principle that, if you wanted to become a player and go running with a mob, you didn't complain when it all went wrong. That's why his job was mainly about prevention, not about settling scores. As a result, the chances were that if Billy was taking that step out of the front line, he was never going to see the inside of a courtroom for anything relating to his activities. Because as far as his guv'nors were going to be

196

concerned, Evans wasn't a problem any more, which meant that he was safe. At least as far as the football side of things was concerned.

'So, who's stepping up then?' he asked matter-of-factly. 'Hawkins?'

A smile spread across Billy's face. 'No! He'll be dropping out with me. We've got a business to run. Hey! Now there's a thought. From now on we'll be on the same side!'

Unable to stand any more of Billy's smugness, Roberts grabbed the car door handle and climbed out. 'I don't know what's going on or what you're up to,' he snarled. 'But we'll never be on the same side. Not in a million fucking years.'

Billy watched and laughed to himself as the Vauxhall drove out of the car park. The day he grew tired of getting one over on the Old Bill was the day he jacked it all in. He was going to enjoy rubbing Roberts' nose in it every chance he got.

He started the car and put it into drive but then pushed the gear lever forward again and lifted his phone.

'Mickey. Hello, mate. It's Billy. Yeah, we need to talk. There's been a few erm ... developments.'

Not for the first time in recent memory, the upstairs room of the St George had been plunged into a stunned silence by a single carefully constructed sentence, and it was a full minute before someone spoke again; Geoff shaking his head and saying, 'Well, I gotta hand it to you two. You sure do know how to grab the attention.'

'You've seen the stuff in the papers,' said Hawk. 'It's just getting too heavy for me. Time's come to get out.'

Chris leant back in his chair and sniffed loudly. 'I knew it.'

'Knew what?' asked Hawk.

'You're selling out.'

Billy looked at him angrily but kept his voice calm. 'No, Chris. Not selling out, getting out. There's a big difference.'

'Yeah, right. Course there is,' he replied sarcastically.

'Leave it out, Chris,' interrupted Stretch brusquely. 'Show the man some respect. He's done more for this firm than anyone else here.'

'Bollocks! When was the last time either of these two was in the front-line? I'm fucked if I can remember seeing either of 'em in action more than twice last season.'

'Oi! You're bang out of order,' barked PJ. 'You don't diss a bloke just because he's bowing out. You fucking know that as well as anyone.'

'Listen,' said Hawk, holding up his hands to calm things down. 'The point is that I made my decision and, when I told Billy, he decided that rather than break in a new face, he'd stand aside and let someone else take over. So if you're gonna gripe at anyone, gripe at me.'

'No one is gonna gripe at anyone,' said Geoff quietly. 'Right, Chris?' He glared across the room for a second and then stood up, shook Billy and Hawk's hands and with a wry smile said, 'Now piss off downstairs and get some beers in. We've got a decision to make.'

When they eventually joined Billy and Hawk in the bar, it came as no surprise to discover that Geoff and PJ had been installed as the new team at the top. And, with Chelsea away the first game of the season, they had the perfect opportunity to prove exactly how the new order was going to work. It was one they didn't intend to waste.

Billy bought them all a beer, and then he and Hawk shook hands with the lads who for so long had been an integral part of their lives. Even Chris had relaxed and almost mumbled an apology before Hawk grabbed hold of him, kissed him on the cheek and told him not to be a wanker.

And then for Billy and Hawk, it was over. At least that part of it.

Part Four

PJ glanced across the tunnel entrance at Stretch as a stern-faced Stuart Pearce strolled between them in the direction of the changing room. Despite the fact that his beloved West Ham were one-nil down, he couldn't help but smile. 'I tell you what,' he laughed as the last of the players left the field. 'When I see Billy and Hawk, the beers are on me. This is fucking top!'

Stretch looked at him and then glanced around at the heaving stands on either side of them. 'I know what you mean, mate. Who'd have thought it, eh? Us down here on the pitch. A few months ago they were doing their best to keep us out!'

The two of them turned and grinned at Geoff and Darren as they came out of the tunnel behind them. Both were wearing similar smiles on their faces.

'All right boys?' they said in unison.

'Sound,' replied PJ. 'I can't get my head around this at all. It's too fuckin' weird.'

'I know,' laughed Darren. 'I walked into the tunnel and there was Roy Keane stood in front of me. It was all I could do to stop myself from lumping the twat. Fuck knows what it'll be like when Judas comes down!'

'He'll take one look at us mobbed up on the sidelines and shit himself,' added Geoff. 'Hope so anyway, the bastard.'

'Not if we're in these poxy vest things he won't,' moaned Stretch. 'He'll probably piss himself laughing. Are they wank or what?'

Geoff looked at him and shook his head. He might have been wearing a black tabard with the legend 'WHU security' emblazoned across the back, but underneath it was a dark blue Stone Island sweater. Coupled with the white Henri Lloyd baseball cap perched on his head, there was no disguising his true passion. 'What's this, then?' he asked, reaching out and lifting his arm to stare at the familiar patch on the sleeve. 'And this?' he added, grabbing his cap.

'I ain't comin' to football without any gear on,' grunted Stretch as he grabbed his hat back. 'I'd feel like a bloody scarfer. Besides, look at you lot. I ain't the only one Sl'd up.'

'The man's got a point,' added PJ, as he glanced around at the others. 'And it ain't arf winding up the Mancs. Big Chris and a few of the others have been standing in front of some of their main lads giving it large all through the first half. Euston should be fun later.'

'Yeah I saw 'im when Beckham scored,' added Geoff. 'I thought for a second he was gonna dive in and slap a few.'

A breathless voice behind them grabbed their attention and they turned to find David Knight hurrying up the tunnel towards them. 'Lads!' he gasped. 'I need you outside.'

The four of them turned and ran down the tunnel after him, heading through the labyrinth of corridors until they were standing outside the visitors' turnstiles. 'Wait here!' barked Knight as he headed over to where five casually dressed young men were involved in a heated argument with a small group of the normal match-day staff.

They stood waiting nervously as the quarrel raged, wondering what to do as it became more and more heated, despite Knight's efforts to calm the situation.

'What the fuck are they moaning about?' asked Darren.

'Who knows?' replied PJ, glancing over to a gathering of policemen who were drinking tea and ignoring everything that was happening. 'But the Old Bill don't seem to give a toss, do they?'

'Bollocks to this,' snapped Geoff as one of the United fans moved forward and shoved David Knight in the chest. 'Come on, these aresholes are talking the rise!'

They hurried over, each one instinctively taking deep breaths to suck in oxygen and get the adrenaline fuelled up and flowing freely. 'Right you lot,' barked PJ once they had pushed their way into the throng and were standing between the two groups. 'Fuck off out of it... now!'

A stockily built youth stepped forward and stood so close to him that PJ could feel his beer-laden breath on his face. 'Or what?' he smirked. The sneering tone and thick northern accent immediately irritated all four of them.

PJ smiled and pushed his head forward until the gap between their noses was all but invisible. His eyes glazed with hate and filled with the desire to strike. 'Or I'll take your face off the front of your head and shove it up your arse!'

Geoff stole a brief glance at Knight. He looked pale rather than angry. This was either his worst nightmare or his dream scenario. He was in no doubt that he'd find out which later on. He returned his concern to the United fans as another spoke up, the tone equally aggressive as the speaker tried to gee himself up.

'Just do the cunt, Pete!' he growled.

Darren suddenly rushed forward and pushed him hard in the chest so he stumbled backwards. 'Shut it you little shit! Or you'll get some as well!'

'Oi!' responded the youth as the other United fans spun around to watch, each of them becoming increasingly nervous as they wondered what they had got themselves into. 'That's fuckin' assault! I'll have you for that!'

'Assault!' exclaimed Darren. 'I'll show you a fuckin' assault you little ponce!'

Geoff glanced across at the policemen, who had finally woken up to what was happening. However, rather than come over and intervene, they were simply standing and watching, seemingly glad that something was going on to help pass the time and relieve the boredom. But seeing them rang the alarm bells and Geoff moved forward to pull PJ away. Too late. Even as he put his hand on his friend's shoulder, the youth's head flew back as the head-butt connected with a sickening crack.

'Fuckin' bastard!' he screamed, his hands flying to his face as blood spurted out through his fingers and down the sleeve of his pale blue Ralph Lauren shirt. Almost simultaneously, Darren landed his first punch, a swinging right hander that struck his target on the side of the head and knocked him to the floor. Darren stepped backwards to avoid him as he fell, flexing his knees and bobbing up and down with his arms outstretched and his palms upward as he glared at the other United fans, waiting for any response. 'Come on then!' he growled. 'Who else?'

With two of their number being hurt so badly, and so quickly, any inclination to fight vanished from the remaining reds and they began to pull away as the police finally got their act together and hurried over. Geoff and Stretch stared at them as they came, waiting for the inevitable grief. But instead, the coppers grabbed the protesting northerners and dragged them away, ignoring their angry threats as they manhandled the visitors out on to Green Street and away. By the time they had disappeared from view, David Knight was leading PJ and the others back into the ground, while the relieved stewards remained outside, just in case of any further problems.

As they neared the tunnel, Knight grabbed Geoff and stopped the four of them in their tracks. 'You ever pull a stunt like that again ...' he began angrily. 'And I'll...'

'Hang on a minute!' replied Geoff calmly. 'What did you want us to do? Stand by until someone gave you another slap?'

'Well no,' he blustered, slightly embarrassed by Geoff's unexpected question 'But... well you can't go around beating up people just because they're complaining. It's not on. There are ways of dealing with situations like that. Better ways. That's all I'm saying.'

PJ shook his head. 'Yeah, it looked like you were doing just fine,' he said sarcastically.

Stretch stepped forward and stared at him. 'If you didn't want us to step in, why the fuck did you fetch us?'

'Look, all I'm saying is that if this is going to work, we need to get a few things straight.'

'I ain't got time for this shit,' said Darren. 'The second half's started.' He turned and headed out towards the pitch, closely followed by PJ and Stretch.

Geoff watched them walk off and turned to Knight. 'Don't worry. I'll sort it, OK? Just remember we're all kind of new to this.'

'Just make sure you do, that's all,' said Knight, suddenly angry with himself that he'd put himself in a situation where he'd been made to look foolish. 'I'm not going to stand by and watch you bastards drag the good name of this club through the shit just because you can't control yourselves.'

As he stormed off, Geoff sighed to himself and then followed after him. He was right. They wouldn't be able to get away with stuff like that too many times. Sooner or later, if the club or Hawk didn't get the arsehole, the Old Bill certainly would. He'd have to speak to the others before the next game but it was something he wasn't looking forward to. Especially since the one who'd been the first to strike a blow had been PJ, his number two.

Still, it was inevitable that sooner or later he was going to have to bring someone to order. After all, that's what being top dog was all about.

With less than a minute to go, and the score at 1-2, Paolo Di Canio dragged the ball back into the penalty box as he searched desperately for a way through a resolute Manchester United defence. Just three minutes ago, he'd pulled West Ham back into the game from the spot and now it was all hands to the pumps as the Hammers searched frantically for a late equaliser.

Standing stationary in front of the protesting away fans, big Chris stared out on to the pitch and willed someone to do something, anything. 'For fuck's sake, one of you! Come on!' he yelled. With nothing in front of him and everything happening at eye level, it was all he could do to stop from running out there himself.

But then, even as the ball bobbed around for what seemed like the hundredth time, and Suker finally managed to scramble the ball into the net for the equaliser, a coin bounced off the back of his head and drove it forward.

'Fucking bastards!' screamed Chris as Suker wheeled away and the ground exploded with noise. 'I fuckin' missed it!'

He turned and stared at the faces of the United fans, searching for the missile thrower, desperate to exact revenge.

Below him, a small group of lads began giving him abuse and laughing at his misfortune. 'You wankers!' he barked, putting his hand to his head and finding it covered in blood. More laughter.

'You little shits!' he growled. 'That's fuckin' well it.' He was about to dive in when a policeman appeared beside him, grabbing hold of his shoulder and wheeling him round. But for once, it was out of concern, not anger.

'You all right, mate? D'you see who slung it?'

Chris stared at him and blinked. For a second he was unable to comprehend what was happening as the effects of the blow finally began to filter through. 'No,' he muttered, barely audible over the noise of the celebrating West Ham fans as the final whistle blew. 'I was watching the fucking game, weren't I?'

'Come on, you'd best get that looked at,' said the copper, gently pulling him away in the direction of the St John Ambulance post. 'Word of warnin' for you mate. Never take your eyes off 'em. Any of 'em. They're all the same. Fucking animals.'

Billy turned off his phone and stared out across the half-lit and totally empty stadium. At that very moment, not more than a few miles from where he was standing, Geoff and the boys were involved in a stand-off with the police outside Euston Station; the closing moves in a game that had seen the CSS and Under-Fives scrapping all day with a United mob that had come down in serious numbers to avenge the piss-taking he and Hawk had organised just a few short months ago.

But from what he'd just been told, Geoff was doing a sound job and United had been sent on the toes more than once. Coming on the back of the hiding that had been dealt out to Leicester and the Babies at the first home game the previous week, it looked like the traditional fear which accompanied a trip to east London was going to be making a comeback.

More importantly, at least as far as Billy was concerned, was the major result they'd had against Chelsea on the opening day of the season. To avoid the attention of the police, Geoff had called it with the Rent Boys at Parsons Green, the old favourite, and had taken a massive firm across London, running Chelsea ragged until the Old Bill had turned up mob-handed and driven the two factions apart. Word on the street was that the boys from the Bridge hadn't been impressed and were claiming all kinds of crap about it not being their main firm and that the serious players hadn't arrived. That was nothing new. Chelsea never could admit to being done. But it all added fuel to the fire and built up the all-important reputation. They were exciting times. And it was all going on without him.

Inevitably after all these years, Billy felt gutted about that, as well as a bit pissed off that they were managing without his influence. He was actually a bit jealous, especially of the lads who had acted as their enforcers inside the ground that very afternoon. Most of them were enjoying the best of both worlds because, after spending the match winding up the northerners, they were now with Geoff and PJ at Euston. Despite his despondency, Billy couldn't help but smile to himself as he wondered what Roberts would make of that.

But it wasn't simply that he missed it, or that he felt obsolete. It was more to do with the fact that in only a few short weeks, without it, life had become almost boring.

The fuss over the article in the *Evening Standard* had died down within a few days, and now that Geoff was dealing directly with Mickey James for any work which needed doing in the pubs and clubs, the truth was that other than taking the money Billy wasn't directly involved in anything that could be even remotely considered 'iffy'. The fact that he had actually got a bit of a buzz from today's game passing off peacefully, at least inside the stadium, showed how tedious things had become. He needed something to get his teeth into; something to get the adrenaline pumping again.

'You OK?'

Billy turned to find Hawk standing behind him, enjoying one last smoke before he headed for home. 'Yeah. Sounds like the lads are having fun at Euston.'

'Not surprising really,' replied Hawk thoughtfully. 'It's been a big day all round, I guess.'

'Fucking boring, though,' said Billy, sighing. 'All these corporate types up here get on my tits.'

'No one said you had to be here. You could have been in the St George with the rest of them.'

'Fuck that!' said Billy, noticing but ignoring the fact that he'd said 'you' and not 'we'. 'I'd have felt like a spare prick at a wedding. I might head off down there now though. You fancy it?'

Hawkins shook his head. 'No, mate, can't. We're supposed to be going to this do tonight, remember? Black tie job, wives in tow...'

Billy sighed and looked at his watch. 'Fuck it. I forgot about that. Shit! Sam's going to slaughter me; I promised I wouldn't be late. We'd best piss off home and get ready. Come on, I'll walk out with you.'

The large function room of the Royal Gloucester Hotel was heaving with people having a good time, the great and the good mingling freely and happily with the less glamorous but equally important.

At the bar, Billy stood counting the number of faces he recognised as he waited to be served. But when they all began to blur into one, he gave up. In his semi-sober state, it was all too surreal, especially since he was still struggling to get his head around the sight of players he'd watched battle to a draw with Manchester United that very afternoon, now dancing around in dinner suits and trying to pull anything in a skirt.

He shook his head and turned his attention back to the bar, trying for the umpteenth time to catch the barmaid's eye and cursing out loud when she ignored him yet again to make a beeline for a well-known and famously single player.

'Billy ...? Billy Evans?'

He turned to find himself staring into the face of a youngish man with fair hair. Although vaguely familiar, Billy had no real idea who he was but knew instinctively from the way that he stood and spoke that he was a follower of the Saturday scene. The guy might as well have had a Stone Island patch on the sleeve of his dinner jacket. 'The one and only,' he replied as he took a cigar from his pocket. 'Sorry, mate, I'm a bit pissed. I know the face but...'

'Pete Simpson,' he said, holding out a lighter for Billy's cigar. 'I was with you and Hawk in Rome.'

Billy clicked his fingers as his brain caught up and he exhaled a cloud of pungent smoke. 'London Terrace Elite. You were with Danny Mason, right? How is the old wanker?'

'He's sound,' replied Simpson, impressed and proud that someone as famous on the scene as Billy Evans had actually remembered him, the number two in one of London's smallest, and least active, hooligan firms. 'I hear you've moved on. Joined the ranks of the old guard.'

'Well, it had to happen sooner or later,' said Billy with a shrug. 'Anyway, what you doin' here? This is a bit upmarket for you, ain't it?'

'I'm here with one of the sponsors. Corporate thing, you know how it is.' He paused for a second and, after taking the briefest of glances around, leant forward, lowering his voice almost to a whisper. 'Listen, I'm glad I ran into you. I've been thinking of giving you a bell for a while now.'

'Oh aye, what you after? A new motor?'

'No! Nothing like that.' Billy watched him as he spoke. There was something about him that was slightly unsettling, almost as if he were worried about the two of them being seen together. He certainly wasn't relaxed. In fact, he looked quite nervous.

'So? What *do* you want?'

Simpson glanced around again and then handed him a white business card. 'Can we have a meet? I might have some erm ... business to put your way.'

Billy took the card and held it between his fingers without looking at it. 'Concerning ...?'

'Not here. Give me a bell and we'll talk.'

'Fair enough,' said Billy, dropping the card into his pocket. 'I'm intrigued.' He was about to speak again when a pair of slim female hands slid under the back of his jacket and wrapped around his waist.

'Come on, fatty. I demand that you come and dance with your wife.' Billy smiled and turned his head to look at Sam's face resting on his shoulder, her glazed eyes and cheeky grin making her look even more attractive and appealing than usual.

'Fatty, is it?' he said. 'That's bloody charming.'

She took his hand and moved off towards the dance floor but, before he had taken a step after her, Billy looked back at Simpson and gave him the briefest of nods. 'Tuesday.'

Just as Billy knew he would, Pete Simpson walked into the safe haven of the St George, looking like an identikit of a typical Saturday lad: Lacoste shirt, Armani jeans and Rockport boots. The only thing missing was a Stone Island jumper. But then again, it was August.

The two of them shook hands and after Billy had bought him a drink, he led the two of them through to the upstairs room, away from the prying eyes and ears of others.

'So,' he began, as he dragged two chairs away from the wall. 'What's the score?'

Simpson shifted uneasily on his feet for a second of two and then sat down. 'I don't really know where to start,' he said. 'I mean, this ain't something I ever thought I'd be doing in a million years.'

'That sounds a bit ominous.'

'It is. And it's a bit erm ... delicate.'

'Why? Davey boy ain't been caught kid-fiddling has he?'

'No!' he blurted out. 'It's nothing like that. Jesus, he's straight as an arrow.'

'Well, what is it then?' Simpson stared down at his feet and said nothing. 'Just spit it out, Pete,' said Billy calmly. 'Or we'll be here all bloody night.'

'Well,' he began quietly. 'It's like this. It just so happens that I'm quite close mates with our chairman. And he's got this problem, see.'

Billy gave him a sly grin. 'What kind of problem?'

Simpson paused for a moment and then suddenly stood up as his nerves got the better of him. 'Look, on second thoughts Billy, forget it. This was a bad idea.' He went to leave but Billy grabbed his arm and held him back. He was getting a bit pissed off with the way Simpson was acting but was also desperate to know what was going on that could cause such obvious unease.

'For fuck's sake, will you just sit down and tell me!'

Simpson looked at him for a second and took his seat again, rubbing the back of his neck as he tried to relieve the stress he had put himself under. 'OK. OK. I'll tell you. But you gotta give me your word this is between you and me.'

Billy held up a hand in acknowledgement. 'On my boys' eyes, nothing you say will go outside this room. Now for fuck's sake get on with it!'

Simpson paused and took a mouthful from his bottle before leaning forward and speaking, his voice barely audible above the noise coming from the afternoon drinkers downstairs. 'We're in the shit. Financially I mean. And we're talking big time, fucking millions. If it ain't sorted soon, the club'll fold. It's that bad.'

'You and about a dozen others, mate,' said Billy, sighing.

'Yeah, you're right. But Derek, he's the chairman, he's been pinning all his hopes on this young Irish kid we've got. Seventeen years old, from Dundalk. I tell you what; this kid's a fucking diamond. Best prospect I've ever seen at our place.'

Billy lifted his head in surprise. 'Is this the Morgan kid?'

'That's right,' replied Simpson. 'Jimmy Morgan.'

'I read a bit about him the other day. Don't he live at your chairman's house or something like that? Yeah, that's right. I remember now. The journo in the *Express* was bloody raving about him. Reckon he's already knocking on a call-up.'

'Tell me about it,' said Simpson, sighing. 'That's the bloody problem.'

'How come?'

'Well not many people know this, but he was actually invited to train with the Irish squad a couple of months back. That's when it all went tits up. For us anyway.'

'Why? What happened?' asked Billy, increasingly engrossed.

'While he's there, this scum-sucking wanker of an agent started crawling all over him, talking about massive wages and sponsored cars; all that bollocks. You know the way those bastards work. Anyway, by the time Morgan comes back to us, this cunt has got him signed up as a client. And the first thing he does is walk into Derek's office and tell him that as soon as the kid turns eighteen he's off to the Premiership.'

'Bummer!' gasped Billy. 'But surely your man already had him signed up?'

'Yeah, I know. You would have thought that, wouldn't you?'

Billy rubbed the side of his head as he tried to keep up with what was being said. 'Hang on a minute. Either I'm missing something here or you haven't explained it properly. How can a kid who lives with your chairman *not* be signed to the club? Is your mate some kind of mug or what?'

'Look,' said Simpson. 'Let me go back a bit and explain. It'll be easier.' He took a drink and leant forward again. 'Clubs like ours have to rely on picking up bargains or kids and selling them on. So if someone calls Derek and says they've got someone worth looking at, he looks. Anyway, about three years ago, he gets this call about a kid in Dundalk. The guy who rang was almost shooting his load on the phone. So Derek sends a scout to check him out. Next day, the scout rings Derek and tells him to get his arse out there. Not just because this kid is bloody incredible, but because no one's ever looked at him before.'

'So Derek flies straight out to Dundalk, has a look for himself and asks the kid on the spot if he wants to come and sign on with us as a schoolboy. 'Course, he's over the bloody moon but the trouble is that his old man's dead, his mum won't leave Ireland and he's got no family over here so it looked a non-starter. Then out of the blue, Derek turns round and says that if there's no other way, the kid could come over and stay with him for a while and see how things went from there. Well, the old woman's a bit doubtful at first so Derek flies them both over to stay for a few days to see how it goes. Now, I don't know what Dundalk's like, I don't really want to know either, but I do know what Derek's drum in Chigwell's like and it's a fuckin' mansion! After a week of that, the old woman's well up for it so she tells Derek that if her boy's happy, he could come over. But only on condition that if he turned out to be any good and stayed, he would live with Derek until he was eighteen. Which also meant that he couldn't be transferred. You OK so far?'

Billy nodded, inviting him to go on.

'Well Derek's missus was a bit iffy at first, I mean, having a fourteen-year-old Mick land on your doorstep can't be much fun, especially when you've already got three kids of yer own. But Morgan's a really nice lad and, in the end, she gave in and gave it the nod. So then they start talking contracts.'

'So he is on a contract, then?' asked Billy.

'Oh yeah!' nodded Simpson as he took a drink. 'Not a bad one either, for a kid his age.'

'So what's the fuckin' problem then?'

'Right, now I don't know all the details here, but these are the basics. When Derek wrote it up, the old woman made him put in a clause which said that if the kid was going to remain in England, Derek had to act as his appointed guardian until he turned eighteen or returned to Ireland, whichever was the sooner. In return for that, Derek asked for a second clause that said if the kid was still playing on his eighteenth birthday, he'd sign a new contract with us. That meant that if he was sold, we'd at least get back some of the money that had been invested in him, if not make a tidy wedge.'

Billy nodded again. 'OK, I'm still with you. So what happened next?'

'Well, the old woman was chuffed to fuck, and so was the boy. All Derek could see was money in the bank!'

He took another drink and carried on with the next instalment as Billy listened intently. 'Well, the thing to, about six months ago, we had a run of injuries and Morgan had to be let loose on the first team. The little fucker only got man of the match on his bloody debut didn't he! Course, the papers are full of it and straight away we started to get the big clubs sniffing around. But all Derek did was blank 'em, 'cause he knew that he couldn't sell the kid even if he wanted to. 'Course, what he should have done was to sort out the new contract there and then and get him to sign it early. But the prick didn't.'

'Why the fuck not?'

'Because he's a tight cunt. We would have had to up his money, see, and over six months that would have added up to a fair wedge. And the bottom line was that with the old woman on-side, he thought he was safe.'

'So is that when this agent came on the scene?'

Simpson nodded ruefully. 'Yeah, d'you know, the wanker even went over to Ireland and told the kid's mum that Derek's been ripping the kid off by keeping him on low wages.'

'Your mate must be well pissed off,' said Billy as he lit a cigarette.

'Oh, that ain't the half of it,' laughed Simpson wryly. 'Our boy turns eighteen in January, which means that we've only got him for a few months anyway. And get this, this bastard has told all the Premiership clubs that he'll be available and has been talking to a couple of them already.'

'But what about this contract the kid's on? That's gotta be worth something. And even if he does do the off, you'll get compensation. The old Bosman rule don't apply till he's, is it twenty-three or twenty-six?'

'Twenty-three, I think,' replied Simpson. 'Nah, according to the legal bods, the contract's worth fuck-all. It'd get ripped to shreds in court. And as for compensation, well that's another problem.'

'Fuck me!' said Billy. 'Is anything *not* a problem at your place?'

Simpson shook his head sadly. 'Seems like it, don't it? The problem with compensation is that it takes time. And it's time we ain't got. But not only that, Derek was in the papers in the summer slagging off the FA about the plan to rebuild Wembley, so now he feels there's more chance of Maggie Thatcher getting the freedom of Yorkshire than there is of an FA tribunal giving us a decent hearing. Besides, even if they did us a favour, compared to the three or four million we'd have got if we sold 'im, the compensation would be fuck-all. Pennies. As it stands, we're shafted, mate. Well and truly.'

'What does the boy say about all this?' asked Billy.

'Oh, he says fuck-all. He's even moved out of Derek's. This agent geezer has got him living with someone else.'

Billy shook his head in amazement. 'I bet he's popular on match days.'

'You better believe it. The little shit's only going through the motions half the time - just in case he gets injured.'

'So what the fuck's this got to do with me?' asked Billy as he trod his Benson & Hedges into the floor.

'Well this is where it gets a bit complicated,' Simpson whispered nervously. Billy shrugged his shoulders and invited him to carry on. 'Like I say, the way things look, the club ain't gonna get fuck-all for this kid when he moves, which leaves us right up shit creek. But there is one way we can at least salvage something.'

'If he gets injured and has to stop playing, right?' suggested Billy. 'Then the insurers will have to cough up.' Simpson nodded slowly. 'So seeing as how I'm hardly likely to be in a position to do him some damage on a pitch, I guess, and stop me if I'm wandering off the plot here, what you want me to do is arrange for young Jimmy to have an accident of some kind.'

'That's about the size of it,' murmured Simpson.

Billy looked at him and furrowed his brow. He appeared as cool as ever on the outside, but inside he was buzzing with excitement. 'What makes you think I know anyone who could pull a stunt like that?' he asked quietly.

'I don't. Not really. But seeing you Saturday got me wondering. And I reckoned if half the stuff I've heard about you from Davey over the years is true, it had to be worth a punt. '

'Or two,' said Billy, with a smile to himself at his joke.

'You what?'

'Irish money. Never mind. Does your mate know you're talking to me?'

'No. He knows I'm talking to someone, and he knows what I'm talking about, just in case you were wondering. This was actually his idea in the first place. But he hasn't got a name. He doesn't need it.'

'As it happens,' said Billy after a short pause, 'I might know someone, but it won't be cheap. Not if you want it done properly. I'll sound him out and call you tomorrow.' He paused again and then leant forward, lowering his voice to an aggressive whisper. 'But let's get one thing straight; I don't want anyone ever knowing we've even talked about this. You got me?'

Simpson raised an eyebrow and sniffed loudly. 'D'you really think I do?'

Samantha Evans lay with her head on her husband's lap as she watched the late film on Sky Movies. Above her, Billy appeared to be equally engrossed but, in reality, he was miles away.

The meeting with Simpson that afternoon had got him thinking. More importantly, it had got him buzzing. And he hadn't felt like that for months.

Despite having a pile of paperwork sitting on the desk in his office, as well as a stack of calls to make, there was only one thing running through Billy's mind as he sat in his Range Rover and that was his meeting in the St George the day before. The more he thought about it, the more of a rush he got.

It had taken Billy about ten seconds to decide that the only person he was going to get to do a job on Morgan was himself. He'd hurt enough people in his time for fuck-all but sport; earning off it would be a whole new experience. And despite the fact that there was a lot more to this than a simple straightener, by the time he'd left for work about three hours ago, he'd worked out exactly how he was going to do it. All he needed now was to sort out the details; which is why he was waiting in a Homebase car park in Wanstead and not sitting in his office in Romford.

He caught sight of Pete Simpson wandering in his direction and drove over to meet him before continuing out on to the main road as soon as he had climbed inside.

'Where're we going?' he asked nervously.

'Nowhere,' replied Billy. 'I just like to keep moving, that's all.'

Simpson nodded and stared out of the window. 'Fair enough,' he said. And then left a long pause before coming out and asking the question which even at that stage, he half-hoped Billy wouldn't be able to answer. At least not in the affirmative. 'So you reckon you've got someone lined up for this then?'

'Yeah. He's sound.'

'How much does he know?' asked Simpson after another long pause.

The basics, that's all, that someone wants someone else crippled. He doesn't even know it's a football thing.'

'Bloody hell, it sounds bad when you say it like that. '

Billy laughed out loud at his naiveté. 'It is fucking bad. What did you think was gonna happen?'

'I don't know. I just didn't think about it like that.'

'Well don't then,' said Billy with a shake of his head. 'Just leave it all up to me and I'll get it sorted. All I need from you is a few odds and sods.'

'Such as?'

'An address, a decent picture. Oh, and a hundred grand up front. In cash.'

'A hundred grand!' gasped Simpson. 'Jesus Christ, that's steep!'

Billy glanced across the car and shook his head 'You reckon! So what did you think it was gonna cost? A tenner?'

'I don't bloody know. I thought...'

'Listen, if I'd have known you wanted it done on the cheap, I'd have gone up King's Cross and got you a couple of druggies for fifty quid. 'Course, after all that shit they'd have been taking, they wouldn't exactly be the brightest buttons, which means that it's a safe bet that they'd fuck it up and we'd all be dragged down with 'em.'

'OK,' sighed Simpson. 'I get the message.'

'Look, Pete, this kind of thing is a specialist job. This kid has got to be hurt just enough so that he has to stop playing but not enough to seriously harm him, right? And it's also got to be done in a way that doesn't attract the attentions of the Old Bill. 'Cause if you do that, the insurance boys will get twitchy and won't pay out.'

'Yeah, but one hundred grand. Fuck me, that's some serious wedge, Billy. And we're skint, remember?'

'But what's the kid insured for?' said Billy with a shrug. 'One, two million? You gotta speculate to accumulate, Pete, otherwise you end up with fuck-all. And your team are history, mate.'

Simpson sank back in his chair and sighed. He knew Billy was right. All he had to do was convince Derek. Still, it had been his idea in the first place. 'I'll see my man and let you know what he says. How quick could your boy get this done?'

Billy smiled to himself. 'I reckon he'd get on it as soon as the cash is in his hands.'

After dropping Pete Simpson back at his own car, Billy headed down the A13 towards Tilbury, a town famous for its docks and infamous for its skinheads, its villains and The Sun - a pub once voted by the tabloid of the same name as the most violent drinking hole in Britain. A label it had lived up to for years until even the local police, hardly the most passive of groups themselves, finally got pissed off with spending every Friday and Saturday night sorting out trouble there and shut it down for good.

He navigated his car along the decaying high street and made for a small group of yards hidden away in a back street on the edges of the docks, driving slowly past them at first before turning around and returning back up the narrow street and eventually bringing the car to a halt outside the second unit. A badly painted number two on the gate was the only indication that anyone was actually using it.

Billy climbed out and looked around. Despite the fact that it was mid-week and early afternoon, the whole area seemed to be deserted. Yet it had an almost tangible air of villainy about it, a tingling aggression that made Billy feel like he was being watched, which he probably was. Even the walls surrounding the yards had an evil look: tall metal panels that provided the tenants with both security and secrecy, the latter being the most important in the majority of cases.

He locked the car and wandered over to the metal gate, his loud thump immediately attracting the booming sound of a large dog barking angrily at the intrusion and shattering the silence. Within a minute, a deep, gruff voice had shouted it down and then demanded to know who was outside. The gate opened without a second's delay as soon as Billy had answered.

From inside, a powerfully built man with a shaven head and arms covered in tattoos stepped out into the street. He was coated, almost from head to toe, in a mixture of oil and dirt. Yet Billy could tell that he wore the golden brown, weathered hue of a man who spent most of his working life outside in the open air. And from the amount of gold hanging around his neck and ears, that work was obviously profitable.

He looked Billy up and down for a second and then a broad smile spread across his round face. 'Well fuck me!' he said, thrusting out a large hammer-like hand as he spoke. His words dripped with a thick Essex accent, rattled out at machine-gun speed, typical of someone who spends much of their time working alone. 'You're either lost or after sommink.'

Despite the grease covering, Billy took his hand and shook it warmly. 'All right, Danny. How's tricks?'

'Fucking top, mate. Couldn't be better. Hey, it's good to see ya. You look good. Bit fat though.' He let out a belly laugh and stood to one side. 'Come in, I'll make a brew. And watch them shiny shoes, it's a bit messy in there. If I'd have known you was coming I'd have cleaned up.'

He waited until Billy was inside and then slammed the door shut before leading his visitor across the yard to a tiny hut outside a large lean-to at the far end. Billy looked around him as he followed. The place was full of old cars in various states of disrepair. Some were complete while others had been painted a bright yellow but were battered almost beyond recognition. Over to one side, an almost brand-new, dark-blue Mitsubishi Shogun sat gleaming in the sun. For some reason, it fitted in perfectly with the surroundings.

'Still banger racing then,' said Billy as he walked.

Danny stopped and turned round to look at him. 'Bloody hell, there ain't no foolin' you is there? Staying on at school did you the fuckin' power of good.' He let out another laugh and began walking again, shouting over his shoulder as he moved. 'I was racing all weekend as it happens. Done two fuckin' cars as well. I tell you what, Billy, these old Granadas are gettin' bloody hard to get hold of. You ain't got none up your place, 'ave ya? I'll have to start using these bleedin' Jap fings soon.'

'No, mate. In fact that's why I'm here. I want to erm ... borrow one.'

Danny led them into the hut and switched the kettle on before sitting down and lighting a cigarette all in one practised movement.

'How's that then?'

Billy took a smoke from him and looked around. The carpet was so filthy it had simply become an extension of the yard outside, and the walls were covered in a collage of porn and scribbled notes on scraps of paper. It was exactly as he'd remembered it.

'I need a motor. Nothing flash but it has to be fast and reliable. And it has to be able to take a shunt.'

'When for?' asked Danny without even the slightest hesitation. Billy held out his hands. 'Not sure, mate. Could be tomorrow, could be next week. Maybe never.'

'And I take it it'll be coming back to me for disposal?'

'Yep. Once I've finished with it, it'll need to vanish - and fast. That's why I came to you. You're the guv'nor when it comes to stuff like this.'

Danny stood up and busied himself with two cups as the kettle began to boil. 'As it 'appens, I got something that might suit. I built it up for some kid wanting to do a bit of ram-raiding. Dumb fucker paid me half up front and never came back. Seeing as it's you, I'll let you have it for two thou, no questions asked. False plates already on it and I'll even deliver and collect it if you want.'

'Sounds sweet,' said Billy.

'Wanna look?' asked Danny as he handed Billy a steaming mug. 'Come on.' He led him through to the lean-to, which contained another four old cars. Two had been stripped out and painted for racing hut the others were complete. Danny walked over to a large silver Ford at the far end, turned and smiled. 'What d'you reckon then?'

Billy studied it for a second. It looked like a perfectly standard early eighties Mark2 Granada, the square box shape harking back to a style of car design long gone and the dull paintwork making it appear totally anonymous - like any one of a million other old cars. If Billy hadn't known any better, he'd have valued it at a maximum of £250.

'Sound eh?' said Danny proudly. 'Check out this fucker.' He bent down and lifted the bonnet to reveal that, in stark contrast to the tired exterior, the mechanical parts were gleaming. 'Nineteen-eighty Granada. Proper Ford RS sports suspension, manual gearbox, limited slip diff and a nicely run-in half race V6 2.8 motor. This fucker'll take off like a greyhound with its arse on fire and hit 140 a piece of piss. See this?' he added, pointing down at the front end, showing off the detail like the craftsman he was. 'There's some serious steel in here. I've even stiffened up the wings so they won't crease. This'll take a tidy front-ender, no problem.'

Billy studied the box section frame expertly welded in under the bonnet and smiled. It was exactly what he wanted. Almost. 'Can you get the windows tinted for me? As dark as possible. And I'll only be needing it for a few hours, so I'll pick it up from here and bring it straight back if that's OK?'

'Sweet,' said Danny with a nod. 'I'll get that sorted. Just let me know when and I'll have it ready.'

'By the way, did you ever find out what happened to the kid?' asked Billy.

'I heard the little twat got nicked doing a break-in. Fucking young 'uns today ain't got no patience.' He dropped the bonnet with a slam and stood up. 'Oh, and just so you know, this'll be stripped out and painted for racing within half a day of you getting it back here. All part of the service. Trust me, no one, and I mean no one, will ever trace it.'

It was almost knocking off time when Billy finally made it back to the office. Jill was spitting bullets at the fact that he'd not only been missing all day but had left his mobile turned off.

After placating her and turning his phone on, he was just about to sit down and begin doing some proper work when his phone buzzed and told him he had a text message.

He pressed the required buttons and studied carefully what arrived. 'Deal OK. Will meet STSP a.m. with stuff. LTID,' he said out loud to himself. 'What the fuck does STSP mean?'

'Same time, same place,' said Jill as she walked in and placed a coffee on his desk.

Billy laughed as he suddenly realised who it was from. He typed in 'sound' and sent it before dropping his phone on the table and leaning back with his hands behind his head and a grin on his face.

Sometimes, every once in a while, life really was sweet.

Billy clicked opened the briefcase and stared at the little packets stacked neatly inside. Each one was sealed and marked: £l000/£20.

'It's all there,' said Simpson nervously. 'A hundred grand. I've counted it about fifty times in the last hour. I tell ya, it's amazing the things that go through your head when you've got that much cash sitting in your motor.'

'Two weeks' wages for Bergkamp. Fuckin' crazy ain't it?' said Billy, reaching into the case and taking out a 10 x 8 colour photograph, the thin young face smiling out without a care in the world. 'So this is our boy then?'

'Yeah, that's him, the little cunt,' replied Simpson, his voice suddenly more aggressive. 'That bastard's sold us right down the river.'

Billy glanced at him and shook his head. Never mind a woman scorned, he thought; nothing gets the arsehole more than a geezer whose football club is getting shafted.

'His address is in there as well. He's staying with his agent's sister, I think. You can do that wanker as well if you like. That tosser's ...' He suddenly stopped talking and turned pale, realising that what he was saying wasn't actually any kind of joke at all. It really *was* going to happen and, more importantly, he was a part of it. 'Well, you-know...'

'Forget it,' Billy cut in. 'What time does he get home from training?'

'There's a rough timetable in the case. Have you got any idea when ...?'

'You just leave that to my man,' said Billy firmly. 'Here, these are for you.' He took five of the packets from the case and held them out. Simpson pulled back from them, aghast.

'What the fuck's that for?'

'Call it commission. Besides, I need you to do something for me.'

'What?' he asked nervously.

'I'll give you a call in a couple of days,' said Billy. 'When I do, drop everything and fuck off out the country for a couple of weeks. Save you getting spooked. By the time you come back, the fuss should have died down.'

Simpson reluctantly took the money and nodded. But as he moved to get out of the car, Billy stopped him. And after staring directly into his eyes for a few seconds, said, 'None of this ever took place, you got me? You ever say a word about it to anyone and you're history.'

CHAPTER 31
Wednesday 6 September 2000
12.30

Billy drove the silver Granada slowly through Tilbury and out on to the dual carriageway leading up towards the A13.

After his Range Rover, safely hidden away in Danny's yard, the old Ford felt positively archaic. But it ran like a well-oiled sewing machine and, even at a steady sixty mph, Billy could feel that there was more than enough power in reserve. In the end, he gave up wondering just how much and floored it. The rear tyres registered a slight yell of protest and then dug in, throwing the car forward at a staggering rate and shoving Billy back into his seat as if someone had put a huge hand on his chest. 'Fuckin' hell!' he gasped out loud as the speedo spun round to 120, only stopping its upward trajectory when Billy lifted off the throttle as the slip road hove into view ahead. He dabbed the brakes to bring the speed down to a reasonable figure and carried on, heading for Chigwell and the job in hand.

For the previous few days, in between his normal work, Billy had been a regular visitor to the affluent Essex town, studying the habits of Jimmy Morgan and working out exactly when and where he was going to execute his hit. Sometimes he'd sat in his car watching the front of the large and obviously expensive house the kid was living in; at other times, he'd wandered around on the common at the end of the road, noting any detail he thought might prove useful and adding it to the timetable Pete Simpson had given him. All of it helped to build up a picture of his prey. By yesterday, Billy had decided that he had everything he needed. Today would be the day. And ever since he'd taken the decision, he'd been buzzing. But it wasn't like any buzz he had ever experienced before. It was much more intense: raw adrenaline mixed with pure anticipation, a potent mixture and one that certainly focused the mind. More importantly, it wasn't shared. Not like a plot-up at football. This was all his. Every last ounce of it. And for the first time, he'd actually begun to understand how people became addicted to things. He could certainly handle a blast of this once in a while.

As he neared his destination, just as he had done a thousand times since yesterday, Billy began to visualise what was going to happen, running over every single detail to make sure that he'd be ready for any eventuality. And by the time he arrived in the quiet Chigwell street, he was totally wired in to what he had to do. As far as he was concerned, Morgan's career was already finished. There wasn't a trace of hesitation or doubt in his head.

He cruised past the now-familiar house and, after noting the position of the various parked cars in the street, drove to the end, turned and positioned the Granada in exactly the place he wanted to be, parking on the kerb, with the common behind him and a perfect view of the front of the house 150 metres down the road. All he had to do then was wait.

It was another hour and a half before Morgan returned but so intense was his concentration that Billy had hardly noticed the time passing. He was just pleased to see that, as usual, the driver dropped him off and was out of the street even before the kid had closed the gates and was through the front door.

The second it closed behind him, Billy started the Granada to get some heat into the engine, sure in the knowledge that within a few minutes Morgan would be back out and heading for the common. His daily dog-walking routine had never varied since Billy had been watching him, and today was no exception. By the time the door opened again, the car was just about fully warmed and ready.

But as the now-familiar black mongrel bound out and stuck its head through the gate, barking furiously in a desperate effort to relieve the boredom of a morning spent doing nothing, Billy suddenly became aware of his heartbeat, it seemed to be getting louder by the second, thudding through his body and blocking out everything else. And for almost the

227

first time, he was suddenly aware of his fear. Not of getting caught, but of getting it wrong. He hadn't ever considered the possibility that this wouldn't work but now he realised just how easy it would be for it to do exactly that. He was only going to get one shot at it. And only one. Everything had to be right. The timing, the speed, everything. Get a single thing wrong and it'd be all over. The chance missed.

Billy closed his eyes and took a deep breath, holding it for a few seconds before slowly exhaling. It was an old trick, learnt on the front line of a hundred rucks, and was designed to calm him down and help get his head together. It never failed. And by the time he opened his eyes again, he was back on it. Focused, calm and confident.

In front of him, Morgan followed the animal out on to the drive, where he clipped on its lead and opened the gate. The dog continued to bark furiously as it pulled him out on to the path and in the direction of both the common and Billy, who, even as they began walking, snicked the car into first and eased off the clutch, allowing the old Ford to creep forward off the kerb and build up momentum - movement, the best way to avoid wheel spin when the moment came. And it *was* coming.

Still blissfully oblivious to the tension building up around him, Morgan continued to walk towards his destiny, which by now was waiting in a small gap between a white Peugeot and a red BMW, less than thirty yards in front of him.

He hated walking the bloody dog. It was a pain in the arse. And he hated living in this shell of a house. There was never anyone around. They were all at work trying to keep up payments for the houses they never spent more than an evening living in. It was crazy. Life had been easier at Derek's place. It had been more homely. And he missed that.

But at least he didn't have to listen to the dog's barking. He simply cranked up the volume on his Minidisk and drowned it out with Eminem.

Billy watched as Morgan got closer and closer, willing him to step into the space where he'd crossed the road almost every day since he'd been watching him. When he was about five metres away from it, Billy gave the throttle the merest of prods to marginally increase his speed to 20 mph, mentally working out the distances and timings in his head with terrifying precision. There was no room for error. It had to be inch perfect.

And then Morgan was at the gap. He paused for a second and after taking the briefest of glances back up the road, stepped out into the space between the two cars. In that instant, Billy eased the steering wheel to the right and floored the throttle. The large silver car leapt forward and slammed into the back corner of the Peugeot, shunting it forward into the BMW and trapping Jimmy Morgan between the two vehicles before he even knew what was going on. Despite the impact, Billy kept his foot hard on the accelerator, driving the solid front end of the Granada further into the French hatchback and squeezing the hapless footballer even harder between the two cars until the rear wheels of the old Ford lost grip and began to spin.

Then, and only then, did Billy lift his right foot from the floor and quickly glance around. The road was completely empty of traffic and he'd spent enough time watching the houses lately to know that they were almost certainly unoccupied. So time, though short, wasn't critical. He returned his gaze to Morgan to see that the kid's eyes were almost bulging out of his head as he tried to work out what had just happened to him and why he wasn't feeling any pain. But the only thing concerning Billy at that moment was the sudden realisation that Morgan was still standing upright. And, aside from the obvious shock, he looked totally uninjured. There certainly wasn't any blood — at least none Billy could see.

He cursed out loud to himself and slammed the car into reverse, backing away with the intention of blasting the Granada in for a second time and inflicting another wave of damage. But, as he reversed off, it eased the pressure on the Peugeot, allowing Morgan to fall slowly forward on to the creased bonnet. And as soon as he saw that, Billy knew he'd done exactly what he'd set out to do. For the young footballer didn't bend at the waist, but at a point half way up his thighs, proof that his legs were well and truly fucked.

Billy edged the car forward until it was alongside the now severely damaged Peugeot. And after stopping for the briefest of final, but pitiless, looks at the prone young body, he accelerated slowly away and headed back to Tilbury.

Jimmy Morgan lay sprawled across the white metal and shivered uncontrollably. He had finally managed to work out that the thing tugging at his right arm was the dog, struggling to free itself from the lead he had wrapped firmly around his wrist when they had set out on their walk. The rest was simply a blur. But if he could have had one wish right there and then, it would have been for someone to turn down the volume on his Minidisk which in spite of the crash was still blasting music into his ears from his back pocket. Because at that moment in, he didn't really care who the real Slim Shady was. He just wished he'd fuck off and let him drift into unconsciousness.

Danny slammed the gates shut and walked round to the front of the Granada. 'What d'you hit then?' he asked as he knelt down for a closer look at the damage. 'Nothing big, I'd reckon. There's hardly a scratch on 'ere. Busted headlight and a few dents. That's fuck all.'

'I was only doin' about thirty,' said Billy, shaking slightly as he lit up and desperately fought the increasing desire to tell him everything. 'It was a bit of a balls-up really.'

Danny stood back up and lifted the bonnet, smiling proudly as he inspected his work. 'Look at that! It ain't moved a fuckin' inch.' He dropped the bonnet back down and glanced across at Billy. 'Listen, if your er... job didn't work out properly, I'll buy this back off you if you want? It'd save me having to build another one up.'

'No, mate. Best strip it. Just in case, you know?'

Danny nodded. He did indeed know. 'Worth asking,' he said. 'D'you wanna give me a hand stripping it then? Some do, just for peace of mind.'

'No, mate.' Billy replied with a wave of his hand. 'I trust you. Besides, I best piss off. I've got a business to run.'

Danny nodded and walked him over to the Range Rover. 'What is it today? Wednesday? Oh yeah. Well I'll be racing that on Sunday then and that'll be it gone. You should come down for a look; you paid for the fucker after all. Besides, you never know, you might enjoy it.'

Billy smiled and shook Danny's hand before climbing into his car. 'Cheers, mate. Good to see you again.'

'Yeah, you too. Don't leave it so fuckin' long next time.' He walked over and opened the gates as Billy started the car and reversed it back out of the lean-to. But just as the Range Rover had almost passed out of the yard, Danny shouted out and stopped him. 'And don't forget, any Granadas you come across, give me a shout.'

The instant Billy heard the gates slam shut behind him, he accelerated away from the yard and began running through the events of the day, satisfying himself quite quickly that he hadn't left anything that might link him to either Morgan or his accident. Even the call to the ambulance had been made on one of the pay-as-you-talk phones Hawk had got for the lads they were going to use on the pubs. And they were totally untraceable.

Once he had finished, and was happy, he ran through it all again, just to make sure. And when he came up with the same answers both times, he lit a cigarette, switched on the soulful sounds of Al Green and finally let himself relax and enjoy the post-job high that was beginning to kick in and envelop him.

Back in Tilbury, Danny drove the Granada into the spot vacated by the Range Rover and made himself a coffee. He sat for a while and then, noticing the time, switched on the radio to listen to the hourly news.

Two hours later, he had completely stripped the old silver Ford of both its glass and interior trim and was busily spraying the almost bare shell with a coat of bright yellow paint. Job jobbed.

Derek Sippings stared through the observation glass at his young player and visibly shook. Ever since he had been called to the hospital, his emotions had been fluctuating wildly between the extremes of guilt and relief. At least twice he'd even been forced to choke back a desperate urge to vomit. But above everything else, he felt an almost overwhelming sense of sorrow. At the end of the day, a young kid's life had been ruined. And for what? The fact that he was involved made it even worse. He hadn't expected it to be like this. In truth, he hadn't known what to expect at all.

He stole a look at a uniformed policeman who was talking to a middle-aged man in a suit, and then walked over to a doctor sitting at a desk filling out some paperwork. After introducing himself, he asked for a true assessment of the injuries. But the doctor shook his head.

'I'm sorry, we can only really talk to the family.'

Derek smiled sadly. 'I'm all the family he's got. At least here in England. He's from Ireland, you see.'

The doctor looked at him and nodded. 'Well, he's got severe crush injuries to both legs as well as two shattered knee-caps, a broken pelvis and we think there might possibly be some lower back damage as well. He's also got injuries to his spleen and kidneys, but we don't really know the level of tissue and muscle damage yet, although it's obviously fairly extensive. In accidents like this, a lot depends on how quickly the ambulance arrives and stabilises the patient. But apparently he was alone when they turned up, so God knows how long he'd been there. Poor bugger.'

'Will he ...?'

'If you were wondering if he'll ever play again, my answer would be a definite no. Strictly between you and me,' he added, lowering his voice almost to a whisper, 'I'll be amazed if he'll ever even be able to walk properly.'

'Mr Sippings?'

Derek turned to find the uniformed officer and the suit standing behind him. 'PC Marsh and Detective Constable Taylor. I thought I recognised you, sir. I'm an O's fan, you see.'

'Nice to meet you,' he replied weakly. 'Sorry the circumstances are so tragic. So what do you think happened, then?'

The policeman shook his head. 'Looks like a tragic hit-and-run. Probably kids in a stolen car. We think it was one of them who called the ambulance but can't be sure because they didn't leave a name or a number and apparently the voice on the tape is very muffled. We're doing some forensics and door-to-door stuff, though. But to be honest, around there, at that time of day...' He shrugged his shoulders and left the statement hanging, the inference obvious.

'We might get lucky with the car,' added the suited copper in an effort to reassure him. 'But the truth is that it could be anywhere by now. And if it was kids, they'll probably panic and torch it.'

Derek stared at him for a moment, then turned back to the glass and Jimmy Morgan. His heart was banging so loud he was sure the two coppers could hear it. Could it really be this easy to ruin someone's life and get away with it? 'So what you're saying is that unless you get lucky and find either the car or a witness, the person who did that will never get caught?'

The suited copper shrugged his shoulders but said nothing. He didn't have to, the expression on the face of PC Marsh said more than enough.

A nurse appeared on the other side of the glass and the three men watched her in silence as she busily checked the equipment and made notes on a clipboard. But in the end, Sippings couldn't bear to watch any more and turned away. The guilt had returned. 'Seventeen years old,' he murmured to no one in particular. 'What a bloody stupid waste.'

Part Five

CHAPTER 33
Friday 3 November 2000
15.30

Billy walked into the arrivals lounge at Gatwick Airport and drew in a lungful of good old English air. Much as he'd loved being in Florida with Sam and the boys, he was glad to be back. Not because he wanted to get back to work, but because after two weeks away, he'd started to miss the day-to-day buzz of life.

He always felt like that when he came back from holiday. It was one of the consequences of Sam's golden rule forbidding any contact with either work or home. For all he knew, he could have been declared bankrupt and he'd never have known.

Yet the truth was that for once he'd been glad she had insisted on it. Because in the aftermath of his attack on Morgan, his life had become increasingly difficult to handle.

That same evening, even while he was still buzzing from the high it had given him, the media had exploded into a frenzy, screaming out for information and grieving over the loss of a player who had been widely tipped to become the new George Best. And it had gone on for days. The papers had provided almost saturation coverage, while it had been just about impossible to turn on the television or listen to the radio without being reminded of it. There had even been talk of a reconstruction on *Crimewatch*, but they had been forced to cancel it in the end when it became clear to everyone that the kid just hadn't been able to remember anything about the attack.

But Billy had. He'd remembered every single detail and had been desperate to tell them. Or tell anybody, for that matter. For the longer it all went on, the more fuel was added to his high, increasing the buzz to a level he'd never experienced before. He had actually started to get off on the fact that people all over Britain were looking for him and hating him. A couple of times he'd even found himself wandering around and smiling at people, wondering if they had any idea that he was the one and that he was shafting them all. It had felt incredible, and he'd felt invincible.

Bur inevitably, as the days passed, the press had grown tired of the story getting nowhere and had moved on to something else. Yet Billy's head had continued to spin with it and he'd struggled on for weeks trying to get a grip on things before finally realising that the only way that was ever going to happen was if he could somehow manage to escape it all for a while. That's why he'd suggested taking the kids to Florida. Not simply to give them all a holiday, but because he needed some time away to get his head straight.

And it had worked, eventually. Because although for the first few days of winding down he'd been a pain in the arse - snapping at Sam and the kids at the slightest provocation - by the time the second week had begun, he had chilled out, quickly returning to his old self: relaxed, cheerful and full of typical Essex-boy confidence.

Now he had returned from Florida fully refreshed and with his mind firmly back on the case and raring to go.

Despite the seemingly constant rain, he could hardly wait.

With typical feminine, post-holiday efficiency, Samantha Evans had everything unpacked and put away by nine o'clock. The dirty laundry had been sorted into piles and the second load was already thrashing away in the machine. She'd also found time to ring both her own and her husband's parents to tell them they were back and catch up on any gossip.

Billy, meanwhile, having fed and bathed the kids, was wading through a pile of mail and answerphone messages, none of which were important but all of which were better than helping out in the kitchen. He was about to wander upstairs to see what the boys were up to, when the phone rang. He answered it to find a familiar voice on the other end.

'Hello, my son!'

'Hawk, you nonce,' he said, laughing. 'How the bloody hell are you?'

236

'Good!' came the reply. 'Really good. Listen, I know you've just got back and all that, so I'll fill you in on everything to do with work on Monday. But all the lads are meeting up at the St George tomorrow. D'you fancy it?'

Billy raised his eyebrows and shot a glance at the kitchen. 'I'll have to ask Sam. I think she's got me down to visit the folks, what with there being no game on.'

'Well that's the thing, once we've had a few beers, we're all going off to meet up with the lads from the LTE. Their boys have got a game and the club are treating it as a kind of testimonial to raise money for that kid who got done in that accident. The poor fucker's being taken back to Ireland on Monday.'

'Oh, right,' said Billy, starting to feel slightly uneasy at being reminded of it all so quickly. 'Haven't they got anyone for that yet?'

'Nah. Don't look like they ever will now. Still, it could be worse, he could have been one of ours. So you coming then or what?'

Despite his confidence, Billy couldn't help but breathe a silent sigh of relief. 'No, sod that. It'll be too bloody depressing. Anyway, that's all a bit public-spirited ain't it? What the fuck's got into everyone?'

'You bloody cynic,' replied Hawk. 'Some of us thought it'd be a decent thing to do, that's all. Show a bit of East End solidarity, like. I mean, they've had a right shit time down there lately. What is it they say? Losing one's unfortunate; losing two is fucking careless.'

'What the fuck are you on about?' asked Billy.

'Oh shit! You wouldn't have heard, would you? About their chairman, I mean?'

Billy felt the blood drain from his face as the words sank in. 'You what?'

'Yeah, they found him in his motor on Tuesday. Sawn-off in his hand and the top of his head spread all over the roof lining,' said Hawk matter-of-factly. 'The papers are saying he topped himself but I've heard a couple of whispers saying that it was a gangland thing. He was up to all kinds of dodgy stuff, apparently.'

Within a few moments of Hawk's call ending, Billy had logged on to the Internet and was searching for everything and anything relating to the death of Derek Sippings.

He read what little he could find and then dialled Pete Simpson's number, only to find he had his mobile switched off and the answerphone on. Billy cancelled the call without leaving a message and sat for a moment staring into space.

Suddenly, he began to sense his stomach knotting. It was a thankfully rare but familiar feeling that had never let him down before. It meant trouble. He grabbed his phone and, after telling Sam he had to shoot out for a bit, headed for the door.

Mickey James leant back against the wooden chair and lifted his pint. 'No, mate. All that stuff in the papers was total bollocks.' He took a mouthful of bitter and, after licking the froth from his lips, placed the glass back on the table and leant forward again.

'Sippings didn't top himself. It was made to look like he did, but he didn't. That was a hit. And according to a copper I know, whoever did it was a pro, and a fucking good one as well. He told me that your man still had the barrels of the sawn-off in his mouth when they found him. And if it hadn't been for the forensics boys being on the ball, they'd never have known.'

Billy looked at him and shook his head. 'Why the fuck would anyone want to wipe him? It don't make sense.'

'Does it ever?' said Mickey. 'He wasn't bent though. Not as far as I know anyway. He wasn't even well connected. The only faces he knew were a few old-time villains at his golf club.'

'And you haven't heard anything on the street about who might have done 'im?'

Mickey shook his head and took another drink. 'Not a clue. Why are you so interested anyway?'

'It's a football thing,' lied Billy. 'We were thinking about putting in a bid for their security contract, that's all.'

Mickey frowned and leant forward. 'One other thing my mate told me though. They reckoned he'd been ... well, they said he'd been tortured before he got done.'

'You what?' asked Billy, suddenly horrified.

'Yeah. He said that's how they knew it wasn't suicide. They found some burn marks on the side of his head, like he'd had electric wires put there or something.'

Billy looked at him, increasingly appalled at what he was hearing. 'How come they didn't notice that straight away then?'

'When I said the side of his head, I meant the side that wasn't attached to the rest of him, if you know what I mean,' replied Mickey sarcastically.

'Oh Jesus! You are kidding?'

'Straight up.' He settled back in his chair and took another drink. 'Bastards, eh?'

Billy took in a sharp breath and glanced uneasily around as the knotting sensation in his stomach suddenly got worse.

He was almost back at home when his phone emitted a series of loud beeps informing him that he had a text message. He grabbed it from the holder and after hitting the required digits, read the message as he drove along. It said simply 'Meet a.m. STSP. Reply exactly as before if OK.'

He cancelled it and rang the number as quickly as he possibly could. But by the time it had connected again, Pete Simpson's phone had been switched off.

'Bollocks!' he shouted angrily before steering the Range Rover to the side of the road and braking to a halt. He dialled the number again but it was still switched off and so he read the message for a second time, realising as he did so that a great deal of thought had gone into putting it together. He checked back through the messages he had sent and, after finding the correct reply, typed in 'sound' and sent it; confident that at some point tonight Simpson would turn on his phone and collect it.

Once he had done that, Billy drove the car away from the kerb and headed for the sanctuary of his house, all the time wondering what the bloody hell was going on.

It was going to be a long and very worrying night.

CHAPTER 34
Saturday 4 November 2000
11.20

Typically for a Saturday morning, the car park of Wanstead's Homebase was packed. And, having sat there for almost half an hour listening to the incessant rain hammering on the roof of his car, Billy was becoming increasingly concerned that when Simpson did eventually turn up, he wouldn't be able to see the black Range Rover among the hordes of other vehicles. He was already late. For all Billy knew, he could have been and gone.

He picked up his mobile and not for the first time that morning dialled the increasingly familiar number, cursing out loud and dropping the phone back into his lap when he was once again connected to an answerphone. He hated feeling frustrated almost as much as he hated waiting. And he hated waiting with a passion. In most instances, he regarded it as nothing more than a needless waste of time which served no purpose other than to simply fuel anger and resentment. In his entire life, he'd never met anyone who'd been glad to have been kept hanging about.

He sat for a few minutes and then lifted the phone again. This time he ignored the urge to try the number, instead typing in yet another in a long line of text messages. This one simply read 'STSP. Where RU? CSS.' But before he could press the send button, he caught sight of Simpson scurrying through the parked cars and the pouring rain towards him, his body language displaying more than a desire to stay dry. He looked scared shitless.

The second he was safely ensconced in the passenger seat, Billy started the engine and, without a word, drove out of the car park and turned north, heading for nowhere in particular and letting the car stay in silence for a few minutes while Simpson got his bearings. Once he was sure his passenger was properly together, Billy turned angrily on him.

'So are you gonna tell me what the fucking hell has been going on or what?'

Simpson sighed loudly and ran both his hands up the side of his head. It was obvious to Billy that he hadn't slept all night; but then again, neither had he.

'How much do you know?' he asked, his voice almost trembling with fear.

'Fuck-all,' responded Billy tersely. 'I've been out of the bloody country for the last fortnight. So come on, tell me! And start from the beginning.'

Simpson looked at him and sighed. 'Everything was fine until last Sunday. The insurance company had paid up, Derek had cleared most of the club's debts and Morgan had recovered enough to be sent back to a hospital near his home town. Your man did a fucking job and a half on him. You do know that, don't you?'

'Never mind that,' barked Billy. 'Just get on with it, for Christ's sake.'

'Sunday afternoon,' continued Simpson nervously, 'me and the lads are watching the Sky game in our local when these two geezers walk in. You could tell they were wrong 'uns right off. Big bastards, you know? Anyway, bold as brass, they comes straight over to us and start asking questions about Jimmy Morgan's accident. Well the lads all clammed up a bit, I mean, we didn't have a fucking clue who these two Micks were, and we'd kind of had enough of talking to journos lately.'

Billy raised an eyebrow and stopped him in mid flow. 'Micks?'

'Yeah. Fuckin' accents were so thick we could hardly understand 'em. Anyway, we're startin' to get a bit pissed off when Davey comes back from the bog. Well you know what he's like with Micks. He fuckin' hates 'em.'

'How come?' asked Billy.

'He was a Para, weren't he? Spent ages out in Belfast. It freaked him out for a long time. Well, he's a bit pissed so he starts winding them up. Going on about Bloody Sunday and all that bollocks. 'Course, we don't know who these blokes are, so we let him get on with it. And they're just standing there taking all this shit he's giving them and not saying a word. Then he starts up the old "No Surrender" song and next thing we know one of them's only got a fucking shooter pressed up against his forehead! Straight up! Well me and the others were off out of there like a fucking rocket.'

'What happened to Davey?' asked Billy, struggling to concentrate on his driving as he tried to absorb what Simpson was telling him.

'Nothing. He said that this geezer just glared at him for a bit, stuck the gun back in his pocket and the two of them walked out and drove off before the Old Bill turned up. Calm as you fuckin' like!' Billy shook his head and turned into a McDonald's car park. He had to stop and listen to this properly if he was going to take it all in. Either that or he was going to crash into something.

'So then what happened?'

'Well, the others are all over the place. I mean, it ain't every day someone waves a pistol about in front of you. But me, I start to put two and two together don't I, and I got a bit panicky. So I rings Derek and tells him what had happened, and that's when he told me.'

'Told you what?' asked Billy nervously.

'That back in the late eighties, Jimmy Morgan's old man had been a high up in the paramilitaries. Or at least he was until he got a late-night visit from the opposition.'

Billy felt his heart leap up into his throat as the full impact of the words sank in. 'Tell me you're joking.'

Simpson shook his head as he looked across the car at Billy. Tears were beginning to form in his eyes but Billy had not an ounce of sympathy for him. Only anger. 'Why the fuck didn't you say anything before?' he raged.

'I told you, I didn't know. Gospel. Derek only found out about it two days before he ...'

'But how couldn't he have known for Christ's sake? The kid was living with him.'

'No one knew,' pleaded Simpson, his voice trembling with fear. 'Not even Jimmy. I don't even know if he does now.

Apparently he was only a nipper when his old man got done and to protect him, his mother had changed her name and moved. But because of who his dad had been, this group he'd been head of has been keeping an eye on him. Just in case, like. Now it looks like they've come over to try and find out what happened for themselves.'

'Hang on,' cut in Billy. 'How come you know all this now?'

'Some Irish journo rang Derek last week and told him everything. He'd somehow put it all together. I guess what with that and your bit, and then me telling him all that about what happened with Davey, well I suppose that's what spooked him. And I know he'd been visiting the hospital every day, and that'd been getting him down a lot. But he must have been in a really bad way to top himself. Poor bastard.'

Billy stared at him in stunned silence for a few seemingly endless seconds. 'Where have you been all week?' he asked slowly.

'I've been keeping my bloody head down, that's where. Staying with my sister up in Watford. Why?'

'So you haven't heard any rumours then?'

Simpson looked back at him with an anxious expression on his face. He didn't like the way this was going at all. 'What rumours?'

'Derek didn't commit suicide, Pete. He was killed.'

'Bollocks,' he replied, shaking his head and sinking back against the door. 'The papers said ...'

'No, Pete, it was a professional hit,' added Billy, his voice calm and deliberate. 'Trust me.'

He watched as Simpson's entire body began to tremble and his face collapsed into a look of total panic as tears welled up in his eyes. This time, Billy did feel pity, for both of them. He lit a cigarette and passed it across the car before lighting a second for himself. The nicotine had an almost instantaneous calming effect.

'Do you think it was these Irish blokes?' he asked shakily.

Billy let out an ironic grunt. 'I think it's a pretty safe bet, don't you?'

'But why?' said Simpson as he drew on his smoke and stared out of the window. 'I mean, how could they have found out?'

'Who knows? Maybe they just put two and two together like you did and came up with a different answer. The right one, as it happens.'

Simpson suddenly sat bolt upright, a look of almost abject terror on his face. 'But that means they could be looking for me! Oh Jesus!'

'Calm down!' said Billy holding up his hands. 'Just calm down!'

'That's fucking easy for you to say,' squealed Simpson. 'You ain't got the fucking IRA trying to track you down, have you?'

'And neither have you,' said Billy quietly, the tone of his voice hiding the fact that his mind was racing at a million miles an hour; trying to take everything in and work out what was going on. 'I'd put money on it. Look, if these blokes were after revenge for Jimmy Morgan they wouldn't be interested in you. They'd be after the bloke who set it all up. It's how they work; they're soldiers. Chances are that if it was them who killed Derek, they're already back in Belfast.'

'D'you reckon?' asked Simpson desperately.

'No doubt about it,' replied Billy, relieved to notice that even as he spoke his passenger relaxed slightly. After all, the last thing he needed was for Simpson to freak out. He couldn't have handled that. He needed to think, to work out how best to deal with this problem.

And it was a problem: a fucking serious one. Because while Simpson might be gullible enough to swallow the obvious bullshit he'd just been fed, Billy hadn't believed a word of it. He knew full well that if these guys were out to settle a score, they wouldn't stop until they were happy. And if they really had tortured Sippings before they killed him, pound to a pinch of shit he'd told them who was next in line. As much as it frightened Billy even to think it, it was almost certain that unless he acted fast, the poor bastard sitting next to him was already as good as dead. The obvious concern was what he'd say if they ever did get hold of him.

'So what do we do now?' asked Simpson, his voice still croaking with emotion.

'I haven't got a bloody clue,' replied Billy as he reached forward and started the car. 'But it might be a good idea to get you out of the country for a while. Just to let you chill out and give me a bit of time to find out how the land lies. I know some people out there who'll be able to help out.'

'But you said ...'

'Stop worrying. I just want to satisfy myself, that's all. I am involved in this as well, remember?'

He felt Simpson relax even further but, before he pulled the car out of the car park, he paused for a second and then looked Simpson square in the eyes. 'But there is one question I need an answer to first. A straight answer, Pete.'

'What is it?'

'Did you *ever* mention my name to Derek Sippings?'

'No, never,' he answered.

'Are you sure? Absolutely sure?'

'On my life. I never said anything to anyone.'

Billy held his gaze for a second and nodded in acknowledgement before turning back to the windscreen and heading for Wandsworth. The slight blush of Simpson's cheeks and tiniest of twitches on the edges of his mouth had just told him exactly what he needed to know.

CHAPTER 35
Saturday 4 November 2000
13.00

The second Simpson had climbed back into his own car and driven off - with strict instructions to go back to Watford and leave his mobile on at all times - Billy grabbed his own phone and dialled his home.

'Hello.'

He paused for a second and absorbed the voice. She sounded tired, but cheerful; typical of his wife. 'Sam, pack some things will you? We're going away again.'

'You what?'

'I said we're going away again. This afternoon.'

'Don't be bloody stupid,' she laughed. 'We only got back yesterday. And I'm at work Monday. So are you!'

Billy fought back the growing urgency in his voice and carried on talking as he started the car and began the journey back to Romford.

'Yeah, I know all that, but we're going away again. Tonight.'

There was a long pause and when his wife spoke again, her voice was slower and sounded full of apprehension. 'What's going on, Billy?'

For a moment, he thought about lying to her, but decided against it almost instantly. They'd been together too long for that and, besides, she knew him too well. Billy had learnt years ago that the best way to deal with his wife was to tell her the truth, just not the whole truth. 'I've got a bit of a problem, love, that's all. And it's best if we get away until I can deal with it.'

The phone went quiet again and Billy waited for what seemed an eternity for her to respond. When it came, her answer was exactly what he expected, and hoped for. 'OK, Billy. You know best. How long will you be?'

With Sam seemingly sorted, Billy's next call was to Hawk. And, judging by the level of noise in the background, he was in the St George, which was rammed out.

'Where the fuck are you?' he shouted above the din. 'It's your round!'

'Sorry, mate,' replied Billy, 'something's come up and I won't be able to make it. But listen, I need to talk to you for a minute. Can you bomb through to upstairs and call me back? I can't hear a thing with all that bloody noise.'

He cancelled his call and concentrated on the business of driving as he waited, desperately trying to avoid thinking about the shit he seemed to be falling into, until the phone rang again.

'What's up?' asked Hawk. 'You sound a bit iffy.'

Billy took a deep breath. 'I've got a problem, mate, and it's a fucking big one. But I need to get away for a few days until I can get it sorted. So can you keep an eye on everything for me till I get back?'

'No worries,' replied Hawk. 'Consider it done. But has this er... problem got anything to do with a couple of Irish geezers?'

The words sent a chill down Billy's back and as he let out a silent curse to both Simpson and Sippings, he instinctively pressed down on the throttle to urge the Range Rover along. 'Why d'you ask?'

'Sal said that these two Micks were in the pub looking for you last night. Big bastards, she said.'

'What did she tell 'em?' he asked, his voice beginning to waver slightly.

'You know Sal. She told 'em fuck-all.' There was a pause and then: 'What's going on, Billy?'

Although desperate to tell, Billy spared his friend that panic and, after telling him to have a beer or two for him, switched off his phone and shook his head.

'Fucking Simpson,' he whispered. 'I fucking knew it.'

CHAPTER 36
Saturday 4 November 2000
13.45

Billy knew instinctively that something was wrong the second he turned into his drive. He jumped out of the car and ran inside to find his wife sitting on the stairs sobbing hysterically, her two sons clutched tightly to her.

'What the bloody hell's going on?' he asked as he knelt down and enveloped the three of them in his arms.

'This little sod,' gasped Sam, clutching Alfie even tighter to her. 'I couldn't find him anywhere and ...' She started to sob again and leant forward until her head was resting on Billy's shoulder. Within seconds, her arms were around his neck, holding on to him as she cried.

He let her get on with it for a few minutes and then patted both of his boys on the head, prodding them in the direction of the landing and watching as they climbed to the top of the stairs and sat down. The two of them were nervously watching and trying to understand why their mum was so upset. Billy gave them a broad wink and was relieved to notice that they both gave him a half-smile in return.

'I was only at the end of the road, Dad,' explained Alfie, shrugging. 'That's all. And I was only talking to him because he called me by my name. *And* he said that he was your mate, so he's not really a proper stranger, is he?'

Billy closed his eyes as the alarm bells started to ring again. He hadn't passed a soul when he'd driven in. 'What did he look like Alfie?'

'I dunno. He was just a bloke. He spoke funny though,' he said with a grin. 'Like that bloke from *The Big Breakfast.*'

Billy lifted his head and stared at him. 'Which bloke from *The Big Breakfast*? Johnny Vaughn?'

'No, the one with the blond hair, like Mum's. You know. '

'No,' gasped Billy. 'I don't.'

'Patrick Kielty,' said Sam, lifting her head and wiping her eyes on her sleeve. 'He means Patrick Kielty. The comedian from Belfast.' She looked up and stared at him, her normally stunning blue eyes rimmed with redness. 'Now, are you going to tell me what the hell is going on?'

After making sure the doors were locked and installing the kids upstairs with a video, Billy led Samantha through to the front room and sat her down.

'D'you remember the do we went to? The West Ham thing? Well, I met this bloke there. He said he might have some business to put my way, so I gave him a ring a few days later and we got together. Well, I thought it was gonna be something to do with motors like, but no, it was nothing to do with that. Complete waste of time as far as I was concerned.'

'Well, what did he want then?'

Billy stole a glance at her and then turned his eyes to the floor. 'He wanted me to arrange something. But honest to God, Sam, I turned him down straight.'

'Arrange what?'

He shook his head and avoided her gaze. 'You don't wanna know.'

'Oh yes I bloody well do,' she barked angrily. 'If this has got anything to do with that Irish bloke who was talking to my son at the end of this street less than one hour ago, believe me, Billy, I want to know. So you best fucking well tell me. And right now!'

He looked at her, amazed and shocked to hear her using the F-word. He'd only ever heard her say it once before and that had been years ago - when she'd mistakenly thought he'd had a bit of skirt on the side.

'OK,' he said. 'If you really want me to tell you, I'll tell you. He wanted to know if I knew anyone who could ... well, harm somebody.' He stared at her as he said it, watching to see how she reacted. But she simply stared back at him, her face expressionless, her eyes still blazing.

'And you told him you didn't?'

'Of course I did! Bloody hell, Sam.'

She paused for a second and glared back across the room at him, desperately wanting to believe what he was saying but not knowing if she was able to. 'So if you had nothing to do with this bloke and whatever it was he wanted doing, why are we suddenly going on two holidays and have got Irish blokes camped out at the end of the road?' She suddenly stopped talking and stood up. 'Don't tell me this has got anything to do with the IRA,' she said, her voice faltering with each word that came out. 'Don't you dare tell me that, Billy.'

He moved towards her but she pulled back from him, fear replacing anger in her eyes and the colour draining from her cheeks.

'It's nothing like that, Sam, honestly,' he said.

'So what the bloody hell is going on then, Billy?' she cried. Tears streaming down her cheeks again. 'Tell me! Because I'm getting scared here.'

Billy stood in the middle of the room and looked at her with his tired eyes, not knowing what to do or say for the best. In the end, he continued the charade. Half the truth sounded better than the whole.

'The bloke I spoke to must have sorted out someone else to do his dirty work, because this lot are looking for him. The trouble is, he's vanished and they think I know where he is. That's all.'

'And do you?'

She closed her eyes and sighed with relief when he nodded. 'Then tell them, Billy. And let's try and get back to normal.'

He looked at her and nodded again. 'OK, Sam. If that's what it takes, then that's what I'll do.'

He wandered out of the room and headed for his study, dropping down onto his chair with a thump and staring at the wall for a few minutes, trying to work out what he was going to do next. But the truth was that he already knew. He'd known ever since he'd found out about Derek Sippings.

What he didn't know, however, was what he was going to do after that.

By the time Billy had got the boys dressed and ready, Sam had redone her make-up and, aside from a slight puffiness around her eyes, was looking almost as attractive as usual.

He gave her a hug and, after passing on strict instructions about staying in public places at all times, as well as keeping in constant touch with him, placed the three of them in her BMW and sent it off along the rain-sodden A12 in the direction of the M25. His Range Rover followed a discreet distance behind to make sure she wasn't tailed as she headed for the Bluewater shopping complex on the other side of the Thames. The decision to send her there had been taken to get her and the boys out of the house and also to give Billy time to get his head together and work out what he was going to do.

But as he drove along behind her, constantly checking in his mirrors to see that they weren't accompanied, an idea began to gel in his head. And as soon as he was convinced that it was almost certainly the only option available to him, he grabbed his phone, clicked in his hands-free kit and dialled Pete Simpson's number. He was relieved to find that, as he'd requested, it was still switched on.

'Pete, it's me. Are you OK?'

'Yeah, I guess so,' he said nervously. 'What's happening?'

'I've sorted you out with some plane tickets and stuff but we need to meet.'

'Where? And when?'

Billy took a deep breath to calm himself. His guts suddenly felt like they were on fire, which was hardly surprising really; given the circumstances and the fact that he hadn't eaten for almost an entire day. 'Are you at your sister's yet?'

'Yeah. Just got here.'

'Right, then get back in your motor and get to my garage in Romford, quick as you can. D'you know where it is? Right, you got a pen? Then here's the address ...'

With Simpson sorted, Billy returned his attention to Sam and the boys, instinctively checking his mirrors as he did so but thankfully finding nothing unusual lurking behind him. Reassured by this, he forced himself to relax as he followed along behind her, using the time to run his plan over and over in his head, fine-tuning the detail as he did so. By the time the first signs for the M25 came into view, he was sure that he had almost every eventuality covered; and, more importantly, that it was going to work.

He lifted his phone again and called Sam in the BMW, telling her that he was letting her go on alone from that point and reminding her that he loved her and she shouldn't worry about him. And then she was gone, up the slip road and down on to the M25. But even before she had joined the traffic heading for the Dartford Bridge and Kent, Billy was accelerating back up the A12 in the direction he had come. At the same time he was searching through the numbers stored on his phone until he found the one he was looking for.

It was the number of someone he'd known for years, both at West Ham and abroad with England, but which he'd only ever rung once before. It was in Glasgow, when he had been with a tidy England mob that had kicked things off with a huge jock firm, and it had all gone wrong when more sweaties arrived and hit them from the rear. In the end, Billy had been forced to call for reinforcements. But even then it had been a last resort, because he had always tried to avoid any kind of contact with the England lads who'd been into extremist politics - something that applied equally to the few he'd had with him at West Ham. Because at Upton Park - unlike at certain clubs where the supporters were known for having an element with a specific political bias - such lads were tolerated rather than accepted. The Hammers were more community-focused than politically aware and, as a result, had traditionally been just like one big happy family - which is why The Squad had stayed so strong for so long. There were no divisions of any kind.

However, that hadn't stopped some of his former lads from becoming involved, not only with the right, but the left as well. But they had always understood that when it came to a choice between The Squad and their politics, the CSS had to come first. Even lads like big Mark understood and accepted that. And he was as extreme as they came. Yet Billy had still kept a distance from him just as he had the others; wary that any kind of association might lead to assumptions about his own beliefs that he never wanted anyone to make.

He looked at the number on the screen for a split second longer and, after letting out a silent prayer of thanks to Sky Sports for picking West Ham as the Monday night match, pressed 'call' and waited until a gruff cockney voice answered with a curt 'Who's that?'

Billy balked for a second at the accent. It sounded different from the usual East End: well educated but abrupt and with an almost sinister undertone.

'Is that Mark?'

'Yeah, who's that?'

'Mark, it's Billy. Billy Evans.'

The voice changed immediately. Less aggressive now, but no less intimidating. 'All right, Billy boy. What's the story?'

'Listen, Mark, sorry to drop this on you, mate, but I need your help. Fast. Who do you know who can find out about two Irish geezers for me?'

Billy had just walked into his office at the garage when Mark returned his call. And it wasn't good news.

'These fellas you're on about,' he began. 'If they're who my contacts reckon they are, then they ain't IRA, mate. They're loyalists. That's our side, Billy. What you been doin' to upset 'em ?'

'It's a long story, Mark,' said Billy. 'But I've got to get hold of them somehow. I need to arrange a meet.'

'Well I've passed on your number. That's all I can do for you. But if it is them, then they're from one of the active groups, so someone will get it to them.'

'Cheers, Mark, I owe you, big time.'

There was a brief pause and then the gruff voice continued, quieter now, the tone sounding almost concerned. 'Listen, Billy, these geezers, they don't fuck about, mate. If you've wronged 'em ... well, just you be careful, that's all. And don't forget that they've got some heavy connections over here. Very heavy, in fact.'

Billy felt another shiver run down his spine and, with a final goodbye, he cancelled the call and dropped the phone on his desk.

Once he had sent home the last of the sales staff and made sure everything was locked up, Billy rang Sam to check she was OK and then settled down to wait for Simpson to arrive.

Then, and only then, did it suddenly begin to dawn on him that he wasn't just running on adrenaline, he was running on autopilot. What's more, he was doing things that he would never normally have done, without giving a thought to the consequences and, in truth, not even caring what those consequences might be. But the stark reality was that he had no option *but* to behave like that. The events of the past twenty-four hours had put him into a position where the element of choice had been taken away. It was literally them or him. And the tragedy was, that if he was going to survive intact, it was going to have to get worse before it would get better. There was absolutely no doubt about that.

But what had also started to nag at him was the realisation that in a perverse kind of way he was actually getting off on it. He'd ridden the emotional roller coaster of the Saturday scene for years but it had never been like this. It had never even come close. This was life-or-death stuff he was involved with, and it didn't get any more intense than that. How could it?

The piercing clamour of his mobile broke into his train of thought and, after rubbing his eyes to relieve the steadily increasing tiredness, Billy grabbed it from the desk and stuck it to his ear. The voice, when it came, was totally unexpected and almost made his heart stop dead with shock, the Irish accent the softer southern variety rather than the abrasive northern tone he'd been expecting.

'Mr Evans?'

'Yes,' he croaked, swallowing hard before he spoke again. 'And you are ...?'

'Looking, Mr Evans, I'm looking. Do you know where Simpson is?'

'No. But I know how to get hold of him,' said Billy, flinching at his own matter-of-factness. 'He knows someone's looking for him. That's why he's gone into hiding. He wants me to help him get out of the country.'

'Will you help us find him then? It'd make life much easier for everyone concerned. Including yourself.'

Billy could feel himself start to shake as he listened to the sheer malice pouring from his phone. 'I don't think that would be a good idea. Not yet anyway. I need to explain some things first.'

There was a pause and then the soft Irish brogue continued. 'Go on. I'm listening.'

After taking a silent but deep breath, Billy closed his eyes and said: 'I want to make it clear to you that I didn't have anything to do with what happened to Jimmy Morgan. It *is* true that Simpson came to me and asked me to help him, I admit that, but I said no. That's not the kind of thing I'm into.'

'Rest assured, Mr Evans,' said the voice after a pause, 'if I'd have thought otherwise you and I would already have met. Don't forget, I do know where you live.'

'Just so we understand that,' said Billy, walking over to the window and silently screaming with relief that he was seemingly safe.

'That's understood,' came the reply. There was a brief pause and then he spoke again, the voice lower and much more menacing this time. 'Now, will you tell me where I can find Simpson? I'm not a patient man, Mr Evans, and I'd hate to have to apply any kind of, shall we say ... pressure to get what I want.'

Before he could answer, Billy caught sight of a blue Ford Escort signalling to turn on to his forecourt, the driver clearly visible through the side window. He took another deep breath and moved back from the glass.

'Call me again in an hour. And I'll have an address for you.'

CHAPTER 38
Saturday 4 November 2000
18.00

Having run down the steep concrete stairs to the showroom, Billy unlocked the side door and walked out into the driving rain to find Simpson still sitting in his car rummaging around in a bag.

'My passport,' he called out through the glass. 'I've left my fucking passport in my flat.'

Billy shook his head and signalled at him to lower the window, calling out when he had done so: 'Stick it round the back, will you? There's more space.'

Simpson nodded and started the car as Billy ran back inside to keep dry. Within a few minutes, the two of them were standing side by side, dripping on the showroom floor. Simpson, with two small bags placed in a neat pile by the door and an excited look on his face, looked for all the world like a little kid about to go off on a school trip.

Billy looked at him and smiled weakly. His stomach was beginning to knot up again. 'You OK?'

'I am now,' he replied. 'I tell you, I don't even know where to start with this. The whole thing's freaked me out. You're a fucking saint, Billy. You've saved me, mate, that's for sure.'

'Forget it,' said Billy, dismissing the comment with a wave of his hand. 'Anyone would've done the same.'

'Yeah right-oh!' He paused for a second and then asked nervously, 'Well, what's the score then?'

'Oh yeah, well I've er ... sorted you out some tickets to Cyprus,' said Billy. 'For a couple of weeks like. You should be OK there until all this has died down. You'll be able to come back then, no problem.'

'You sure?' asked Simpson nervously. 'I was actually thinking of asking for a transfer at work. Move up North maybe. Make a clean start.'

Billy shrugged his shoulders. 'It's your call, mate. Anyway, what was it you were saying about your passport?'

'Shit. Yeah. I've left it in my bloody flat. Well I didn't think I'd be needing it when I went to Watford, did I? I'll have to get it though, or I won't be going anywhere. What airport am I going from?'

Billy looked at him and frowned. 'You what?'

'Which airport? I mean, if it's Heathrow or Luton, I can pick it up on the way. Gatwick or Stansted, I'll have to do a special trip like.'

'Oh,' said Billy, finally realising what he was on about. 'It's er... Luton. Yeah. Luton. Don't worry. I'll drive you up. You can leave your motor here. It'll be safer. You got the keys by the way? Just in case I have to shift it?'

'Sure,' replied Simpson eagerly, digging around in his pocket and throwing them over. 'You can drive to the airport in it if you like. Save you the petrol money.'

Billy was about to speak when the noise of his mobile ringing echoed through the building. His heart leapt into his mouth and he glanced at his watch. It hadn't been an hour yet. It couldn't be them calling back. Not yet.

He walked through to the bottom of the stairs and then ran up. His breath came in short, sharp gasps as he burst into his office, not because of any lack of fitness, but because his chest felt so tight it was all he could physically manage.

Billy lifted his phone and nervously glanced at the screen, almost melting with the relief of seeing 'Sam Mob' rather than 'private number'. He hit the button and greeted her warmly, and, after assuring her that everything was going to be OK, listened intently as she told him that the boys were enjoying themselves and that she intended to stop off at her folks on the way home; something he was especially glad to hear, as it would give him more time to do what he had to do.

She was still speaking when a noise jolted him around and he turned to see Simpson standing in the doorway behind him. He shut his eyes and took a deep breath, willing his heart to start working again. 'I gotta go, Sam,' he said. 'I'll call you in a while, OK? Kiss the boys for me.'

'Don't ever sneak up on me like that again,' he gasped as he put the phone down. 'You gave me the fright of my fucking life.'

'Sorry,' said Simpson sheepishly. 'I didn't mean ...'

Billy held up his hand to stop him speaking. He couldn't prolong this any longer. His heart was banging so hard it was scaring him and he hadn't slept or eaten for so long he couldn't even remember what either was like. But the two combined were making him feel lightheaded. And there was too much at stake for this to be cocked up just because he'd lost the plot and wasn't on the case. He had to do it, and he had to do it now or he wouldn't be able to do it at all.

'Come on,' he said. 'We need to get you out of here.'

Billy walked over to the door and turned off the office light, leading the two of them through Jill's office and following the same routine in there. But when they got to the top of the stairs, he stopped and closed his eyes. 'I don't fucking believe it!'

'What's up?' Simpson asked.

'I've only forgotten my fucking phone, ain't I? You go on, I'll be down in a sec.' He moved over to let Simpson past.

But even before he had got a proper grip on the rail, Billy had struck, hitting him right between the shoulder blades with both hands and every ounce of strength he possessed. At the same time, he hooked Simpson's legs away with his right foot. The two actions combined to send his body spinning forward for at least a metre before gravity kicked in and dragged it earthwards, smashing it lengthways against the sharp steps and filling the entire building with the music of pain: an irregular and excruciating symphony of thumps, grunts and cracks that can only ever be created by someone tumbling down a flight of concrete stairs.

Billy slowly followed the body down as it fell, hoping and praying that each blow it suffered would be the one that solved his problem and made it safe for him to go home and sleep at night. He didn't care if it was a broken neck or a blow to the temple, just so long as it meant that the truth about his involvement in Jimmy Morgan's accident was silenced for good.

By the time the battered body reached the bottom with a final, sickening thud, Billy was almost on top of it, listening and watching for even the slightest sign of life but noticing with a grim satisfaction the quantity of blood seeping out from under the head.

He was just about to kneel down and lift an eyelid to check for any signs of a reaction when he was interrupted by the distant call of his mobile, snapping him back to the reality of what he'd done and why.

He ran up the long stairs to answer it. The journey made him feel lightheaded again and the legend 'private number' told him who was on the other end even before he'd pressed the button to receive the call.

'Mr Evans, have you found him?'

Billy closed his eyes and desperately fought to compose himself. Shoving Simpson down the stairs had been the easy bit; pulling this off was going to be far more difficult. 'Yeah,' he wailed. 'I found him. But there's been an accident. He fell and...'

'What kind of accident?' asked the voice, higher in pitch this time; maybe even a bit agitated.

'He's dead,' said Billy, feigning shock as best he could. 'He fell down the stairs and he's dead!'

'Where are you? Have you called anyone yet?' The urgency in the voice was now obvious. The calm, considered responses of previous calls had been replaced by what could even have been a degree of panic.

'My garage ...' gasped Billy, 'in Romford. He's ...'

'I know where it is. We'll be there in twenty minutes. Don't do anything. Just wait.' The line went dead and Billy sat down on his desk with a thump. It hadn't sunk in yet. But he had a sneaky feeling that he might just be on the verge of safety.

CHAPTER 39
Saturday 4 November 2000
19.40

By the time the dark blue Shogun arrived at the garage, Billy had put Simpson's bags back in his car and moved it around to the side of the building where it could be clearly seen. He had even slid the keys back into his jacket pocket and, for good measure, hit the side of his own head against a wall a few times to redden it up and make it look as if he'd been fighting.

And then he had sat down to look at the body, the first dead person he'd ever really seen up close. Aside from his jacket, it had remained untouched and lay exactly where it had fallen. The legs stuck out at odd angles, pointing up the stairs, while the head lay on the floor where it had come to rest, surrounded on two thirds of its perimeter by a rapidly drying pool of blood.

The more Billy had studied it, the more amazed he had begun to feel that he could have caused so much damage with so little effort, or compassion; because it was true to say that he didn't feel anything at all. No sadness, no regret, no nothing. He didn't even feel relief. He just felt remote, like it was all happening to someone else. And he was glad he felt like that. Because as soon as these two had left him, he was going to call the police, spin them an edited version of the tale he was going to tell the Irishmen, and then he'd finally be able to get home and sleep.

Billy waited until the lights had been switched off on the Shogun before he opened the door and gestured the two men inside. They were nothing like he'd expected. To look at, they were just normal: fairly tall, well built and well dressed. One had black hair, one brown. Appearance-wise, that was it. They were the type of anonymous people he passed in the street or even sold cars to each and every day. But they had an air about them - one that made Billy feel decidedly uncomfortable. It was as if they could read what he was thinking even before he was thinking it - not nice at all.

He swallowed heavily as he locked the door behind them, suddenly unsure of what to do. Should he shake their hands, offer them a drink? What was the etiquette for dealing with the average terrorist?

'Where is he?'

Hearing the voice again shook him. It was still as soft, still as malicious, but this time it was also human. Tangible. Dangerous.

He led them through to the stairs, where the taller of the two men bent down and grabbed hold of Simpson's hair, pulling his head up to give the second man a good look at the face. When he nodded, almost imperceptibly, the tall man simply dropped it. The thud made Billy wince.

'So, Mr Evans, would you like to tell us what happened?'

Billy looked at the shorter of the two men and shrugged his shoulders, knowing his voice was going to shake when he spoke but desperately trying to fight it. 'He ... erm ... well...' He stopped and took a deep breath before starting again, slower this time, more deliberate. 'I don't know much about what's been going on lately because I've been away. But as I said, he asked me to help him get away a few weeks ago and now that I'm back, and knowing that you wanted to ... well, see him, I rang him and tried to find out where he was staying. But he wouldn't tell me and insisted on a meet here. What could I do? I tried to trick him into stopping until you called but he wouldn't have any of it. In the end, we struggled and ...' He stopped talking and held out his arms as he shrugged his shoulders. 'I don't know what else to say.'

The two men looked at each other without speaking. Even Billy could tell that this was a development they hadn't really expected.

'Did he ever say anything about what happened to Jimmy?' asked the taller of the two.

'Not a word,' said Billy shaking his head a little too quickly. 'And I never asked. It was a terrible thing though,' he added as an afterthought. 'Young lad like that...'

The glare from the shorter man made it clear that Billy had said enough and so he fell silent, following the two men as they turned away from the body and walked back through the showroom and out to the waiting Shogun. As he was about to climb in, the shorter of the two, the man with the voice, turned back to Billy and smiled.

'Did you know Jimmy Morgan had a brother?'

Billy shook his head nervously. 'No. I had no idea. Why?'

'Bear that in mind, though, won't you?'

'Er, yeah, sure,' replied Billy.

The Irishman continued to stare deep into Billy's eyes for a moment and then climbed into the car, pulling the door shut behind him as the engine started with a roar. But before it pulled away, the darkened window next to Billy purred down and the man with the voice looked at him and smiled. The cold eyes showed not a trace of emotion.

'Thanks for yer help, Billy. And you take care of yerself. Good care.'

Although he'd had a nightmare couple of days, Billy Evans felt as relaxed as he had done for many a month. And with a garden full of people celebrating Guy Fawkes night despite the pouring rain, he had every reason to feel pleased with himself. The pressure was finally off.

Even the police had been sound when he'd spoken with them last night, allowing him to go home and get some sleep before going in this morning and making a statement; putting on record the fact that he'd gone into work last night and found this bloke in there on the rob. The fight had just been a tragic accident, him tripping like that as Billy tried to hang on to him. Terrible.

The Old Bill had actually thought it was quite funny, what with him running a security company and all. Not much of an advert they'd said. God knows what the local papers were going to make out of it. But that was the least of his worries. Besides, there was no such thing as bad publicity, everyone knew that. Although in this case, the truth might have been slightly damaging to say the very least.

The only thing about the whole affair that had nagged at him for a while was all that stuff that the Irishman had said - about the Morgan kid having a brother. That hadn't made any sense to him at all. Still, after the last few weeks, and with a bellyful of beer, who gave a fuck? Not him, that's for sure.

He walked over and put his arm around Sam as she and Julie finished clearing up the mess from the barbecue. She was a different woman from the one he'd seen so panic-stricken yesterday. But then again, she'd always had a capacity for blanking out bad stuff. Even the worst kind. Billy suspected that much of that came from his former involvement with The Squad. It couldn't have been easy watching him walk out the front door every match day, year in, year out. But he'd never asked her about it, and certainly never intended to now.

She suddenly turned around and gave him a kiss full on the lips. 'You know we're almost out of lager, don't you?' she said.

'What!' yelled Hawk, suddenly appearing beside him. 'That's bang out of order. What kind of party is this? No bloody lager!'

Billy looked at him and laughed. 'You really are pissed as a fart, aren't you?'

'Who cares?' said Hawk. 'You're only young once.'

'Bloody youth's wasted on the young,' said Billy. 'It should be the other way round.'

Hawk looked at him and shook his head. 'What the fuck are you on about?' he said, before realising what he'd said and holding his hand up to his mouth and adding a loud 'Oops. Sorry, Sam.' He turned back to Billy and they both started to giggle; like two little kids who'd been caught doing something they shouldn't have.

'Billy, I'm going to nip out and get some more lagers,' called Sam.

'No,' he shouted back in reply. 'Don't go out in this rain Sam. It's bloody mad. We're all right. We'll just start on the shorts, won't we, Hawk?'

'You bloody well won't,' cut in Julie. 'We're at my folks for dinner tomorrow and I'm not having him throwing up all day. He can go on the diet Coke. He could do with some of that anyway,' she added, walking over and patting him on the stomach. 'He's getting as fat as you, Billy.'

'I'll be back in ten minutes,' shouted Sam as she disappeared around the side of the house and vanished from view.

Billy went to go after her but stopped to talk to one of the neighbours, and by the time he'd made it around to the front her BMW had gone. He shrugged his shoulders and walked back to the garden, only to be called into the house by Julie, who was waving his mobile and mouthing 'phone' at him.

He wandered over and took it off her. 'Billy. Speak now or piss off!' he said rudely.

'D'you remember what I told you yesterday, Billy, about Jimmy Morgan having a brother?' Billy swallowed and stood bolt upright as the soft Irish voice rendered him instantly sober. 'Have you worked it out yet?'

'I... I don't get it,' he stuttered in reply. 'Why are you ...?'

'You see, where we come from,' continued the voice, sounding as if it were reciting something rather than discussing it, 'we look after our families, Billy. If something bad happens to a loved one, we like to think that something bad will happen to the person responsible. That's fair isn't it, Billy?'

'You're Jimmy's brother aren't you!' exclaimed Billy as the realisation finally hit him. 'Aren't you!'

'We're *all* Jimmy's brothers, Billy. Not just me. That's the whole point,' purred the voice. 'You harm one of us; you have the rest to deal with. Do you understand what I'm saying to you now?'

'But Simpson's dead. You saw him!'

'Oh, Billy. Come on now. Simpson wasn't responsible. He was just a loose end that needed to be tied off. Just like the chairman. No, Billy boy, the driver, that's who was responsible, the driver. Do you understand me now?' There was a long pause and then he added, 'An eye for an eye, Billy. That's what they say.'

Billy stood staring into space as the line clicked dead. 'Oh Jesus!' he muttered, grabbing his keys from the hook and running out to the Range Rover. He blasted it away up the road and dialled Sam's number as quickly as he could. He was stunned to find that it was actually ringing.

'Where are you?' he said, trying desperately to keep his voice calm.

'I'm almost on the A12. Why?'

'Where are you going then?'

'To Sonny's'

'What, the Paki shop across the A12?'

'Yeah, what's up with you?'

'Bollocks!' he shouted, slamming the brakes on and spinning the car round to head off in the opposite direction. 'Why haven't you gone to Asda?'

'It's 5 o'clock on a Sunday. It's closed. What's the bloody matter?'

'Nothing,' he blurted. 'I'm just following after you, that's all. I'm worried about this rain.'

'Billy!' she yelled. 'You're pissed as a rat. Pull that bloody car over before you get nicked!'

'No, Sam. I'm worried about you in this rain.'

'Billy, stop that bloody car or else. I mean it!'

'OK,' he lied. 'You're right, I'm doing it now. There, I've stopped, all right?'

She carried on berating him as he blasted after her, desperately searching for the back of the BMW and almost gasping with relief when he finally saw it among a line of cars ahead. The Range Rover's height gave him an excellent view above the ten or so saloons between them. He was about to tell her to pull over and wait for him when he stopped himself. She'd go mad if she found out he was there. And how would he explain it?

Instead, he looked around and searched desperately among the few cars on the road for a dark blue Shogun. But when none could be seen, he relaxed a little and decided to follow her to the shop. She'd go mental when she saw him, but at least he'd feel happier.

The line of cars slowed to a crawl as they approached the junction with the A12 and Billy watched from his lofty position as, every so often, one would nip out into the traffic stream and turn left on to the dual carriageway. But, with the rain hammering on his roof and almost defeating the best efforts of the wipers to remove it from his windscreen, it was taking an age and it was fully five minutes before the BMW made it to the front of the queue.

Suddenly, smoke began to bellow from somewhere up ahead and Billy watched it for a few seconds before shaking his head. 'All you'd need,' he thought. 'Bloody engine to let go in this weather.'

Keeping his eyes on the cars ahead, he reached down to turn on the radio, but the smoke continued to bellow upwards and he began to catch the slightest whiff of burning rubber. He sat up and stared ahead, leaning forward to get a better view and noticing for the first time that the smoke was pouring up from the car directly behind the BMW. And for the first time, the knotting sensation in his stomach began to warn him that something was wrong. Seriously wrong.

He pushed open the door of the Range Rover and stepped out into the rain, walking along the side of the stationary cars and staring at the back of the BMW as it suddenly began to inch its way out into the A12 traffic.

When the first blast of a car horn screamed in protest, Billy finally began to grasp the reality of the situation and broke into a jog. At that instant, the white reversing lights on the large Jaguar saloon that was immediately behind his wife's car flashed on and it shot back into the car behind with a loud crunch, only to immediately shoot forward again and ram the BMW ever closer to the traffic hurtling past - traffic which was, by now, howling in protest and missing the BMW by inches.

By now, Billy was sprinting and, as he came alongside the flanks of the Jaguar, he dived for the driver's door in an effort to wrench it open but missed as it shot backwards again, ramming itself even harder into the car behind and driving that even further backwards. Almost immediately, it shot forward again, exploiting the extra space it had made for itself and driving into the BMW with such force that the white convertible flew straight out into the traffic. Billy screaming out loud as a blue articulated lorry hit it square on and blasted it away from sight in an explosion of noise and shattered glass.

Instinctively, he left the Jaguar and ran after it, shouting out and pleading with the lorry driver to stop, as the cab of the huge vehicle rode up over the BMW and crashed down upon it, the impact all but flattening the car within less than a second.

As the twisted metal dug into the tarmac and finally dragged the lorry to a halt, Billy slowed to a walk as he tried to take it all in, barely hearing a sound of the chaos going on behind him as he approached the spot where, only seconds ago, his beloved wife must have experienced the very worst kind of terror.

When he drew level with the cab, and what remained of the BMW, Billy moved towards it and knelt down. He stared at it for a moment before slowly reaching forward and pushing his hands in among the hot and twisted metal, desperately searching for one last touch. But he never found it.

CHAPTER 41
Sunday 5 November 2000
22.30

Danny Howarth was busily grinding off the badly trashed front end of an already banger-raced Mk5 Cortina when he suddenly realised that his dog was barking furiously.

He glanced at the time and after placing the grinder on the floor - leaving it running to give the impression that someone was still working - wiped his hands on his jeans and picked up a large spanner before moving quickly over to the door. He leant against it for a second and then gradually began to ease it open before flicking the light switch on the wall and jumping out into the rain with a shout.

Instantly, the place was flooded with a bright, white light and Danny stood in the middle of the yard looking furiously around with the spanner held out in front of him, ready to attack whoever was trying to break in. But there wasn't a soul to be seen; just the dog barking furiously at the gate.

He wandered over as a loud double-thump reverberated around the yard. He calmed the dog by placing his hand on its head as he strained to hear a sound over the noise of the still-screaming grinder and the driving rain.

'Who is it?' he yelled, smiling to himself when the answer came and dropping the spanner on the floor.

When the car was inside, he studied it carefully. The front end wasn't too bad but the back was a mess. They'd been lucky to get to Tilbury without the coppers pulling them over - something to thank the rain for anyway.

'How'd it go, then?'

'As expected,' came the reply, the soft Irish accent sounding far more relaxed than normal. 'The Jag here, it was good. You built a good car, Danny boy.'

'Hey, just pleased to be of service, lads. Especially after... well, you know. I still feel a bit of a fuckin' idiot about all that.'

'Bloody hell, we've been through all that a hundred times,' said the Irishman as Danny led them through to the lean-to and out of the rain. 'You're the man when it comes ter stuff like this, ain't yer? So it stands ter reason, if someone wants a car buildin' they're gonna come to you, ain't dey? But you don't ask what they want it fer, do yer? Jesus, we're just glad that when we started making our enquiries, word got to you and you made the connection.'

Danny looked at them and shrugged. 'Yeah, it came as quite a shock to find out who the kid's old man was. He stayed wiv me once, did I tell you that? He was over here on erm ... business.'

The two Irishmen looked at him and smiled. 'Yeah, you told us before. Now, will you be runnin' us to the airport in the mornin' or should we get a cab?'

'Lads!' said Danny, holding out his hands. 'What are brothers for?'